Crescent

Crescent

STEFANIE MULDER

PARTRIDGE
A Penguin Random House Company

ISBN:	Softcover	978-1-4828-3043-9
	eBook	978-1-4828-3044-6

Print information available on the last page.

To order additional copies of this book, contact
Toll Free 800 101 2657 (Singapore)
Toll Free 1 800 81 7340 (Malaysia)
orders.singapore@partridgepublishing.com

www.partridgepublishing.com/singapore

For Oma Coby:
Grandma, if you hadn't bought me that golden notebook,
this writing adventure would never have started.

Ubi concordia, ibi victoria.

PROLOGUE

Michael Larson sat behind his desk. His warm morning cup of coffee was cupped in his hands, and the warmth of the liquid spread through his body every time he took a sip. He inhaled deeply, taking in the caffeinated smell while letting his mind wander; he was daydreaming about the success of his latest job but also about the trouble he was having raising his teenage son. He slowly turned in his desk chair toward the window behind him. He angled himself in such a way that he could look out the window and see who was entering the building below him. Without putting much thought into it, he studied the people below in a daze.

Men and women in suits entered the building to start their day at work. In the center of the plaza, a women and her child sat on the ledge of the fountain, and a postman exited the building with a stack of packages. A small figure ran across the other side of the plaza. This figure caught Michael's eye.

His chair squeaked as he leaned forward in his chair to watch this person stumble up to the front door of his building. Though what Michael could see from the seventeenth floor wasn't much, he could determine that this person was there to see him.

Everyone who visited Michael was afraid of him. Even his own boss, who had been persuaded to hire him, had now separated their two divisions, much to Michael's delight. He couldn't say that he hadn't had any influence in that decision. Most of Michael's visitors were cautious around him, though most wouldn't admit it if he asked. Every single one of their words was picked out carefully to please him.

Some were more jumpy than others, which Michael found rather amusing. He chuckled to himself as he sat in his desk chair bringing up the memory. A few short minutes passed before a hesitant knock came on the door.

Michael sighed, taking another sip of his steaming coffee and turning his desk chair back around. "Come in."

An older, stubbly man peeked his head around the door. The man gulped and pushed some thin strands of graying hair away from his eyes. His wrinkled eyes were shaded with worry, and his hands were shaking slightly. "Sir, we have another case."

"That's good." The sides of Michael's mouth curved upward. He glanced at the man's shaking hands distractedly before looking at his computer. "You can e-mail me the information. Thanks for your investigation."

"There's something you should know. I don't think you'll be as happy with this one. You won't be able to send out as many people," the man said while fidgeting with his tie.

Michael turned his attention back to the investigator. He placed his cup of coffee on the desk and stood up slowly. "I didn't hire you for nothing." He strode over to the man, towering over him. "Is it a case or not?"

The man visibly held his breath. "It is …"

"Then what's the problem, Hector? I don't see the problem here."

Hector pushed his glasses up the bridge of his nose. "The pack won't be able to help …"

Michael frowned, his slight smile from before gone before anyone could acknowledge it. "And why is that? Ben and his team are the best we have!"

"Well …" Hector hesitated, again not wanting to tell the truth—a truth that would most likely upset Michael.

Michael clenched his jaw. A dull sound echoed through the office from his impatient foot tapping. "Tell me, Hector. Who has it?"

The investigator gulped. "Nate Mannaro."

"Mannaro has it?" Michael frowned. A dark expression crossed his face. "Ben works for us. Why didn't he tell us he has it?"

"I'm sorry, Mr. Larson, but I suspect Ben doesn't know his son has it." Hector glanced at his watch. He wanted to get out before Michael lost his temper.

"Well, that's just great!" Michael started pacing. "We need to send Ben after his own son. He'll never agree to that."

"I guess you can always find a reason to go after the boy," Hector suggested.

Michael stopped pacing and straightened his suit. "You're right. I want you to find out everything about this kid. Where he lives, which school he goes to, who his friends are; find out everything."

Hector slowly started to make his way to the door. "What should I do after all the information has been collected?"

"Wait for an opportunity to present itself," Michael said as he walked back to sit behind his desk. He grabbed his coffee and took a long gulp.

The investigator looked doubtful. "Why are you so sure that it will?"

Michael smiled his wicked smile. "It always does, Hector."

CHAPTER 1

The door banged loudly as I pulled it closed behind me. I quickly clicked the lock into place, watching as the little marker turned from vacant white to occupied red. I pulled down the hook that was attached to the door and hung my bag on it. Zipping it open I pulled out a plastic bag, which I placed on the toilet seat after I had closed it with my foot. I tried not to gag on the awful smell that came from a drain next to the toilet; it would have to do. I'd rather change in here than in some random alley on the streets. At least there weren't any beggars or homeless people here.

I pulled off my jacket, the suede material feeling itchy against my fingers. Not knowing where else to put it in the small space, I dropped it on the floor. I didn't care what happened to it anyway. Next I clumsily changed from my skirt to my jeans, which instantly felt much better. I dropped the skirt next to the jacket, and as soon as I had changed into my T-shirt, my sparkly top joined the pile.

Out of all the clothing articles, my shoes were the hardest to change. I didn't want to get my socks wet on the filthy floor, which turned out to be a challenge in the enclosed space of the stall. I think I banged my head twice and my elbow approximately twenty times.

Honestly I didn't really care. I was just glad I wasn't wearing the designer skirt my mom bought me anymore. I had tried to get out of the house in my casual clothes, but my mom had been waiting right at the door and had made me go back to change. She said I didn't look proper and I needed to dress like an appropriate young lady. According to her I could run into someone important on the streets. Someone important, meaning one of my mom's preppy friends that would judge her based on how I dressed. I couldn't care less. Plus, it wasn't like I was wearing supershort shorts or anything.

I bent down to pick up the clothes, which had turned suspiciously damp from the floor. I cringed, trying to stuff them into the plastic bag as fast as I could, without touching too much of it. I tied the bag closed and turned around to grab my other bag. It was the only thing my mom hadn't made me go change. It was just a normal, cheap backpack, the original blue color already faded and dirty.

I jumped as I heard a door creak open and fall shut. It wasn't like the stall door; it sounded heavier. More like the entrance door to the entire bathroom. I felt my heart beat in my throat. What if one of my parents had followed me out here? They would be pissed enough seeing me in an ordinary shop bathroom like this, and it would bring a whole new amount of trouble if they figured I had changed in here.

Trying not to make a sound, I attempted to look through the crack of the door. Nobody seemed to be there. Maybe I was imagining it? I certainly hoped so. I waited another few minutes, standing completely still in case someone was there. No other sounds followed the original door slam. Deciding it was safe, I quickly threw my backpack over my shoulder and unlocked the stall. The door swung open with a loud creak. I stepped out and closed the door behind me. The tattered bathroom was completely deserted.

I walked over to the trash can and stuffed the plastic bag with my mom's choice of clothes in it. The bag barely fit, and I had to squish it in all the way. The clothes completely filled up the bin but at least now someone would see it as trash. I quickly washed my hands and dried them with a paper towel, which I then placed on top of the bag with my clothes, just in case it wasn't obvious enough. I smiled to myself; mission accomplished.

Shifting my bag on my shoulder, I walked over to the entrance of the bathroom and opened the door. I jumped as I caught sight of what was on the other side. A broad man was standing just in front of the door opening, his arms crossed and a stern look on his face. I winced as he cleared his throat loudly.

"Took you long enough," he said in a thick Italian accent. He narrowed his pudgy eyes at me. "You can't use the bathroom without our permission. Only customers can use the bathroom." He put his hands on his wide hips, his hands leaving a doughy mark on his stained apron.

"I'm so sorry. I just really needed to use the bathroom. I assume you must be the owner?" I asked, trying to sound as innocent as possible. He looked unimpressed. "I'll leave right away, sir. Sorry to bother you."

Without waiting for an answer, I walked around him toward the front of the store. No offense to him, but it was a really crappy restaurant. I hated being so rude to him too; it reminded me of how my mom acted toward people who didn't have the money we did. Except this time I had no other option. I couldn't risk him calling the police, or even worse, my parents. I would never hear the end of it.

"Are you not going to buy any pizza?" I heard the storeowner yell after me as I pulled open the front door. A small bell rang as it opened and the wind gushed in.

"Sorry, sir. Next time though!" I yelled over my shoulder. I quickly stepped out and closed the door behind me.

"If you ever come back …" I heard the chef threaten behind me, but his words were cut off as the door closed. I closed my eyes and inhaled deeply, trying to relax. I really hated acting like that. Under normal circumstances I would have gladly stayed for a piece of pizza, but I had some shopping to do before I had to be back home for Colin.

Inhaling again I recognized the familiar smell of hotdogs and pollution that hung strongly in the air. I could feel the spring breeze creep gently across my body. It made me realize, once again, how much better my own jeans felt than the designer skirts my mom always bought me. It had been a good choice to change out of it. I didn't want to come across like one of those preppy Upper East Side teens, especially not in the store I was going to.

My mom would, of course, notice I had changed. The detail about the pizza restaurant didn't need to be mentioned. She should have figured I would change. Didn't she know me well enough by now?

Walking down the sidewalk reminded me about how much I enjoyed the streets of Manhattan, today being no exception. The people, the smell, the feeling—simply put, I'm a true New Yorker at heart.

Stopping in front of an old tattered store close by, I examined the address on my phone one more time. It seemed to match the address of the store. Taking a deep breath, I entered to see what was inside.

As expected, it was a skater store. Skateboards hung on the walls, hoodies hung loosely on racks, and T-shirts were strewed all over the place. The place smelled weirdly damp, and a cloud of smoke hovered in the back of the store.

I headed to the counter, arriving to see a twenty-something guy slouching in a beanbag. He was dressed like a stereotypical skater, with a beanie on his head and a half-shaven beard. The guy was playing around with a cigarette, and puffs of smoke were rising up toward the ceiling.

"How you doing, cupcake?" he said as he caught sight of me. He straightened out and crossed his arms. "What's a girl like you doing in a store like this?"

"I'm here to pick up an order," I replied calmly, hiding my scowl. I eyed a stack of boxes on the counter. One of those had to be mine.

The skater frowned. "I don't have any orders from preppy Upper East Siders."

I crossed my arms, ignoring his comment. Of course, he had noticed the one thing I was trying to avoid. "I called yesterday, and your friend assured me it would be here."

The guy chuckled and stood up from the beanbag. "That's where you go wrong, missy. My *friend* assured you. I wasn't here yesterday due to some other business, so I can't help you. I don't know what my employees promised you, and quite frankly I'm not responsible."

"You're the owner. Doesn't that make you responsible?" I asked in disbelief. Leaning his elbow onto the counter, the guy twirled his cigarette. He gave me an expectant look, as if to ask what I was still doing there. "Can't you just check the order list? My package should be in there somewhere."

The skater stretched out and yawned. "I suppose I could help a young lady like yourself out," he said while walking over to the pile of packages. He grabbed a clipboard and scanned the list. "And your name is …"

"Renn," I said as I leaned forward on the counter. "Renn Daniels."

The guy immediately smiled at the sound of my name. The annoyed look dropped from his face. "You're Colin's sister! Should've said so; makes things easier." Handing me the topmost package on the pile, he winked. "Tell Colin happy birthday for me. From Ricky."

I smiled. "Will do."

A phone rang from somewhere in the store, and Ricky lightly rolled his eyes in response. He pulled an old flip phone out of his pocked and held the mobile up to his ear. "Hello," Ricky answered, saying the word with a break between the two syllables. His eyebrows furrowed together, presumably in recognition of the person calling.

I looked down at my feet, not wanting to pry. Plastic bottles and cigarette packs littered the floor. The plastic layer of the floor was coming loose against the counter, and half of it was discolored from the original dark gray color.

Ricky's good-bye on the phone caught my attention again. He looked annoyed, as if he had better things to do than the errand that the person on the phone wanted. I looked up at Ricky, and as soon as he met my gaze, he stalked around the counter to me.

"Now, if you don't mind," he said as he placed a hand between my shoulder blades. He started to steer me out and walked me to the front entrance of the store. "I have some business to take care of. That's what sucks about having two jobs. I don't recommend it; it leaves no free time." He opened the door for me and gestured me out with his hand. "Now, please beat it. I have things to do, people to see. I'm a busy guy. Thanks for your consideration, and tell Colin I said hi."

Giving me one final push, he shoved me out onto the street. He slammed the door closed behind me before I could mutter a protest. The last I saw of Ricky was his hand, flipping the open sign to closed.

"Thank you," I muttered to the closed door. Sometimes I wondered what type of people my brother hung out with. Ricky was nice, but ... strange, to say the least. Just like all the other guys Colin befriended.

I started to head home. I picked at a piece of the cardboard box that was coming loose. Scribbly handwriting labeled the package with my name and an order number. A smiley was drawn on it, and "Ricky's Skater Store" was stamped onto it in red ink.

I looked up at a blasting, beeping sound. The little red traffic light man was blinking, counting down from ten. I was halfway across the street when the countdown reached zero. New Yorker cabbies immediately started honking and shouting out of their windows. I ignored them. Wind whooshed past me as I hit the curb on the other side, a motorcycle racing past right where I had been a second earlier. I was used to it.

Passing a bagel cafe, memories flooded back into my mind. I used to go there for my birthday or any other special occasion with my friends. Well, friend rather than friends. It wasn't that I couldn't make friends; I just preferred down-to-earth people who didn't care about popularity. Sadly for me those people were hard to find at the strict, preppy, uniform-wearing school that I went to. Everyone cared about their popularity status, teachers and parents included.

My eyes raced to a sign behind the glass door of the cafe. "Closed for renovations," it read; "back in the fall." Beneath the sign hung a picture of a sports bar that the bagel place was turning into. So much for my childhood memories.

I walked the rest of the way in silence, thinking about nothing in particular. Cars rushed past on the streets. Reaching Madison Avenue I stopped. To my left I could see my building looming, but in front of me, I could see Central Park green and alive in the distance.

I considered ditching my brother's party and just strolling around Central Park. There was nothing I'd rather do. The trees, the ponds, the ducks—everything about it never failed to capture my attention.

I automatically started to cross the street, but I stopped myself. Even though I hated it when my parents tried to stay on top of their social ladder, I couldn't do that to Colin. Not on his birthday at least.

With a sigh I turned and started to head toward my building. This party that my parents were throwing was nothing like Colin would ever do. He would much rather skate around with Ricky than shake hands and drink cocktails..

Not that I blamed him; I hated it too. Instead of having parties like a normal teenager, I had to go all-formal to please my parents. They'd do anything to stay on top of their Upper East Side social ladder. This included, of course, dressing up their children and pretending that they were already planning to go to law school.

It was just something that came with this life my parents had chosen. I don't even know how my parents had reached this status; they weren't investors, leaders of big companies, or had a huge inheritance to build on. My dad had a middle-class job, and my mom didn't even work. But somehow they still seemed to buy everything that the rich Upper East Siders did, including a penthouse and designer clothes.

The doorman stopped my train of thought. "Hello, Ms. Daniels, how are you today?"

"I'm fine, Stan," I said, smiling. "How are you?"

The heavy oak doors creaked as Stan pushed them open. He followed me into the lobby. "I'm very good, Ms. Daniels, thank you. Would you like me to carry that package for you?"

I sighed. I hated it when people thought I couldn't carry a simple package just because my parents had money. "It's okay; I can handle it. Thanks though."

"No, I insist. It's my job after all," Stan began, offering once again. His red doorman suit wrinkled as he leaned toward me with his hands out, ready to receive the package. I shifted the box to my other side, ignoring his efforts.

I sauntered past the seating area toward the elevator. The lobby was completely empty except for a person standing next to the elevator. I couldn't make out who it was, only that it was a guy. I heard Stan's hurried footsteps follow behind me. "I can carry it myself, Stan," I said over my shoulder with a hint of irritation in my voice.

The doorman wasn't giving up. "Really, Ms. Daniels, I'll do it. And while I do that, your mother insisted ..."

I spun back on my heels. My hair blew into my face as another resident opened the entrance door. The fake jewels on the chandelier clinked. I narrowed my eyes at the doorman. "What did you say about my mother?"

Stan frowned and straightened his suit. "Well, your mother insisted ..."

"Insisted what?" I scowled. I couldn't believe this was happening again. Stan didn't even have to explain; I knew where the conversation was headed. Why was my mom attempting this again, even after I had gotten so mad last time?

Stan fidgeted. I could sense that he was nervous. Like he was going to tell me something he wasn't supposed to.

"Your mother may have insisted you didn't come up with that package to look more proper. She also may have said that you would have changed out of your day clothes"—he hesitated and eyed me suspiciously—"that you're apparently not wearing anymore, and you were to change into a cocktail dress before you entered the party ..."

Fury spread through my body. I glared at Stan, who was fiddling his thumbs to avoid my gaze. I took a step toward him.

"Which dress?" I spat out.

"The one on the couch over there," Stan said, pointing behind him. "She brought it here before the guests started to arrive."

Clenching my teeth I tried not to burst into a rage. "Thanks for being loyal, Stan, but I do not need your help today."

"Sorry for the trouble, Ms. Daniels." Stan nodded.

I nodded back and continued toward the elevator. The mystery figure from earlier was still there. He had been observing the whole time, and when I reached him, he smiled.

"Shall I carry that package for you?" he said, imitating Stan's Jersey accent.

I glared at him, but not being able to stay serious for long, I started laughing. "Shut up, Nate."

CHAPTER 2

"Have I ever told you how annoying this elevator music is?" Nate said as he pressed the button for the fifteenth floor. The button instantly lit up and the doors closed. I felt a sinking feeling in the pit of my stomach as the lift began to rise. "You would think an expensive building like this would do a better job at picking out their elevator music. Or, you know, just not have any music at all," Nate continued, his dark eyebrows knitting together.

I leaned back against the wall of the elevator, taking in the soft tune. I never really paid attention to the music anymore, especially since I had been taking this elevator every day for most of my life. However, Nate always seemed to notice it, even though he had been to my house millions of times before. I glanced at my best friend. "I think you mention it every time you come over."

"It just reminds me every time ..." he replied, his words trailing off. His green eyes sparkled with amusement. "I'm sorry, but not everyone has to take an elevator up to the elevator to their penthouse. Some of us actually live in normal houses, like, ones without a doorman. Or double elevators."

I stayed silent, not acting on Nate's sarcasm. I felt strangely drained and exhausted; too many thoughts were running through my head at the same time.

Nate cleared his throat, one of his many horrible ways of attempting to change the subject. "What's in the package?"

I shrugged. "I guess you'll have to find out."

Nate stared at me for a second. I felt his eyes on me, watching me intently. "Are you okay? You seem a bit off."

"I'm fine."

Nate took a step toward me, stretching his arm out to lean it against the wall next to me. "Really? 'Cause you're not talking as much as usual. And usually you make some kind of remark when I complain about the elevator music. That's the only reason I say it anyway."

I looked at him. "To annoy me?"

Nate chuckled, his eyes sparkling. "I suppose so."

"What a great friend you are."

"The best." Nate grinned. "But are you going to tell me what's going on?"

I hesitated, running my hand through my hair. Some of my brown locks fell in front of my eyes, and I pulled the hair back behind my ear. "My mom …"

Nate shook his head. "Stop right there. We'll talk after the party, I promise. But for now, forget about it and enjoy Colin's birthday." He winked at me as the elevator doors opened. "You can do the whole girly pouring out your heart and emotions thing later."

I rolled my eyes at him, which made him laugh.

"Fine." Nate sighed falsely. "I'll take you to Brooklyn."

I smiled, liking that a bit better. I followed Nate across the hall to the penthouse elevator. One of the perks of having rich parents; they buy expensive houses. We stepped into the elevator, and Nate pressed the button to the twenty-fourth floor, which just happened to be the top floor.

Nate sighed, more seriously this time. I watched as he twisted a string bracelet that he had on around his wrist. "Can I tell you something?"

I nodded.

"Well," he said, eyeing me, "it's not bad having the money you have. I get where you're coming from, don't get me wrong, but life isn't easy for me either."

I smiled. "After the party you can take me to Brooklyn, and after I tell you my problems, you can do the whole girly pouring out your heart and emotions thing," I said mockingly.

Nate stared at me, not moving a muscle. "Very funny."

"I'm serious!" I exclaimed with a laugh. "You can tell me all of your secrets …" I hesitated. "If you have any, that is."

The elevator made a loud *ping* sound, and the doors began to open. Nate muttering something about me having no idea was the last thing I heard before loud orchestra music filled the small area in the elevator. People roamed all around my living room; all of them were wearing suits and dresses, making me fall out of place surprisingly quickly. Nate's jeans and plaid shirt didn't fit into the formal category that well either.

Scanning the crowded room, I spotted my brother, who was leaning on the handrail of the midsection of the stairs. He stood elevated above the throng of people, observing how they were drinking cocktails and eating small appetizers. Colin was the only person in the room besides Nate and I who wasn't dressed up. He was wearing his usual leather jacket and red pants, making him look like a fish out of water. I instantly started heading toward him, Nate following close behind.

I made it halfway through the apartment before I was stopped by a lady whose face was so wrinkle-free that I was sure it couldn't be natural. She looked slightly familiar, but only from having had to shake her hand at a previous party. Her leather dress hugged her body like a skin suit, and she was wearing a jewel necklace that looked more expensive than my entire closet.

"Renn!" she exclaimed, putting her hand on my arm. "Congratulations with your brother. He's getting so old, twenty-one, my dear. I can remember him so vividly as a toddler."

Like she could remember, I thought to myself. It's not like she really cared about Colin, and she had probably just seen his baby picture that was on display somewhere near the front door. I glanced back at Nate, who was rocking on the balls of his feet awkwardly. He gave me a sympathetic look.

"You really are a lovely girl," I heard the woman say as I turned my attention back toward her. She ran her fingers across my cheek, and it took all my energy not to recoil from her touch. "You should really do something about your hair though. You need to accentuate your natural waves. And some makeup wouldn't do you any harm either. Some blush would prevent you from looking so ghostly."

"Thanks," I replied bluntly.

The woman opened her mouth, but seemed to rethink what she was going to say. "That wasn't a compliment, honey."

I stared at her, trying to calm myself down. "I figured," I said carefully, not wanting to sound too rude. The woman stayed silent, so I excused myself and quickly made my way past her and the rest of the guests. I heard bits and pieces of conversations, and everyone seemed to be talking about everything and anything but

Colin's birthday. When I got to the stairs, I jogged up the steps. I looked back at Nate, who had continued to follow me. Most of the people here knew him as my friend, but there were also some teachers from our school present. Luckily he hadn't been stopped by any of them.

"Happy twenty-first birthday!" I cheered at my brother when I reached his side. Colin smiled, but it didn't show in his eyes. He clearly didn't look as happy as he was trying to come across. Some of his shaggy blond hair had fallen in front of his eyes. Half of his hair was dyed black, which didn't help much with the enthusiasm factor either.

"So ..." I started, trying to get a conversation going. "How does it feel to be twenty-one?"

Colin shrugged, looking back over the crowd. "Not much different," he replied with a bored tone to his voice.

I opened my mouth to say something, but Nate, who took a step toward Colin, cut me off. "Happy birthday, man!" he said, sticking his hand out toward my brother. Colin shook his hand, and they did one of those awkward guy hugs. Except it didn't seem so awkward to them as it looked to me.

"I guess I can take you drinking sometime then?" Colin asked Nate. He turned around to lean with his back against the railing, and Nate had taken a seat on the stairs in front of him.

Nate gave him a confused look. "You know I'm seventeen, right?"

Colin shrugged, crossing his arms. "Yeah, so? Seventeen is almost eighteen."

"True ... but it's still illegal."

Colin laughed. "Yeah." He nodded slowly. "So?"

"I bought you something!" I spoke up, changing the subject. I was surprised he hadn't noticed the package yet. I held it out for him. "I went through some trouble to get it, but you deserve it for your twenty-first."

Colin took the package from me and examined the label. "You didn't have to do this, Renn. If Mom and Dad found out ..."

"I don't care about Mom and Dad." I crossed my arms. "They probably already know about it anyway, and I can make my own decisions. Now open your present before I get Nate to do it for you."

Nate smirked as Colin took a seat on the stairs. Nate craned his neck, lifting his head from the banister to watch from behind as Colin opened the package. He conjured a pocketknife out of nowhere and cut the tape. Colin was that type of person who always had a pocketknife handy. His face lit up instantly as soon as he unrolled the cardboard.

"You got me a personalized skateboard?" he exclaimed while turning the board over in his hands. "This present is better than anything Mom and Dad have ever given me." He chuckled coldly.

I grinned. "I had some help from someone at the store, but at least now you have a one-of-a-kind board. And Ricky says happy birthday."

"The idiot," Colin said, laughing. "I'm surprised he remembered."

"He must have had some help remembering. I'm sure it didn't come from him," Nate said from behind Colin.

Colin looked back at Nate with a confused look on his face. "How do you know Ricky? He barely comes out of his shop. And if he does, it's to skateboard."

"Don't be so surprised. I know people too."

"Come on. You barely know people at your school besides Renn," Colin said with a playful smile. It felt good to see Colin smile. After the last couple of months, he hadn't been his happy self. It was a relief to see him smile. At least he was still capable.

Nate hesitated. "I know some people. It's not like you're any better. You graduated, what, three years ago? You're still living with your parents."

"True, but I go to the skate park, where I meet people, and I've been helping out at Ricky's store to earn some extra cash. Since my parents will only pay for college if I follow their dreams, I have to pay my way to my own dreams. I meet enough people that come by in Ricky's store."

"Huh," Nate replied, a smile playing at his lips.

"If you want to meet some people, you should go down to the skate park with Colin," I told Nate.

Colin nodded in agreement. "Yeah, no kidding. You can meet some of my friends. They're not all that bad; some of them are actually nice."

Nate pressed his lips together. "Thanks for the offer."

"No, seriously," Colin said, standing up. "I'll give you some tips on skipping class if you'd like, and then you can come hang out with us."

"I'll think about it."

"Anytime. You should really be skipping some more classes at your age." Colin stepped around Nate, heading up the stairs. "But if you don't mind, I'm going to go put this up in my room now in an attempt to escape this terror of a party." He excused himself, leaving Nate and me alone on the stairs.

Eyeing the crowd I spotted a big cake sitting on the counter. Nate followed my gaze. "Want to go get some cake?"

I started down the stairs. "I'd be more than happy to, considering it's the only good thing in this apartment."

CHAPTER 3

After another hour or so, the party slowly started to come to a close. Colin hadn't come down from his room, so all the guests had taken to saying good-bye to me instead. I politely shook their hands, muttering thank-yous and good-byes as they left. Most of the conversation went the same way as the conversation with the Botox lady had gone, the men telling me Colin was a "fine young man" and the women commenting on how I should really try on some different outfits.

Nate leaned against the counter watching me, a plastic plate and fork in hand. I'm pretty sure he was on his third piece of cake by now, but I couldn't blame him. The cake was good. I wouldn't have expected any less from my mom; the cake was multilayered, with a crème spread in between each layer. It was decorated with frosting, sugary decorations, and blue icing that read "Happy 21st Birthday, Colin." However, I'm sure Colin hadn't had any of the cake.

As the last group of guests said their good-byes and made their way to the elevator, I saw my parents, and they did not look happy. Spotting Kelly and Andrew himself, Nate quickly stuffed the last piece of cake in his mouth. "I think I should get going …" Cake crumbs fell out of his mouth as he talked.

I frowned. "I thought you were going to take me to Brooklyn."

"I will." Nate squeezed my shoulder. "Just hear your parents out first. After that you can give me a call and head over."

"And why should I call first? I thought you said you didn't have any other friends to hang out with."

"Just in case," Nate said while putting his plate on the counter. He looked up at me with a familiar smirk. He always gave me that look when he was up to something or playing with me. He had been giving me that look since kindergarten. "Maybe I'll go hang out with my girlfriend."

"Your girlfriend?" I could hear the tone of disbelief unintentionally slip into my voice.

He made a face at me. "What? Why would I not be able to have a girlfriend?"

I raised my eyebrows at him as he walked past me toward the elevator.

"Fine, I don't have a girlfriend. But that makes me a loner since you're my only friend, which instantly also makes you a loner. So I wouldn't be rocking that judgmental look of yours too quickly." Nate's eyes twitched to the side, glancing at something behind me. I didn't have to look back to know my parents were approaching.

"I have to help my dad with something anyway," Nate continued. "I'll see you soon."

Giving me one last encouraging smile, Nate stepped into the elevator with the last of the remaining guests. My heart sank down with the elevator as I stood alone in my apartment. I inhaled deeply, letting the cool air fill my lungs. Then I turned around to face my mother, who had her hands on her hips. A few single blond strands stuck out of her otherwise neatly pulled-back hair.

"What do you think you're doing showing up in casual clothes to a party like this?" she exclaimed, her voice shrill. "Seriously, Renn, carrying a package? That's the doorman's job," she continued. I'm pretty sure she didn't even know that Stan was his name. She probably just saw him as another employee.

Kelly turned to her husband. "I'm going to launch a complaint against that guy; he doesn't do anything we say!" she continued in the same breath. She crossed her arms, making a superior *humph* sound.

I slammed down the cake I was still holding, making the plastic tremble on the counter. "That won't be necessary, Mom. Stan offered, but I refused to accept his help." I pushed myself past her to walk away, but her thin fingers grasped my arm. I winched as one of her rings scratched me.

My mother's shoulders raised as she took a crisp breath. "And why is that? Renn, I've told you before: we have money. You pay people like the doorman to do things like that for you."

"Well, I don't want to accept that either," I said, trying my best to hide the slight tremble in my voice.

A sour expression crossed her face. It was an expression that I knew all too well. "Say something about this, Andrew!" She turned to Colin, who was just making his way down the stairs. "Or Colin, talk some sense into your sister!"

Colin's eyes widened when my mom noticed him. He quickly shook his head, keeping quiet. Some of his blond hair fell in front of his eyes. My eyes raced to my dad as I heard him suck in a breath, hesitating. He looked confused as he searched for words. "Renn, let your mother ..."

"Let my mother what?" I interrupted, cutting him off. "I'm not going to let my mother decide my life like she does with Colin. I'm sixteen. If I don't make any decisions myself, I'm going to be stuck here forever. And you know the only reason that Colin is here and hasn't gone off to college is because you want him to study law, and that is the one thing he doesn't want to do." I turned on my heels, grabbing my coat and bag off the rack on my way to the elevator.

I was almost there when a firm grip grasped my wrist. I looked back rapidly to start another rage, but my anger drained slightly as soon as I met Colin's eyes. All of his happiness that I had noticed before was gone; he only looked sad. I mentally hit myself. Why did I have to go and ruin his birthday? He deserved so much better; he looked like a lost puppy. Sometimes I wondered if Colin was really twenty-one; he looked younger, and his eyes always showed more sadness than a guy his age should have.

"Don't leave," he whispered while leaning toward my ear. "Hear them out for once. It'll make them happy."

I stood there, with Colin holding my wrist, considering my options. My mind felt like slush. All I could think about was leaving, escaping this nightmare. Leaving down the elevator felt like a much better option. But then the same thing would happen that always happened. I would leave, feel terrible, come back thinking things might change, and then they don't and everything happens all over again a few days later. What would be the harm of hearing them out for once? I would do it for Colin at least.

"Renn, consider what your mom is saying," my dad said, stepping forward before I could think of anything to say. "What's the point of having money and not spending it?"

I placed my bag on a nearby table. I took a deep breath, trying to calm myself before I said anything I would regret later. "Why do you always take sides with her? You don't even care about living here; you'd be fine living outside of the city. You're just here for her."

"Renn, don't—" Colin whispered sternly, but I ignored him. I wasn't going to stick around just to pretend like I was the bad guy.

"Seriously, Dad! Make your own decisions." I felt my voice rising. I tried to lower it, but when I continued to speak, it only came out harsher. "Don't let her decide your life like she does with Colin and me."

Disappointment shot through my mother's face. It was another emotion that I often saw on my mother. I remember the first time I ever saw it: in first grade when she asked whom I wanted to invite to my birthday party. I had told her I wanted to invite Nate—nobody else. She asked about my other friends, but I told her I didn't have any. The same look she was wearing now appeared on her face. I think it was because I didn't want to invite any of her friends' kids.

"Renn, I'm just trying to figure out what's best for you," she said quietly.

"Then why can't you see I'm not happy?" I pleaded, lowering my voice as she had hers. I couldn't say I didn't feel a little bad. "Why can't I just be a normal teenager?"

"You are a normal teenager, Renn. Wearing a dress for a party once in a while won't hurt," she replied gently.

I crossed my arms. I could feel the anger bubble inside me. "We always have parties, Mom! You just want to stay on top of your self-created social ladder."

My mom's face turned dangerously red. "I did not create a social ladder, nor do I wish to be on top of that."

"Yes, you do!" It felt like the rage bubble had popped. All my emotions from the past years seemed to come up to the surface, gasping for air. "You always want us to be formal, not do anything that causes us to use energy, you want us to throw stupid parties, and you pretend like you own our future," I sputtered out.

My mom turned to Colin. "What do you think of this?" she asked forcefully, her eyes trying to hint the answer that she was trying to get. Colin came to stand next to me and nervously scratched his head.

"She may have a point …" he said, rocking on the balls of his feet.

My mom's eyes turned misty, glinting in the light. "She may have a point?" she repeated softly.

"Maybe if we give them more freedom?" my dad said, looking at my mom carefully. "Stop with the parties?"

Kelly turned to her husband. "I am not stopping with the parties. My friends enjoy them!"

Out of the corner of my eye, I saw Colin roll his eyes disappointedly. He was hurt too, but he didn't say it.

"Can't you see my point, Mom? It's all about you."

My mom ran her hand through her hair, making it stick out of her bun. It gave her a frantic look. "That's it! You're grounded! Three weeks, no exceptions. Bring it up again, and I'll double it."

"Don't you think that's a bit harsh, Mom?" Colin interrupted.

My mom took a step forward and lifted a finger at him. "You too. No exceptions."

Colin's eyes widened in surprise. "What did I do?"

"You agreed with your sister," Kelly said with a slight smile of accomplishment. "You can say good-bye to that skateboard too."

"Dad, you're not going to say anything about this?" Colin gasped in disbelief. I knew he had always agreed with me, but he had always been afraid to admit it. He looked at Andrew. Our dad stood there with a blank expression. "Not even a reply?"

"Enough, Colin." My mom turned to look at both of us. "Both of you, go to your rooms."

"That skateboard is the best present I have gotten in years!" Colin took a step forward, blocking my direct view of my parents. He casually moved his hands behind his back, and then he started pointing at me. My parents couldn't see it; he did it in a way that only I could. I tried not to look too confused so that my parents wouldn't tell that anything was off. He pointed again, more forcefully this time. I turned to look over my shoulder at the elevator behind me. The elevator. Colin was pointing at the elevator. Of course he was.

I slowly grabbed my bag, trying to make the least amount of noise possible. I inched myself toward the elevator, taking only small steps at a time. Colin took a step to the side, blocking me from my parents' view. My mom was too occupied with Colin, and it was no surprise to me that my dad didn't notice. He wasn't the observant type.

"You have never given me anything as good as that!" Colin was saying, his voice close to shouting.

"Colin, I said enough!" Our mom yelled furiously.

I pressed the button on the elevator, and the doors immediately opened. I shifted my bag on my shoulder as I stepped into the elevator. I fought myself, trying not to want the last word for once, but I couldn't help it. "No, Mom." I clenched my fists to stop my hands from shaking. "You have said enough."

My mom's eyes widened, and her cheeks flushed. "Don't you dare go down that elevator, young lady!"

"Watch me." I smiled. I was more than glad to be getting out of there. Looking past my mom, I saw Colin smile.

"Good luck!" he yelled. "Love you!"

"Colin!" My mom's shrill scream filled the room. "Andrew, do something about this."

My father sprinted toward the elevator doors, but they were already closing. He wouldn't make it in time.

"Come back," he yelled through the last open sliver of the door... "I know it can be hard sometimes, but …"

The doors closed before he could reach me. I didn't care. I didn't even want to know what my dad was going to say. My knees buckled, and I sank to the floor. Silently I let the tears roll down my cheeks.

CHAPTER 4

I heaved myself up from the ground as the elevator arrived at the fifteenth floor. The doors slid open, and I crossed the hall over to the building elevator. Eyeing the panels I noticed that all three elevators were still on the first floor. I groaned; this was just what I needed. I pressed the down button, desperately hoping my parents hadn't followed me.

I rocked on the balls of my feet while tapping my fingers on the sides of my thighs. The elevator that was coming up to get me was going dangerously slow. It felt like there was an hour between each time the floor number showing on the panel increased by one.

I couldn't run into my parents. It would be pathetic, and I was not in the mood for another lecture. My mom would drag me to my room by my hair. She would put me on lockdown, and it wouldn't surprise me if she hired a personal bodyguard to follow me around between my room and school. I rubbed my eye, and my fingers came away wet. I sniffed, trying to get rid of the remaining tears.

I glanced behind me at the penthouse elevator, and I saw that the doors were still open. My hands started to feel clammy. It would only be a matter of time now before my parents would be able to come after me. Why hadn't I thought of that? A soft *ping* sounded, and the elevator doors started to close.

Thoughts swarmed in my brain, but I couldn't seem to fit the pieces together into one idea. There was a flash of green light to my right. An exit sign hung above a door. It was the emergency exit, meaning a staircase. I took a deep breath, trying to regain it. My vision started to spin. Was this what a panic attack felt like? Was I starting to hyperventilate? I couldn't tell.

Exit sign. Stairs. I ran my hand through my hair. The stairs went down to the first level. Colin and I used to run up and down them when we were younger. The door wasn't armed with an alarm. I could run down. I looked down at my hands. Through my blurry vision, I couldn't tell if they were shaking. My eyes focused on a piece of hair that was stuck between my ring and middle fingers.

Stairs, right. I looked at the penthouse elevator. The doors were halfway closed. It seemed like time had slowed and like I was moving through water. I would never make it down fifteen flights of stairs in time. The elevator behind me was on its way up. It would arrive when my parents would, and they would meet me down at the lobby at the same time. It would never work.

Before I knew what I was doing, I raced forward, sliding my foot between the almost closed doors of the elevator. I grunted, feeling the pressure of the doors trying to close the empty space on my foot. For a moment I thought the doors would close anyway, crushing the bones in my foot on the way. But then I felt the pressure release, and the doors opened, waiting for someone to press a floor button. I stepped inside and pressed all of the buttons from fifteen through twenty-four. Something had to hold up my parents. I felt a lump start to form in my throat. I tried desperately to push it away, but it persisted.

When I stepped back into the hall, the doors of the newly arrived, building elevator opened. I quickly got in and pressed the button to take me down to the first floor. The last thing I saw before the doors closed was the elevator panel on the other side of the hall; the elevator was rising up from the sixteenth floor, and it stopped again at the seventeenth floor.

I leaned back against the elevator wall and ran my hand over my cheek and up to pull some hair behind my ear. My fingers came away wet, smearing some of my fresh tears across my face. I desperately tried to stop my tears, but they kept coming—like there was no switch to turn off the flowing faucet. *I won't cry*, I scolded myself. *Not until I get away from this place.*

The doors of the elevator opened, and I hastily walked out. Instead of entering the lobby, I collided with an elderly couple. I glanced up at the panel and saw that we were only on the eighth floor.

"Sorry," I muttered, taking a step back.

The old woman smiled. It made her wrinkles disappear momentarily, and there was a sparkle in her eye. "That's okay, honey. No worries."

As soon as the old couple entered, the doors closed, and the elevator started to descend. I avoided looking at the old lady, but I could feel her gaze on me. The old man leaned against the wall of the elevator, a cane in hand. He was wearing one of those berets that old men wear, and he had a frail face, which gave him a tired look. The woman, on the other hand, looked far from tired. She carried a handbag, which had two knitting needles sticking out on one side. From what I had seen earlier, she had wrinkles, but they seemed to be hidden by her energy. It was like she had an aura of happiness around her, infecting everyone she met by her presence. Everyone except her husband, who had probably spent his whole life with her trying to calm her down when she got too excited. A small gold band was worn on each of their left-hands' ring fingers.

I dared not look at the old lady; I was resisting every urge to look up to see if her infectious smile would cheer me up. After another moment of silence, the woman spoke up.

"You're such a beautiful young lady." Her voice was soft. "What a bummer to see your beautiful face ruined by such tears."

When I looked up at her, she smiled sadly. The old man glanced at me but seemed more interested in the elevator button panel. I heard his soft raspy breathing echo through the enclosed space.

I sniffled a bit, shifting my weight from one foot to the other. "I wasn't crying." I looked down at my feet. The carpeted ground was covered in patterned spots. They reminded me of teardrops, like one of my tears had rolled off my face and made the imprints on the floor.

The old lady let out a slight laugh. "Your eyes are all red and puffy. I remember when my kids were younger; they never wanted to admit that they had been crying, especially when they reached their teenage years. Kids always think it's embarrassing to admit that they are upset or are crying over something. They're afraid others will laugh, so they lie about it. But mothers can always tell when their children are upset and have shed a few tears."

"Yeah, well … my mother can't." I fidgeted with the necklace I had around my neck. It had a charm in the shape of a heart. I had gotten it from my mother when I was four. I barely remembered it, but it seemed to be the only loving memory I had of her. I had even gotten the chain lengthened when I grew and the necklace didn't fit anymore. I remembered that my mom had kissed the charm before tying it around my neck, saying that the heart was a reminder that she was always there for me. A lot had changed since then. I resisted the urge to rip it off then and there. Even though I hated the way my mother acted, I still wore it as a silent wish. A wish that my mother would return to her old self, the way she had been when I was younger.

There was a soft *ping*, and the elevator doors opened. I let the old couple exit first, and then I followed them out into the lobby. The old woman stopped when I passed her. Her husband noticed.

"Leave the poor girl alone," the old man grumbled as he headed in the other direction. A dull sound followed every time his walking stick tapped the floor. It ticked like a metronome that was set to 45 BPM. I turned to walk away, but the old woman grabbed my hand. I could feel the papery skin of her frail hand through my fingertips. She squeezed my hand, her grip surprisingly firm. When I held her hand, it felt like I would break her bones if I squeezed too hard, but she was strong. Her looks deceived her more than just her kind smile did.

A light shone through her eyes. "Life is full of obstacles, but in the end, it's all worth it. Everything works out. I've known you for longer than you know. I've lived her as long as you have, and seen you running through the halls when you could barely walk. You are a special girl. More than you think. You will achieve greatness, and yes, you do face troubles along the way. It is hard, but you have the strength to overcome them. You're no ordinary girl." The lady sighed. "Trust me."

"I might not be so sure about that," I said quietly.

The woman turned and started to walk away. Unlike her husband she was light on her feet, not making a single noise as she walked. "You'll see," she said back over her shoulder. She met her husband in the middle of the lobby, and when she reached him, she linked her arm in his. This seemed to give him some energy. His footsteps became less of a *thump*, but the tapping sound of his cane remained.

I watched as the elderly couple left the building. They seemed so happy, arms linked, not having any problems. Of course they had their age to worry about and probably also a variety of health problems, but they cared for each other. They looked out for one another like it was second nature. Even though the man was slightly grumpy, he had been happily married to this lady for who knows how many years. I didn't need to ask him to know that he was as happy as his wife, even though he might not show it.

The lump in my throat formed again, and my vision became blurry. I wished my life were that simple. I would do anything just to be happy. Like Nate's life, for example. Everything was so simple for him; he didn't need to worry about anything besides the latest homework or video game. His father let him do whatever he wanted, and his dad didn't think he was completely insane.

The *ping* of the elevator made me jump. The hairs on the back of my neck shot up, giving me goose bumps. I immediately spun on my heels, hoping desperately that my parents weren't the ones coming out of the elevator. I could already imagine the spikes of my mom's heels clicking loudly on the floor. But the doors of the lift were closed, and nobody was there. I let out an anxious sigh. I was more than grateful that it was a false alarm. I'm pretty sure I was starting to imagine things.

Entering farther into the lobby, I scanned around, finding it completely empty. Even Stan the doorman was gone. Pulling out my phone, I pondered about where to go next. I considered calling Nate. Automatically I started to dial the number; I knew it by heart. I'd known every phone number he'd ever had, just to make it easier when I called or texted him. It was a frequent activity of mine.

I pressed the call button, but I closed it before the first ring. I'd let him have some peace before dumping all my problems on him. Even though he was my best friend, what guy would be interested in sappy girl problems? No guy that I had ever heard of. I'm pretty sure Nate only listened anyway to be a good friend. He knew I had no one else to talk to about this, so he probably just went along with it to be nice.

An image from earlier popped into my head, from when he had offered to keep me company later and listen to my problems. Nate was a nice guy. He always seemed to know what to say, and he was up for anything. To this day I still wonder why he decided to hang out with me. He was plenty capable of being the popular guy, but he had no interest. Instead, he opted for hanging out with loser Renn. It was something I was greatly thankful for, and I wouldn't have it any other way. We knew everything about each other. Guys were much easier to talk to anyway. I had no interest in girly gossip.

I decided to go to Central Park first. I'd stroll around and filter my thoughts about what I would say to Nate. I wanted to spare him the rant. Plus, I didn't need to rush to his side immediately. I could handle it on my own for a bit. I scanned the lobby one final time before heading toward the door. There wasn't a witness in sight to tell my parents where I had taken off to.

Pushing open the door, the breeze hit me instantly. Cars honked loudly, and a siren wailed in the distance. Yellow blurs of taxi sped around, and hotdog venders were shouting the weirdest promotions. I headed to the corner of the street, to the crossing where I had stood earlier that day. The sight of Central Park made me stop. I stuck out my hand, and a taxi immediately pulled over. The smell of leather and tobacco overwhelmed me when I slid into the cramped seat.

I shifted in my seat and placed my bag on the floor. "To Brooklyn," I told the driver.

I leaned back as the engine started. The motor vibrated as the car started up. Sighing, I watched Central Park disappear in the distance.

CHAPTER 5

Buildings and trees passed in a blur of colors as the taxi sped around Manhattan. I tried to keep my thoughts to my surroundings rather than to my problems. Soon enough, the blurs were replaced by metal structures, with water looming underneath. Cars honked as the evening traffic kicked in.

I looked through the window and stared out at the dark blue colors of the East River. I could see a few tiny figures jogging past the banks of the river from where we stood. Sometimes Nate and I would follow the same path, strolling around the various playgrounds and sitting on the benches overlooking the river. We would talk about random things, like the ever-changing color of the tree leaves with each season or a couple we had observed while walking past. Nate snuck out of school once in a while, usually during lunch break, to stroll around here and calm his thoughts. He took me with him once, but I've been too scared of getting caught since. However, that day was the first time I really saw what people loved about New York. It gave you a vibe that you wouldn't get anywhere else. No other place would feel the exact same. The feeling would always be slightly off.

Stuck in traffic on the Brooklyn Bridge, I started to regret getting in the taxi. Why couldn't I let Nate deal with his own problems first? He had asked me to call first, and that was something he rarely did unless he had something important to do. He probably wasn't even home anyway.

My mind started to wander, reminding me of the fact that I knew where the Mannaros kept their spare key. I sighed deeply, knowing it was something I probably should do. I could let Nate be for at least a few hours, right?

But then my mind started to continue the thought. Telling me why I couldn't go without seeing Nate. I knew it was true, and I hated it. I wanted to be able to deal with my own emotions, but there was a sinking pit of sadness in my stomach that wouldn't go away unless I talked to him. I sighed, realizing that I needed someone to comfort me. I wasn't able to be comforted at home, so I sought it in Nate. No matter what problem I had, I could go to him with anything; and I knew that if he told me it was going to be okay, I would feel better.

I had considered running away before. I thought about it all the time. I thought about the different places I could go and went through a mental list of tactics where I could get money to live on. One option was taking Nate with me. He would even be crazy enough to do it, but I don't think his dad would be so happy.

The truth was something I didn't want to admit, but I didn't want to leave Colin behind. He had taken the role of the parent in my life when my parents weren't able to. He was the one who went out to get ice cream with me when I got a good report card. He had always been there for me, no matter what. To this day I still don't know if this forced him to grow up too fast. I always thought it was just something he was good at—taking care of other people. But lately, ever since Colin had reached this important stage in his life where he had to make future decisions, he had broken when he didn't get the support he needed. I blamed myself for not being there for him. That's why I couldn't leave him. If I couldn't help him, I could at least be there.

I just wished my life were as easy as other people's. My life wasn't normal. People offered to help me, but if I couldn't pay them, they told me to get lost. You couldn't tell who your real friends were. There were always those people who pretended to be your friends. Those were the people that left you stranded when you lost everything and needed the most.

Nate wasn't one of those people. He listened, comforted me, and let me have a shoulder to cry on. He'd always listened to me go on about my problems, while he probably had his own problems too. I'd try to talk him, but he didn't let much slip. Nate wasn't one with an easy childhood either. His mom had passed away when he was very young. Whenever I brought up the subject, he would dismiss it with a lame excuse. No matter how hard I tried, I never got him to budge. I always got the same reply. Car accident. I was seven. Don't remember too much. The end.

The cab inched forward, going at the approximate speed of a snail. I sighed and pulled my phone out. Three missed calls from my parents. Two texts—one from Colin and one from Nate.

"Be careful, Renn," Colin's read. *"Come back soon, okay? Let me know how you're doing. Don't let me go through you leaving for too long :). Love you."*

The tears felt hot to my skin. My gut wrenched in pain. The smiley face Colin had put in his text came across as a reassurance for me that it would be okay if I stayed away for a bit. But deep in my heart, I knew it was fake. Colin had put it in to make sure

I didn't feel bad, while he wanted me to come home more than anything. I made a promise to myself. I wouldn't stay away for too long. I would spend the night at Nate's, blow off some steam, and come back the next morning. One night would be okay.

I wiped away some of my tears and took a look at Nate's text. I felt my eyebrows knit together as I read, *"Hey, I just got a message from Colin."* Colin did think of everything. *"I don't know where you're headed but please be careful. Remember to give a call if you head over here ... Anyway just be careful.'*

Why was Nate putting so much emphasis on wanting me to call before I came over? What was wrong with coming over like I always did? It was okay if he had something to do, I got that, but wouldn't a quick text be sufficient?

My phone beeped loudly. I looked down to see that I had clenched my phone so hard that the volume had turned all the way up. Why did it matter to me so much? That was a question I had been asking myself for years now, about a variety of subjects. So what if Nate had a girlfriend? It was none of my business.

Of course he would have told me, right? My stomach filled with a sinking feeling. What if Nate was hiding something from me? It made me anxious just thinking about it. What could be so bad that he couldn't tell me? I told him everything; he should know that he could do the same. Even if it was, say, a drug problem. I would help him get the help he needed.

Leaning against the hard cushions of the backseat, I tried to calm myself. I was so upset that I was starting to make things up. I had to stop stressing myself out. If Nate had something to tell me, he would. When he wanted to, and in his own time.

A bump in the road shocked me out of my thoughts. Another few bumps passed as the taxi exited the bridge. Cars drove off in different directions, and the traffic lessened. My cabdriver slowed down while driving through the streets, entering a neighborhood close by.

I jumped as the car made a screeching noise. The driver grumbled something as he banged on the dashboard.

"Is something wrong, sir?" I tried to look over the back of the seat, but the plastic divider blocked my view.

The man shook his head. "No, nothing's wrong. Everything is perfectly fine." He grumbled some more. Then the taxi lurched back and forth a few times, making my stomach churn.

I eyed the speedometer. The arrow pointed at 12 miles per hour and was slowly inching backward. "I can get out if you want."

The driver spit out a bitter laugh. "No, that's okay. This garbage will be up and running in no time."

I shrugged. "I can pay you the money …" I jumped again as the car shook and a cloud of smoke came from the motor. The car lurched and jolted uncontrollably. Then everything went silent. The taxi stood still, and the screeching stopped.

The driver cursed silently and turned to me. "Your address is a few blocks that way. Not hard to find. You owe me twenty-five bucks."

I gave him the money. "Thank you," I said as I got out. The driver wasn't listening anymore. He was grumbling into an old phone. Probably the repair shop.

I slid out of my seat and got out of the car. The door creaked loudly when I slammed it shut behind me. I could see the effect of the motion vibrate through the vehicle. I turned around and headed down the street. I knew the place by heart. Nate and I frequently strolled down the street when we were bored of staying inside his house.

I pulled my jacket more tightly around me as I walked. A cold wind made goose bumps run up and down my skin. The temperature was decreasing fast. It had seemed like a warm day earlier, but when the sun disappeared, only coldness remained. The sun was slowly making its way down the horizon in the distance.

I passed an old abandoned park. Nate and I used to play on the playground when we were younger, but it was in a bad state now. Kids rarely played there anymore. Bits of rust peeled off the old slide. The swing set creaked as the wind moved it.

I felt my phone vibrate in my pocket. Pulling out my phone, I saw that it was my dad calling again. I quickly pressed the cancel button. I wasn't ready to face my parents just yet. If I talked to them now, I would most likely burst into rage. That wouldn't help my case. Maybe I'd call them later, or just the next morning.

I turned my phone over in my hand a few times, running my fingers down the side and over the volume buttons. I decided I would call Nate since I had my phone out anyway. If he wanted me to give him a call, why couldn't I?

I dialed the number and waited patiently as the phone rang. I walked another couple hundred feet but the phone kept ringing. Ringing until it was the only sound you heard and thought would never end. When it did finally stop ringing, I had already turned into Nate's street. It beeped quickly three more times, changing tones as it progressed. Then a computerized voice started to talk. *"Your call is now being forwarded to an automatic voice message. Please leave a message after the tone."*

I exhaled deeply as the phone beeped once more. "Hey, Nate, it's me." I felt a few drops of water land on my face. I looked up. The sky was starting to turn a dangerous shade of gray. I started to jog toward Nate's house, hoping I wouldn't get caught in the storm. I tried to keep my breathing even as I continued to talk into the phone.

"I just wanted to let you know that I'm headed to your place. I'm a few houses away, so I'll be there soon." I hesitated in an attempt to catch my breath. My jog was slowly starting to turn into a sprint as the rain picked up. The heavy drops made dark splashes on the light concrete.

"I know that doesn't really help; I should've probably called earlier," I continued. "I just really need to talk to someone. I … um, I'll be there soon."

I closed my phone and quickly stuffed it in my pocket. Water drops were smeared across the screen. Lightning flashed in the distance. The street was totally quiet except for the loud tapping of my feet. It was strange for a Saturday afternoon, but who knows, maybe there was a game on TV or something.

Rounding the last corner, I could make out Nate's house. I could tell from here that Nate's father's car was gone. Even though the car was from the eighties and was a broken-down piece of junk, the vibrant red color couldn't be missed. Nate's dad usually only took his car to work, and he frequently worked weekends. Maybe Nate wasn't even home. Nate had said that he had to help his dad with something, so maybe Nate had gone with Ben to work.

I ran past the last few row houses before Nate's. I was drenched to the bone. My hair was stuck together in strands that clung to my face. My bag was heavy on my back, presumably filled with water by now. When I got to Nate's house, I sprinted up the stairs in twos as quickly as I could without slipping.

All the lights were off inside the house, and the blinds were shut. I bent down and lifted up the side of the doormat. Underneath lay a small key chain, with a key attached. I never understood why the Mannaros hid their spare key under the doormat. There were probably many other places you could hide it with a less likely chance of it being stolen. Yet it never had been taken, and Nate's house was one of few on the street that had never been robbed.

Water ran off of the mat and over my hands. I grabbed the key and moved to stick it in the keyhole. I grabbed the door handle to stabilize myself. The rain had turned heavy quickly, and it was starting to make my eyesight go blurry.

Light flashed, and a crackle of thunder followed swiftly. I jumped in response, making my hand slip off the door handle. The door creaked loudly as it opened slightly. For a moment I stood in shock, key in one hand and rain pouring down on my head. When my hand had slipped off the handle, it had turned the catch out of place, but I hadn't expected it to open. I hadn't even put the key in the keyhole. Even though the Mannaros kept their key under the doormat, they weren't stupid enough to leave the door unlocked when no one was home.

I stepped inside and closed the door behind me. I could hear the patter of the raindrops from inside the house. They made the house seem hollow, empty. Everything was silent expect for the patter. The floorboards creaked under my foot as I took a step forward.

I flinched as a loud creak sounded from inside the house. I stood frozen for a moment, knowing for certain that the sound hadn't come from me. Which meant someone was inside the house.

"Nate?" My voice echoed through the deserted hall. "Ben?"

No reply came. I placed my hand on the wall and trailed it along the rough surface as I walked. I couldn't make out anything in the hall except for a dark shape of the stairs ahead of me. When I had walked far enough that the stairs were on my left, I knew that the living room entrance must be on my right.

And I was right. Soon enough my hand ran over the doorframe and into the air. I placed my hand on the wall inside of the living room and started to search for the light switch.

Another creak sounded, closer this time. I could feel my heart beat in my throat. My hand shook as I searched for the light switch.

"Where is it?" I whispered to myself through clenched teeth. I knew that the light switch was here; I had turned it on a million times before. Why couldn't I find it?

The noise of a low whimper made me stop in my tracks. All the muscles in my body froze. I couldn't move; my breathing became rapid and heavy. Everything seemed quiet, but I was sure I heard something.

The floorboards groaned, as if being put under heavy weight. The whimper sounded again. I looked around, but it was too dark to see anything. The hairs on the back of my neck stood up, goose bumps forming on my skin. The whimper hadn't sounded human; it was more animallike. But Nate didn't have a dog.

Panicking, I quickly ran my hand along the wall to find the light switch. I felt sick to my stomach. My shaking hand passed over something plastic. I moved it back and felt around. I flicked the switch. Nothing happened.

My stomach churned. Something was terribly wrong. Why wasn't the light turning on? I knew I was facing the living room, but that was it. A buzzing sound rang through the apartment. Then the light flicked. Once. Twice. Three times. I could make out some of the furniture.

It was dark again. I heard something move. I tried to move, but my body wouldn't follow. All my instincts told me to run, but I was stuck on the spot.

The light blinked once more, this time staying on. Relief spread through my body, but it didn't last long. As soon as my eyes adjusted and caught sight of what was inside, panic and fear replaced relief, running through my body like wildfire.

Standing in the living room, next to the couch, was a wolf.

CHAPTER 6

I stumbled backward, my body's rushing attempt to get away. My heel got caught as I tripped into the stairs behind me. Pain shot through my lower back as I fell on one of the steps. A wolf. What was a wolf doing in Nate's house? My chest ached; I couldn't seem to catch my breath. I tried to move; the door wasn't that far away. My limbs were unresponsive, and I couldn't feel my legs. It felt like I was moving through water.

The floorboards creaked as the wolf took a step toward me. Its yellow eyes stared straight into mine. An emotion shot through the wolf's eyes, if that was even possible. They had the slightest tint of green in them, and the piercing look warned of danger.

I tried to scream for help, but the words hung in my throat. I placed my hands on the steps behind me in an attempt to push up, but I was shaking so much that the strength wouldn't come. I tried to remember if I knew anything about wolves, but of course not. I had probably read a book about them in grade school, but the information hadn't been important. Now I definitely wished I remember something. A fact like what caused them to attack.

The wolf took another step forward, creating waves in its fur. If I hadn't been so scared, I would have noticed its beauty. It had a strong figure, with thick brown fur covering it head to toe. Its bright eyes seemed to examine me with fear—or anger. My wolf knowledge didn't extend far enough to know the difference.

It took another step forward. It was past the couch now. Only a few more steps, and it would reach me. I couldn't breathe. I felt around my pocket for my phone and clenched it tight. I didn't dare take my eyes away from the wolf.

I watched as it licked its muzzle. Then it opened its mouth, baring some huge canines. A low growl escaped through them. If the wolf had been okay before, it definitely wasn't happy now.

Panicking, I looked down at my phone. I tried to dial a number, but I couldn't remember Nate's. Or Colin's. Or even my mom's. I tried to hold still, but my body was rapidly taking in oxygen. I looked down. My eyesight was blurry. I couldn't seem to make out any of the numbers. My fingers shook as I tried to go to my contacts list.

Before I could get any farther, another growl left the creature's body. I jumped, dropping my phone. I could faintly hear it drop in the background, but I was too distracted by the wolf.

All of its muscles had gone rigid. My body seemed to follow; all of my limbs stopped shaking, but my heart didn't get the memo. It raced in my chest, and my breathing didn't slow.

Then the wolf kneeled down, bowing its head. Only its eyes looked up, still gazing at me. I held my breath. If it was going to lunge, I would never be able to move in time.

The wolf shuddered, its thick fur dancing. It leaned back farther so that most of its balance was on its hind legs. Its front paws lifted off the ground. That's when it happened. My whole body seemed to stop. I couldn't breathe, and my heart was caught. I couldn't think straight. Only one clear thought was running through my head. The wolf was starting to change form.

Right in front of my eyes, the wolf was proving the impossible. Animals couldn't transform into different creatures. Shape-shifters didn't exist. It was unbelievable; maybe I was starting to hallucinate. Isn't that something that extreme fear does to you? What in the world was a shape-shifter doing in Nate's house? Did he know about this?

I watched the creature in awe. It stood on two feet now and continued to morph until it had turned human. And that human was my best friend.

Nate rushed forward, clamping his hand over my mouth just in time to stifle a scream. My vocal cords finally worked, and the sound got muffled in Nate's palm. I thrashed around, trying to move, but Nate held me in place. I tried again to push him away, but he was too strong. I wasn't going to give up. My mind buzzed, and the first good idea popped into my head since I had entered Nate's house. I didn't have another option.

Nate's hand tasted gross and salty as I sank my teeth into his palm, biting him. Nate flinched, and he pulled his hand back, examining it. He frowned. "What was that for?"

In the second of his confusion, I pushed him away and scrambled. "Get off me!" I screamed. I ran toward the direction of the door. I banged into the wall, but I didn't care. I needed to get out.

I flung the door open and raced down the steps. They were slippery and wet. Drops of rain splattered on my face as I sprinted down the street. I didn't even pay attention to the direction. I could hear Nate's footsteps echo loudly on the steps behind me. "Renn, come back! I can explain."

I continued to run. I didn't even want to hear Nate's lie. There was no rational explanation for this. It wasn't possible. My breathing became heavy, and my feet ached. I felt like falling apart. But I needed to get away. I would not stop running. Even though Nate was probably ten times more fit than me, I would run until he gave up.

"Renn, I'm sorry!" Nate wouldn't give up easy. "Please, just give me a chance."

"Shut up!" I screamed back at him. My voice came out shrill and shaky. Water streamed down my face. I couldn't tell if it was rain or tears. I saw that Nate was close on my heels as I rounded a corner. I tried to pick up speed, if that was even possible. Nate was soaked too; his T-shirt clung to his chest, and his hair was drenched. He looked like a wet dog.

Dog. Wolf. Nate was a wolf. Not just any wolf, some weird, shape-shifting wolf. I don't even know what he was, but it was something that only came up in fantasy stories. My feet tapped the floor loudly. I passed house after house, sometimes seeing Nate in the reflection of one of the windows. It only gave me energy to keep running. This was insane.

"Renn, stop!" Nate shouted after me. His voice was stable, and he didn't seem to be struggling for breath.

"Get away from me!" I could feel a lump start to form in my throat. Or maybe it was already there, and I hadn't noticed. I didn't want to cry, but I could feel tears making their way down my face. None of this was normal. Nothing in my life made sense.

I could hear Nate's footsteps close behind me as we rounded another corner. I couldn't tell if I was slowing down. Tears and rain were blurring my vision.

"Renn, please, just stop running," he pleaded. "Hear me out."

I shook my head. "No."

"Look, I know you're upset," he continued. "This is why I didn't tell you, Renn. I knew you would run. Everyone would."

"Stop talking," I gasped.

"Renn, I'm sorry. I know this is hard to take in …"

"Hard to take in?" I screamed over my shoulder. "It's hard to take in that my parents decide my life. It's hard to take in that my grandma died a few months ago." I struggled to get enough breath for the next few words. "But this isn't even close to being comprehendible."

"Renn, I know, I understand. I'm sorry." He hesitated. I didn't have to look behind me to know he was contemplating on what to say. But I knew him too well. I knew what he was going to say before he said it. Nevertheless my world seemed to come crashing down when he spoke.

"Renn, I just didn't want to lose you."

My knees buckled mid-run, and I collapsed, all of my muscles giving into the pain at the same time. This was all too much. It felt like fainting, but I was still conscious.

I expected to hit the hard concrete, so I braced myself for the impact. But Nate was there like he always was. I hadn't noticed how close he actually was while we were running. He caught me in his arms, and I collapsed into him, momentarily forgetting everything that had happened.

He cradled me, slowly bending down to take a seat on the curb, placing me next to him. His shoulder supported my head, and I ended up in the crevice of his neck. Everything came out in a blur of emotions, and I sobbed. I tried to speak, but Nate shushed me.

"Don't talk. Everything is going to be okay." His strong arm supported me, and he moved his hand to pull some hair out of my face and behind my ear. "I'm so sorry, Renn."

I gasped, attempting to get words out anyway. I could feel more tears well up in my eyes. "Just don't ever scare me like that again." My voice barely came out. It was a soft whisper. But Nate heard. Either he heard, or he knew me too well.

He squeezed my shoulder and smiled sadly. He looked down at me, his green eyes meeting my gaze. "I won't. I promise."

CHAPTER 7

Pulling away, I sniffled and wiped away some of my tears. I inched away from Nate slightly so that I wasn't touching him anymore. I wasn't ready to forgive him just yet.

Nate sat on the ground next to me, staring at the street. He had a strange expression on his face that I couldn't seem to make out. His usually brown hair looked a shade darker through the rain. Drops of water clung to his face and dripped off his chin.

I looked up at the sky. A few drops landed on my face, but it wasn't much. The rain had almost passed. The clouds were starting to break in the distance, and only a slight breeze remained. The breeze pushed some crumpled brown leaves across the street. Puddles remained next to the sewers, and water accumulated under car windows from the water rolling off them. The faint sound of driving cars could be heard in the distance, but that was it. The rest was silent.

"So …" Nate started, but his words trailed off. He looked down at his hands, avoiding my gaze.

I crossed my arms. "You owe me a big explanation."

Nate shrugged. "Figures." He picked at one of his fingernails. "I wasn't really planning on you finding out about this whole thing."

I stared at him, momentarily lost for words. Nate looked tired, exhausted even. There were dark circles under his eyes. It looked like he hadn't had a proper night of sleep in ages.

"So, what are you? Some shape-shifting wolf creature?" I asked, even though I knew what answer I would receive. I had seen it with my own eyes.

Nate sighed heavily and scratched his head. He looked away, still not meeting my gaze. "The scientific term would be werewolf."

My jaw dropped. "A werewolf?"

"Yes." Nate sighed.

"A werewolf? So you're not even human? What species would that fall under?"

Nate turned to me with a glare, his green eyes blazing. "Yes, Renn, I'm a werewolf. I'm perfectly human besides for that fact that I turn every full moon."

I looked up at the sky again. The streetlights had just turned on, and the sky was getting dark. The moon was barely visible through some clouds. It was close to being full, but definitely not a full moon. "It's not a full moon tonight."

Nate rolled his eyes, and they widened as he did. "No, Renn, it's not. I noticed."

"Well, I'm sorry. I'm not familiar with all of this whole werewolf process. Heck, I didn't even know they existed until ten minutes ago." I felt my voice rising.

"I understand that you have questions. I just need to figure this out."

I felt my jaw tense. "*You* need to figure this out? How long have you known about this? Your whole life? And you didn't bother telling me?"

"Renn …" Nate started. He looked upset, but I pretended not to notice.

"I'm your best friend, Nate! Why didn't you tell me?" Everything was trying to process in my brain. My best friend was a werewolf. Great. I watched as Nate stood rapidly.

He ran his fingers through his hair. It was something he frequently did when he was frustrated. "Stop making this so hard for me, Renn! Don't you think I wanted to tell you? Don't you realize how difficult this is for me? I know exactly what I want to say. I've been rehearsing it, in my head, ever since I met you."

I groaned, receiving a weird look from Nate in response. "Then why didn't you tell me?"

"There are laws, Renn. If I could have, I would have told you the day we met. I would tell everyone and scream it from the rooftops, but I don't think it's accepted in society that there is a teenage werewolf running around." He started to pace in front of me. "There are days I just want to tell you everything. About me, my dad, this world I'm living in. The problem is that I can't," he continued.

"Why can't you?" My voice came out in a whisper.

"Like I said, there are laws. Humans aren't supposed to know about the occult. It's against the law to tell someone."

"I can keep secrets, Nate."

"I'm sure you can." There was a hint of sarcasm to Nate's voice. I ignored it. This wasn't the time to joke. Nothing about this was even remotely funny.

"Now that I saw it with my own eyes, you can tell me everything, right?" I asked. I'll admit, I was curious. There was no way Nate was going to get away with this without telling me anything. "If I discovered it myself, you technically didn't tell me, right?"

Nate frowned. "I suppose so."

"If I discovered it myself, then it's not against the law."

"Laws are tricky, Renn. You always get caught, no matter how hard you try."

"Why are you so hesitant to tell me? Is there a problem?" I stuck my hand out. Nate grabbed it and pulled me up.

He shrugged. "Of course there's a problem. I'd rather not get in trouble with the law."

"But no one will know that you told me."

Nate placed his hands on my shoulders and started to steer me back toward the direction of his house. I hugged my jacket more tightly around me as we walked. The cold evening air went right through my jacket and chilled me to the bone. "You have no reason not to tell me, Nate." My teeth clattered as I walked. Nate glanced at me, but I smiled in response, trying not to show that I was cold so that he wouldn't change the subject.

"You're not going to give up, are you?" Nate shivered. I could see his skin through the wet spots on his shirt.

I rolled my eyes. "You can't just drop a bomb like that on me without explaining the rest."

The corners of Nate's mouth curved upward. "Are you sure you're up for that much storytelling? It'll blow your mind."

"I'm sure my mind can't be blown more than it already is. Is the story really that long?" I joked.

"You wanted to know everything." Nate grinned. "But yeah, if you want all the facts, it's a long story."

I smiled, knowing a pleased look would appear on my face. "Tell me everything."

We reached Nate's house, and he stepped back, letting me up the steps first. "In time I'll tell you everything," he said while opening the door. It was still unlocked from earlier.

"Why in time? Can't you just tell me everything now?" I asked, turning the light on in the hallway. Entering the living room I saw that everything was just the same as it had always been. Relief flooded through my body.

"Well, as I said, it's a long story." He walked into the kitchen. I sat down on the familiar couch, curling my legs under me. I waited silently as I heard Nate open the cupboard and grab something. Soon enough the earsplitting sound of the teakettle filled the room. I heard Nate pour water, and he came back inside shortly, sliding the kitchen door closed with his foot. He walked over to the couch and handed me the cup. I cupped the tea in my hand, the steam warming up my face. I slowly blew away some of the steam.

"First questions first." I started, taking a sip of tea. The boiling water stung as it slid down my throat, but it eased the prickling feeling of coldness. I looked at Nate. "How do you keep your clothes on while changing into a wolf?"

Nate, who was drinking, coughed, choking on his tea. He laughed, smearing the back of his hand across his mouth, clearing away the liquid. He looked away as his face turned a shade of red. "That's an interesting question to ask first," he said while placing the tea on the table in front of him.

I shrugged, taking another sip of tea. "I'm curious."

Nate picked up his tea again, downed its contents, and placed it back on the table. His face was slowly turning back to its normal color. "Well, we have special clothes, I guess." A slight grin played on his lips. "I never really put much thought into it, but I think my dad had a warlock put a spell on it or something."

I didn't even notice I had dropped my tea until the glass shattered across the floor and tea spattered the side of the couch. I barely had time to look at the broken glass before the words started to flood out of my mouth. "A warlock? What do you mean a warlock?" I shouted at him. "What other weird creatures exist?"

Nate stared at the broken china on the ground, avoiding my gaze. "Maybe we should clean that up," he said.

I stared at him. "Nate, tell me the truth. Stop ignoring my question."

Nate stood, moving toward the broken cup. "You know, we should really clean that up. Someone could get hurt if they stepped on it. Plus, my dad would kill me if he found a tea stain on the side of the sofa." He made a move to bend down and pick up the glass, but I reached out and grabbed his wrist. Nate looked down at my hand. "That hurts."

"Nate." I felt the heat rising to my cheeks. "What did you mean when you said warlock?"

"Did I say warlock? I didn't hear myself say warlock. Why would I say warlock?"

I glared at him. "You said warlock all right."

Nate pulled his wrist free from my grasp and let himself fall onto the couch next to me. "Fine, you got me; warlocks exist. So do all those other creatures that you read about in books and see in movies."

"What is that supposed to mean?"

"Well, it's not like I was bitten, and the only species around are humans and werewolves. There's more."

I thought back about all those books I loved to read and the movies I had watched as a kid. The monsters that always used to creep me out and keep me awake at night were actually roaming around. "Wait," I said slowly. "Does that mean Dracula exists? Vampires exist?"

"Not Dracula per se, but vampires, I guess." He leaned back onto the couch, reaching up to pinch the bridge of his nose.

"You mean there are blood-sucking people walking around on this earth?"

"Yes … Well, they stay hidden. If they don't have a daylight tattoo, they should know better than to go walking around in the daylight and be turned to ashes." Nate sighed.

"Daylight tattoo?" I felt my eyebrows knit together. Nate seemed so casual about all of this. This terminology was all new to me, and he wasn't doing a very good job explaining things.

"Look, Renn, I'm not a vampire expert. All I know is that if they have access to a sorcerer, they get a daylight spell put on them or something like that. It leaves a mark on them, kind of like a tattoo. It lets them walk in the daylight."

"So they stay away from garlic too?" I hesitated, repeating what Nate had said in my head. "Sorcerers?"

"No, the garlic idea is a butchered tale. There are instances when humans come across the occult, and they get scared. Tales are made up, and they can't tell the reality from the truth. That's when stories like Dracula are invented.

"Hundreds of years ago, when people and the occult used to life alongside each other, things didn't go well. The humans felt threatened, so they started to turn against each other. Evildoers provoked them, and there were horrible wars. After peace was restored and all that, the leaders at the time decided to split into sections, and from then on the humans were kept out of the occult world."

"But how are wars hidden? How do humans not notice?" This made no sense. I'm pretty sure I would notice if someone had two teeth marks in the side of his or her neck.

Nate chuckled. "You'd be surprised. The human leaders at the time decided that it would be best not to tell anyone of what had occurred. Some people had their minds erased. Others decided never to speak of it again. It's all very complicated and would require a whole history lesson to explain." Nate slid himself off the couch and started to pick up the pieces of glass. I watched as he carefully picked up the shards and placed them in the bottom of the cup, which was surprisingly still intact.

"Huh." A gasp escaped through my lips.

"You have to understand that people went through horrible times. There were losses; cities taken over. People wanted to forget the past. It's easy to forget if you try. It's the same with noticing small details about the occult walking around. If you don't want to believe, it's easy to miss the signs of reality." Nate stood and disappeared into the kitchen. The glass shards clanged loudly as they landed in the trash can. When Nate returned to the room, he turned away from me, toward an old piano in the corner.

I watched as he took a seat, and the cover creaked loudly as he opened it. The Mannaros had had the upright piano for as long as I remembered. Sadly, Nate rarely played anymore. I used to beg him to play for me, but I had given up a long time ago because he always refused. Now I wondered if he just played to distract himself. His playing always seemed to distract me.

I had always wished I could play too. Nate used to try to teach me short songs, but I wasn't the musical type. It was much better listening to him.

I took another sip of my tea as Nate's music filled the room. The music started slowly, notes playing individually but flowing into each other at the same time. Nate's posture instantly relaxed, and he started to move to the rhythm. His shoulders were relaxed but powerful.

I'd never heard the song before, but it took me in instantly. The rhythm flowed like a current of water, smooth but intense. It made me forget about everything for a moment. All my worries momentarily pushed out of my mind.

I stood up and walked over to the piano. Without taking his eyes off the keys, Nate scooted over, making space for me on the bench. I watched as his fingers flew over the keys, not missing a single note. I stared at the keys, letting the slow beat of the music overwhelm me. The sound echoed through the whole of Nate's house.

I could feel Nate's eyes studying me. He continued to play, slowing down only slightly to avert his gaze. "I know what you're thinking," he said. "You're wondering how we stay hidden."

"You know me well," I replied softly.

Nate smiled. He looked down to play a few notes and then looked back up to meet my gaze. "Well, besides from the obvious fact of trying to act as human as possible, here in New York we have a law that we aren't allowed to let humans know about our existence. It's a universal law, but it's been enforced in New York due to some past complications. That's where my dad works. They have a special department, which they call the occult section. It's where they keep themselves busy with things like that."

"So, there's this guy that runs a whole city of magical creatures."

Nate nodded. "Basically. His name is Michael Larson. He's a strange guy; his methods are off. He keeps his focus on some artifact and hired others to deal with the law. It occurred to him that he's after something valuable, so he has my dad and the pack looking for it."

I stared at Nate. "Your dad and the pack?"

Nate sighed heavily. He played a few last notes on the piano and then stopped, closing the lid. He leaned his elbow on the cover and put his head in his hands. "I told you there was a lot to tell." He yawned. "But yes, there is a pack, and my dad is the leader or alpha, whatever you call it."

"So, you're saying that there's a whole pack of werewolves here in New York?"

"Renn, there's a whole occult section in the government; there's more than just a pack."

I rolled my eyes. "I'm sorry. I'm still trying to wrap my head around everything. Is that a problem for you?"

Nate smiled, but it didn't follow through his eyes. "No problem." He hesitated. "You know Ricky, the owner of that skater shop you went to earlier?"

I nodded, getting a bad feeling in the pit of my stomach. I had a feeling that I knew where this was going.

"He's in my dad's pack, and he helps the government. It's where he gets the money to run his shop." Nate grinned when he saw my expression. "I told you and Colin that I knew people too."

"So, you're not part of this clan?" I asked.

Nate shook his head. "No, I'm underage. I suppose that next year, when I turn eighteen, I can join the pack." He looked upset. "I'm probably not going to though," he said, looking off into the distance. "The government and Michael do some crazy stuff."

We sat silently for a minute. I yawned. This conversation with Nate had made me come to a conclusion. Maybe my problems weren't as big as Nate's. Everything with my mom barely seemed like anything. I would tell him about my family another time. I felt Nate's eyes on me as I yawned again.

"Well, you can sleep on my bed; I'll sleep on the couch," Nate said, also yawning himself. "If you want to know more of the story you'll need a good night's rest."

I pouted. "But you haven't even told me how you became a werewolf. Or a vampire for that matter. What if I get attacked in my sleep?"

Nate shook his head and stood up. He pulled me up from the piano bench and started to steer me in the direction of his room. "Nobody will attack you in your sleep. If it's any consolation, there is a warlock spell on the house that prevents any intruders. Only people that we know can come in."

I trudged up the steps. I tried to make my footsteps sound as heavy as possible. "You know that doesn't help? It needs more explanation. Like what is a warlock? What type of spell? And I've heard you mention sorcerer, so how come a warlock put a spell on the house? I don't get it. There's more to the story, and you need to tell me."

Nate opened the door of his room and let me enter first. "There's so much more to tell, Renn; you have no idea. Say, for example, if you want to know about my family, there is also more to the story."

"Of course I want to know!" My mind was racing with questions.

Nate pushed me on the bed. "I'll tell you tomorrow."

"Nate!" I yelled, sitting up on the bed. Nate was already outside closing the door.

"Goodnight, Renn," he said as the door clicked shut.

Silence. It felt surprisingly good after the day's events. I sighed, thinking that I was going to be awake for a long time. I was way off. As soon as my head hit the pillow, everything went dark.

CHAPTER 8

I squinted at the early morning light coming in through the window. It was sunny, and I could see the Manhattan skyline in the distance. Birds chirped, and everything else was quiet. Well, not exactly.

I rubbed my eyes, listening to the sounds coming through the closed door. Even though I was a floor above, I could hear people yelling. I could just make out the voices of two people, and one of them was definitely Nate. Stretching my arms I got out of bed. I shook out the covers and placed them neatly back on top. Stepping toward the door, I started to recognize the second voice. It was a rough voice that only one person I knew had.

I quietly opened the door, trying to make the least amount of noise possible. I carefully placed one foot after the other on the wooden floor of the landing, making sure no creaking noises followed. I took a seat on the top step of the staircase and listened. I could hear the conversation more clearly from there.

"Why did you tell her, Nate? You know it's against the law! Why would you jeopardize yourself, and my job, like that?" Ben nearly shouted. He sounded angry, and there was a trace of disappointment to his voice. It was an unfamiliar emotion for Ben. He always got along so well with his son.

"Dad, I already told you; it wasn't supposed to happen. She came without notice. I told her to call, but she didn't. I can't do anything about that," Nate replied, also not extremely happy with his father.

I frowned at the comment Nate made about me. I had called; he just hadn't answered. It wasn't my fault that I had walked in on him as a wolf. I had done what I was supposed to do. Hearing the sound of a blender, I realized that the conversation had stopped. Well, at least Ben had stopped replying to Nate.

I walked down the stairs and stepped into the living room. Nate sat on the couch, with one of the most frustrated looks I had ever seen on him. His hair was a mess, so he had obviously just woken up. He smiled an extremely fake smile when I came in. He had bags under his eyes, and the usual sparkle that was there was gone.

The blender in the kitchen turned off, and a man in his early fifties entered the living room. He held a smoothie in one hand that was the most disgusting shade of green I had ever seen. I could see small chunks floating around the liquid from where I stood. I quickly averted my eyes and cringed. Ben's hair was graying, but there were still traces of brown left—the same brown color of Nate's hair. It reminded me of the wolf's fur. Or Nate's fur, I guess.

Ben smiled at me, giving me a curt nod. "Hello, Renn, how are you this morning?"

"I'm fine, thanks," I replied. I had always liked Ben. He was calm and never made a big deal out of anything. Well, almost never.

Ben took a drink from his smoothie. "That's good," he replied, his voice sounding distant.

From the corner of my eye, I saw Nate run his fingers through his hair again, deep in thought. Eyeing Nate himself, Ben frowned. He took another sip from his drink, leaving a trace of green goop on the side of the glass. He took a seat in the armchair and motioned for me to sit down too.

Ben sighed as soon as I had taken a seat. "So, you know about the werewolf thing?"

Nate shot up from the couch, his face flushed. "Dad, just drop the subject already! I made a mistake. Renn isn't going to tell anybody."

Ben only shrugged. "There is a law, Nate. We have to do something about this, or we're all in trouble."

"Nobody will be in trouble if you don't tell them."

"Nate, I work there. They'll find out, and you know it," Ben said sternly.

Nate glared at his dad. "Not if you keep your trap shut."

Ben stood, facing his son. "Watch your words, young man. Or do you want to go tell Michael yourself about what you did?"

I quickly took a step forward. "If there is anything I can do to help, I'll do it."

"There is nothing you can do, Renn," Ben said, putting his glass on the table. He grabbed his jacket from a chair by the dining table and put it on. "It's better I tell them so that there are no big consequences. There might be a few, but that is completely up to my boss to decide."

With one last look at Nate, Ben strode out of the living room and out of sight in the entrance hall. Keys clinked together as he opened the door. The door slammed shut loudly behind him.

"If you don't tell him, nobody will know!" Nate shouted after him. Sighing, Nate sat back down on the couch. He looked up at me, his fingers making their way through his hair again.

I took a seat next to him. "That's up to you," I replied, looking at him.

"What more do you want to know about my life? My dad is obviously pretty serious about this werewolf stuff, but I don't see the problem in telling you." Nate yawned as he waited for my answer.

I pondered this. "How do you become a werewolf? Do you have to get bitten or something? Do you turn at full moon or just whenever you want?"

Nate smiled in response to my questions. "We turn on the night of the full moon. It's the only time our body forces us to turn. Other than that we can choose when we want to turn, like yesterday, for example, when I had to help one of the wolves out, so I changed and ran there. But that is only possible when you're in control."

"Which means?" Nate really had to start explaining his terminology.

"Well, for starters, it is a wolf instinct, so if you're not in control, you can't change at will, and during a full moon these instincts take over." Nate twisted the rope bracelet that he had on his wrist. "Control can be taught, but only a few have ever mastered it. So, sorcerers invented these." He held out his wrist, showing me his bracelet. "They put a spell on a token of yours that prevents you from losing control during the full moon. This way we don't turn vicious and attack people. Most werewolves have these, as they're in the family. I believe it's actually another law here in New York that Michael has enacted. Every werewolf in the state needs a token, or they're not allowed in."

"For the safety of the people?" It seemed to make sense to me.

Nate grinned. "You got it." He smiled again. "But other than that, we become werewolves because it's in our genes; no bite, nothing. It's something that is passed down through the generations. It's in our blood. My dad is a werewolf, Grandpa was a werewolf, and so on. It's not like vampirism, where you get bitten."

"See!" I exclaimed. "I was right. I could have been attacked and turned overnight."

Nate laughed. "True, but it's unlikely. Plus, like I mentioned last night, we had a warlock put a spell on the house to protect it. It was a gift from Michael when my dad became the pack leader."

"The same warlock that enchanted your clothes?"

Nate grinned. "We have our connections."

I sat silently, which made Nate laugh. He was laughing too much today. "You want to know why my dad is the alpha?"

I nodded rapidly.

"Well," Nate hesitated, eyeing me carefully. "He killed the previous alpha."

I felt my eyes widen so much that they felt like they were going to pop out of my head. "He what?" I exclaimed.

Nate's expression was blank until he exploded into a fit of laughter. "That was amazing." He laughed some more. "Should've seen your face!"

"Nate!" I slapped his arm.

"Ow." Nate rubbed the spot where I hit him. "I'm kidding." He grinned. "It's just a coincidence. My dad is experienced, that's why. This has nothing to do with it, but apparently my mom's family was powerful to the werewolves a long time ago. Not sure why though; I never really asked my dad. It's what I overheard once." Nate shrugged, apparently not really knowing an answer himself either.

"But I was right," I repeated, ignoring the remainder of Nate's grinning.

Nate looked up at me, his eyebrows furrowing together. "What do you mean?"

"I could have gotten bitten by a vampire, even though you have a protection layer on your house?"

Nate rolled his eyes. "We're back at this again?"

"Well, if werewolfism is in your genes, then what is vampirism?"

Nate crossed his arms. "Well, like I said earlier, I don't know much about vampires. I've heard that they get turned through their bite, but they don't complete the transition until they've fed. If they don't feed, they end up in this weird, in-between state, where they eventually die without blood, because human food won't satisfy them. Once they are fully turned, that's that."

"Huh." I looked up at the ceiling. "What about warlocks? And what are sorcerers?"

"Warlocks and sorcerers are both born the way they are. Sorcerers are humans that can practice magic. Warlocks are the nonhuman versions of sorcerers. They don't practice a specific kind of magic, only general spells. Sorcerers often do spells that involve going against nature, like making a bracelet against the transformation. While warlocks do things such as protection spells. The simple stuff. Often sorcerers have traces of warlock blood in them, and therefore they can be taught magic and end up becoming more powerful than the warlocks."

I nodded slowly. I pursed my lips, considering the next question. "So, when was the first time you turned into a werewolf?" I asked but immediately regretted my question when it had left my mouth. Nate looked away, and his expression turned dark.

He frowned. "Speaking of my mom …"

I shook my head rapidly. "If you don't want to tell me, that's fine," I added quickly.

Nate shook his head. "No, it's okay." He cleared his throat. "All kids that are werewolves get signs before the turn. Turn moody, things like that. Parents can usually tell when their child is about to change. An average werewolf turns for the first time when they're about four. I didn't get any signs, nor did I turn at that age. My mom's side of the family are werewolves too, but the genes can skip a generation. This happened to my mom. She wasn't a werewolf. It's like this strange flaw in nature.

"Anyway, I didn't change when I was four, so my parents thought I was like my mom. They just assumed the genes had skipped another generation."

I thought about this. "And your dad didn't mind being the only werewolf in the family?"

"No, my dad didn't like being a werewolf at all. He hated the idea of being able to lose your mind and hurt innocent people. He was glad that I wasn't like him. He's accepted it now and uses it to his advantage to help people with his job. But deep inside he probably still despises it." Nate sighed, and a grim look appeared on his face. "So anyway, my dad didn't suspect anything. He started working for the government, and we were happy. Then when I was about seven, my dad went on a business trip, and my mom was home taking care of me. Everything was perfectly fine until I turned."

I watched Nate's hands turn into fists. He looked miserable, and his eyes became misty. I got a bad feeling in the pit of my stomach. Nate was never this close to tears.

Nate gulped, and his breathing came out unevenly. "I killed her, Renn. I killed my mom."

CHAPTER 9

"I … I thought she died in a car crash …" I stammered. Even with everything I had learned the past twenty-four hours, I hadn't seen this coming.

Nate looked awful. Every trace of happiness from before was gone, leaving something broken in its place. His bottom lip trembled. "I lied." His voice shook. "I couldn't tell you the truth because I would expose myself. But … I … Renn … I killed her … my mom."

"Nate, it's not your fault. You were young, and it was the first time you turned." I placed my hand on his shoulder in an attempt to comfort him, but he shook it off, recoiling from my touch.

"I bit her, Renn." Nate spoke softly. "Even though humans don't turn when they're bitten, they get poisoned. I poisoned her so much that it killed her."

"Nate, stop hurting yourself like this …"

"Renn, you don't get it." Nate stood, interrupting me mid-sentence. "I remember the look on her face. I was weak, so she was able to pull me off. New werewolves don't turn for full nights until they reach their teens, so because it was the first time I turned, I turned back. She collapsed on the ground and held me. She stroked my hair, and the look in her eyes ... it'll haunt me forever."

"Nate ..." I started, but Nate ignored me again.

"My dad came home that evening, and I remember it so well. I was sitting on the ground, holding my mom, bawling my eyes out. I was scared to death, sitting in a pool of my mom's blood. An injury I had caused. My dad was frozen in shock. Seeing the bite mark I had made ... the look on his face said it all. He picked me up, and the two of us sat next to my mom the whole night, not knowing what to do. It's the only time I've ever seen my dad cry."

Nate sat back down, and I placed my head on his shoulder. I felt a few tears fall on my head.

"And it was entirely my fault," Nate said softly, sniffling.

"Nate, your dad forgave you, and he loves you. So did your mom, and she knew it wasn't your fault," I said while squeezing his shoulder.

"Yeah, well ..." Nate hesitated. "Every year on her birthday, he doesn't seem all that happy with me," he spit out bitterly.

"He is, Nate. Trust me." I ruffled Nate's hair, making it even more of a mess than it already was.

Nate smiled slightly. We sat in silence for a minute. Then he stood. "I've had enough of these stories for a while. You go change, and I'll go make breakfast," he said, changing the subject.

I nodded, and Nate headed toward the kitchen. I heard him blow his nose, which made me sigh in response. Nate had killed his mom. It was all still slowly processing in my brain. It wasn't something that made me not want to be around him; it just made me realize that not everybody's life was as simple and perfect as it seemed. Nate had had a rough childhood. It seemed so much worse for him than it would ever seem for me. So what if I didn't receive the perfect birthday present or didn't get to do the things that I wanted? At least I had both of my parents that loved me, or at least attempted to love me.

I stood up and headed up to Nate's room. Once there I opened one of his closets and grabbed the extra set of clothes that I kept at Nate's house. Entering the bathroom I examined myself in the mirror. My long, light brown hair was a mess, and random strands of hair stuck out all over the place. I fingered the ends of my hair, twirling them around my finger. My hair was slightly wavy, which was the only thing that would have looked good if it wasn't so messy. I had faint bags under my eyes, giving me an exhausted look. Two blue eyes stared back at me, the same blue eyes as Colin. A lump formed in my throat. I pushed it away. There was no time for crying now.

Grabbing the extra set of toiletries I kept there, I got to work. I washed my face and brushed my teeth. My teeth clenched together as I ran a brush through my hair. There was a clump right next to my ear, which looked like someone had grabbed it and tied a knot into it. I never quite understood how my hair got so tangled. Changing into the sweats and the T-shirt, I looked in the mirror. I couldn't help but nod in satisfaction. I looked much better.

When I walked back into the living room, I smelled eggs and bacon. The scent filled the room. Nate was just setting two glasses of orange juice out. He smiled as I put my extra clothes away in my bag.

"You look much better," he said. "No offense."

I stuck my tongue out at him. "Thanks a lot."

Nate laughed and gestured at the food. "I made breakfast."

Taking a seat on the couch, I put the plate on my lap. The heat stung my skin through the fabric of my pants. I picked up my fork and examined the eggs. They looked delicious. I cut a piece off with my knife and took a bite.

"It's really good!" I laughed. "Are all werewolves such good cooks?" I said, taking another bite.

Nate shook his head. "Nope, just me. My dad sucks at cooking. If he ever offers you one of his smoothies, don't take it. They're awful, I don't even know what he puts in them." A disgusted look appeared on his face. Then he laughed. "So, what do you want to do today?"

I thought about it. "I really don't know. You choose."

"Well …" Nate swallowed another bite of his breakfast. "You came here to talk about your problems, but you got mine instead. We can go up to the roof and talk if you'd like."

I frowned. "I don't know, Nate. Haven't we had enough problem talk in the past two days? We can go up to the roof, but I don't want to bother you with my stupid problems."

"Your problems aren't stupid," he said, taking another bite. "If you want to talk, we can talk."

I sighed. "Okay, but it's going to be light. I'm not going to be sad today. I don't want to be sad today."

Nate shrugged. "Fine by me." He picked up his plate and put it back in the kitchen.

"You finished fast," I commented, amused. "You must have been hungry."

Nate nodded, coming back out of the kitchen. "I was actually. Didn't have any dinner last night." He walked over to a laundry basket that was sitting on the dining table. He grabbed some clothes out of it and headed toward his room. "Be right back!" he yelled at me over his shoulder.

I sat on the couch and took another bite of food. So much was running through my mind. I wanted to know more about the magical world, but I also didn't want to bother Nate. I didn't want to make him as upset as he had been. Nate wasn't one to share deep feelings, especially something like killing his mother.

I sighed. I would leave the subject until late and hoped that my curiosity didn't get the best of me. I would just tell Nate what happened with my parents and keep the subject away from his mom.

That's when it clicked. It felt like two puzzle pieces had connected in my brain. That's why Nate always wanted me to fix things with my mom and why he was always so keen on helping me. He missed his mom terribly. Nate would never forgive himself if he let me leave my parents.

The loud echo of Nate's footsteps on the stairs surprised me out of my thoughts. I smiled at him, and he smiled in return. "Now what?" he asked. He waited for an answer, but he didn't get one.

"You're not much help," he continued with a raised eyebrow.

I shrugged. "I thought we were going up to the roof."

"Of course; I just wanted to make sure." Nate's phone beeped, and he took it out of his pocket. "Who knows? Maybe you changed your mind," he said while continuing to work on his phone. "I'll go get …"

"You'll go get what?" I asked. When Nate was younger, he always used to stop in the middle of his sentences. I had hated it. He had broken the habit awhile ago, but sometimes it still appeared.

Nate was silent. He stared at his phone. "Unbelievable," he muttered. Then a form of panic crossed his face. "I, um … different plan … we … I'll go pack … you wait," he stammered.

Nate ran back up the stairs to his room, his footsteps following him loudly.

"Nate!" I yelled after him. I followed him in a sprint. I glanced into Nate's room when I reached the landing. Nate was running around, grabbing random things I couldn't make out. I spotted his phone on the floor, and I bent to pick it up. When I turned it back on, I saw that a text was open, and I read it quickly.

"I'm so sorry, Nate," It said. *"They're coming after the two of you. I underestimated them. I don't know what they'll do, but it won't be good. I'm so sorry. Run while you can. Take care of yourself."*

I read it again to make sure. Someone was coming after us. Who would want to come after Nate and I, and for what reason? I went back a page to check the sender. Nate's dad had sent it. That could only mean one thing. Ben had told the government, and they were coming after us.

Nate sped back down the stairs, and I followed. He threw two duffel bags on the table and continued into the kitchen. He glanced at me. "You read the text?"

I nodded but soon realized that Nate was busy looking into some cupboards. "Yeah … So, what do we do now?" My voice shook slightly. The impression that I had gotten about the occult government wasn't very good; who knew what they were capable of?

Nate didn't answer right away. He took some food out of the refrigerator. He answered when he walked back into the living room. "We do as my dad said. We run. We leave this place and hope they forget about us." He slammed some stuff into a bag. "Why did he have to do that?" I heard him mutter to himself.

I walked over to him. Nate didn't notice. He was busy arranging things in his bag. "Do I have to help?" I asked.

Nate looked at me for a second. He started to shake his head but stopped. "Actually, could you go grab all the stuff that's yours? Then we can take that too."

"Of course," I answered and walked to Nate's room, grabbing my bag on the way. My clothes were already in there, so I looked around for some other things that I kept at the Mannaros' house.

I scanned the room, and a picture of Nate and me caught my eye. I picked it up and put it in my bag. I walked back to the door, but bumped into a desk on the way. A stack of papers fell to the ground, followed by a small crash and the sound of breaking glass.

I knelt down and removed all of the papers. Underneath some of Nate's latest school reports was a picture frame. I picked it up and carefully turned it around, shaking off the loose pieces of glass. In the picture was a small boy with striking green eyes and spiky brown hair. Holding him was a woman with the same lovely eyes. She was beautiful.

I had seen this picture before, but had never really taken much notice of it. The boy was six-year-old Nate. I had seen many pictures of Nate as a small boy, but something about this picture was different. The woman was Nate's mom. I had barely seen pictures of his mom, but I knew it was her. Was this the last picture Nate had taken with her? I glanced behind me to see if Nate was there, even though I knew he was downstairs. Everything was quiet. I decided to take the picture with me. Who knew where else it would end up if I didn't take it?

I grabbed my bag off the bed and glanced at the picture one last time. Something in the picture caught my eye. Nate's mom was wearing a ring. Not a wedding ring with a diamond or anything, but a silver ring that was clasping a marble. Usually there was nothing particular about a ring with a marble, but this one was different. I didn't know how, but it had a strange kind of glow to it, like it was important. I chuckled to myself. It was a picture of a ring. I was probably just paranoid about the whole situation I was in.

I put the picture in my bag and walked to the living room. Nate had tidied the place up a bit, and the duffel bag on the table was stuffed full. A hand grabbed my shoulder and turned me around. Nate pulled me into a hug.

"Renn, I'm so sorry," he muttered into my ear. "I hate myself for putting you in a situation like this."

I awkwardly pushed myself out of his grasp. "It's fine. It's not your problem," I replied, taking a step away. Nate shook his head, but I ignored it. "It's okay, really. I don't mind," I said. "But another thing, where do we go?"

Nate frowned, deep in thought. "We can't stay too long because my dad said they were coming for us. So we have to leave. I'll call a cab, and we'll leave Brooklyn."

I nodded, and Nate pulled his phone out of his pocket. He dialed a number and paced around waiting for an answer. After a while someone answered, and he told him or her the address. I assumed he got forwarded to get a taxi. I picked up one of the duffel bags from the table and placed it by the door. I put my own bag around my shoulder. Nate closed his phone with a click.

"The cab will be here in about five minutes. It's better if we go wait outside," he said, picking up the other duffel bag.

After one last look through Nate's house, I headed out the door and down the steps. I heard Nate lock the door behind me and also head down the metal steps.

"Where do we go?" I asked as Nate came to stand next to me.

He put the bag on the ground and crossed his arms. "What about your place?"

"Isn't that what the government expects?" I said. "They're probably already there."

Nate looked off into the distance. "That means Central Park and Fifth Avenue are also off the list." He laughed. "They probably have the whole of Manhattan covered already."

I sighed. "So the city is off the list. Any other places?"

"No, not really. We probably have to go to the other side of the state, if not out eventually," he replied.

An idea popped into my head. "Where were you born?"

Nate gave me a strange look. "Where was I born? What does that have to do with anything?" He hesitated and then chuckled. "Smart, Daniels, very smart. As you might know, I was born on Long Island, the Hamptons to be exact."

"Southampton?" I asked with a smile.

Nate nodded. "Southampton it is." He sighed. "Only some of my Mom's family is left there, but we lost contact with them after she passed. They don't like my Dad very much so there's no reason for me to go there. I'm betting Michael will look into other family first before heading there. He will eventually but it will give us some time to figure things out for now."

The taxi arrived less than a minute later. When we got in, the thick scent of hotdogs filled my nostrils.

"Southampton, please," Nate told the driver.

The driver groaned. "Seriously? That takes like … um …" Obviously not the smartest guy, he tried laughing it off. "A long time."

"Well, that's where we need to be," Nate replied.

The driver sighed heavily. "Well, it's going to cost you like …" I caught him frowning in the review mirror. "Money."

CHAPTER 10

"I told you that an opportunity would present itself." The sides of Michael's lips curved upward. His eyes had a wicked gleam to them. Luckily for him, everything seemed to be working out.

Hector coughed. "You have experience?"

"It's always the same with these kids." Michael sighed, but his slight smile was still present. "The number of offenses we have against the law that come from kids is beyond more than one would expect. You can just tell. Take my son, for example. You can always predict what is going to happen."

The car came to a halt, and the two men unbuckled their seat belts.

"What does Josh have to do with this?" Hector asked carefully. The sunlight from outside reflected on his glasses. A bead of sweat gleamed in the light.

"Josh has nothing to do with this, of course." Michael laughed. It sounded unnatural for him. "You're an investigator. You should be able to figure out things like this." Michael continued. "*It was an example.*" He slowly over-pronounciated the last few words, saying them individually instead of in one sentence.

Hector moved to open the car door, but Michael held up his hand, glancing at the investigator. "Stay in the car."

Hector took a crisp breath, but did as he was told. Michael got out of the car and straightened his jacket when he stood. He walked over to the Mannaros' house. A few people were walking in and out of the residence. There were also two wolves sniffing the perimeter. Ben stood at the side, watching everyone do their work.

"I assume the area has been locked down in case there are any observing neighbors?" Michael came to stand next to his employee.

Ben nodded. "A sorcerer has put an invisibility spell on everyone. Onlookers will see nothing out of the ordinary."

Michael looked around. "I take it that they aren't here anymore?" He asked, his hands in his pockets.

Ben glanced at his boss. "It seems that they have left."

"It seems that they have left? Well, apparently, because they are obviously not here anymore, are they?" Michael crossed his arms. "Did they know we were coming?"

"Not that I know of," Ben replied, avoiding Michael's gaze. "Maybe they just went out for a few hours. They'll be back."

"Will they now?"

Ben nodded. "Most likely." He looked over as one of the wolves passed him.

"Ben, the thing is, I don't think so." Michael held out his hand. "Give me your phone."

Ben looked at him. "Why?"

Michael narrowed his eyes. "Give it to me, Mannaro."

Ben slowly took his phone out of his pocket. "I don't see how this will …"

Michael snatched the phone away before Ben could finish his sentence. He pressed a few buttons and read something on the screen. "You told them we were coming."

"I work for you. I would never do that," Ben stammered. "I did no such thing."

Michael turned the phone around to let his colleague read the message. "Yes, you did." He threw the phone back. Ben barely caught it.

"Okay, here's the deal, Mannaro," Michael said, stepping toward Ben. "You and your pack are going to find Nate, or you're fired."

Ben's eyes widened. "Michael, I'm sorry, but Nate is my son! You would have done the same."

Michael shook his head. "I wouldn't have done the same for Josh. He deserves whatever's coming for him." He hesitated. "You are going to find Nate, understood?"

"They're a bunch of kids, Michael. Things like this happen. It's no big deal."

Michael rolled his eyes. "It's no big deal until the girl starts to tell people, and then we have a giant case on our hands with people finding out about the occult. We all know what happened in the past; humans don't cope well with information like this. We need to take the necessary precautions to make sure nothing gets out of hand. Even if it includes finding the girl and erasing her memories."

"Renn is a good kid." Ben looked like he was about to plead on his knees.

"Find your son, Ben. Soon."

Ben looked up and shook his head. Michael ignored it. He scanned the area, letting his gaze fall on a wolf walking by. He stuck out his foot and kicked its side. The wolf turned around fiercely and growled, but stopped as soon as it noticed it was Michael.

"Stand up, wolf," Michael said, motioning with his hand.

The wolf morphed into a guy in his early twenties. He had a pained look on his face, and he held his hand to his side. "Yes, Mr. Larson?" He grimaced.

Michael rolled his eyes. "Stop yammering. I didn't kick you that hard. What's your name?"

The guy grinned as he moved his hand away from his side. He smiled, but his eyebrows were still furrowed together. "Name's Ricky."

"So, Ricky, do you have any idea where our two runaways have taken off to?" Michael asked with a side-glance at Ben.

Ricky slowly shook his head. He gasped at the movement. "Nope."

Michael raised an eyebrow. "Any clue at all?"

The skater looked around. "Not really. The only thing we found was a smashed empty picture frame on the ground. Their scent has faded, so they probably left about an hour ago.

"Stupid traffic." Michael groaned, but quickly composed himself. "You're not much help. Go, move, do something useful."

Ricky turned around and quickly walked away. He limped slightly. None of the wolves liked Michael, except for maybe Ben. Even that wasn't a "like" relationship; it was more of a tolerating one. Michael knew this and tended to use this to his advantage. He did, after all, have the power to get them fired. Michael turned to Ben. "Find Nate, or you're out."

Ben crossed his arms, but stayed quiet. Michael chuckled as he walked back toward his car. He got into the passenger seat. "These wolves can be so useless," he muttered.

Hector shrugged. "I guess it's not their fault."

Michael glanced at Hector. "So, you're absolutely sure Nate has this marble? If not, then the only thing we're doing is setting up a wild-goose chase. And you know who won't be happy if we don't find it soon."

"I'm sure, Mr. Larson." Hector smiled. "I did a lot of research, and all signs point to Nate. The marble has been going around his mom's side of the family for ages. I even came across some pictures …"

Michael held his hand up to stop Hector mid-sentence. Hector looked confused, which made Michael smile to himself. "Pictures, you say?" Michael pushed a button, and the window next to him rolled down. "Come here, Mannaro!"

Ben walked over to the window. "Yes?" he asked, looking fairly annoyed that Michael hadn't left yet.

"What picture was in the broken frame?

Ben frowned. "What does that have to do with anything? It's none of your business."

"Just tell me." Michael stared straight into Ben's eyes.

Ben hesitated. "I'm pretty sure that it was a picture of my wife with Nate." There was a hint of sadness to his voice. "I don't see how this is important to you. Nate probably took it with him as …"—Ben swallowed—"something to remember her by."

Hector leaned forward to look past Michael. "Was she wearing any jewelry?"

Ben gave the investigator a weird look. Michael also looked troubled; he wanted to punch Hector in the stomach. He was only brining more suspicion toward them.

Ben stared straight at Hector. "Who are you again?"

Michael held his hand out before Hector could say anything else. "Just answer his question. He's into jewelry." Michael pretended to roll his eyes. He needed an answer.

"She was wearing a ring," Ben answered hesitantly. "Look, I don't see how this has anything to do with Nate breaking the law …"

Michael chuckled. "I try to do my best to look into everything, Ben; you know that." He smiled as kindly as he could. "Mind telling this jewelry freak what type of ring? It'll make him happy."

Ben still had a weird look on his face. "Just a silver ring with a marble. It was a family heirloom."

"Thanks, Mannaro. That will be all for today."

Ben nodded and turned around. He started walking back to his house.

"Find your son!" Michael shouted after him. He slowly closed the window. "You were right," he said turning to Hector. "They do have it."

"What now, Mr. Larson?" Hector asked as Michael started up the car.

"Well, the marble isn't here because I had some of my guys search the house. Nate isn't stupid; he probably knows about the marble and took it with him. I hope, at least." Michael sighed. "I'll get some guys to cover Manhattan. We'll go to the Upper East Side. After that we'll search Nate's family."

"Will do, Mr. Larson." The car started speeding up and rounded the corner.

As the two men crossed the Brooklyn Bridge, Michael spoke up again. "I hope they're there. We have to find it before his threat against us is enacted. That would end badly for everyone."

CHAPTER 11

I slowly opened my eyes. I squinted at the sunlight coming in through the window. I looked around and noticed that I was leaning on Nate's shoulder. He was awake and staring out the window. The thick scent of hotdogs hung in the air. Hotdogs. Within an instant all my memories came flooding back.

We were on our way to Southampton. We were running away because the government was after us. They were coming after us because Nate had told me his secret. My best friend was a werewolf. It was funny how one secret had the power to turn your life upside down. I guess that's why secrets are called secrets. People have secrets for a reason. It's not always good to know everything.

"Did you have a nice nap?" Nate asked. He must have noticed that I was awake.

I nodded and sat up. "It was refreshing."

"Refreshing ..." Nate repeated with a grin. He was in a fairly good mood considering the circumstances we were in. "We're almost there. We'll be there in about ten minutes."

I nodded but stayed silent. The rest of the ride stayed the same, silent, no one speaking a word. I didn't know what to say, and I assumed Nate didn't either. What was there to say? We were both in a heap load of trouble, with no solution. The only thing we could do was keep hiding until the government gave up on us. This could take a week, but most likely months, years even. I knew that Ben would never give up, and as long as he worked for the government, if he found us, we would get turned in.

How did I even get into this mess? Whose fault was it? Was it my fault for walking into the house without permission? Or was it Nate's fault for not picking up the phone? I chuckled to myself. It could even be Ben's fault for telling the government.

I didn't like the guy. Michael Larson was his name? I'd never heard of him before, but Nate had told me that he was an idiot. He was mean, arrogant, and kept himself busy with something other than his real job. Nate told me his real job was to make sure humans didn't come near the magical world. According to the Mannaros, that was not what he was doing. He was busy with some artifact.

Who cares? I hadn't even heard of him before. I mean, after Nate showed me a picture in the newspaper, I did recognize him from some TV spots with the governor, but I had always assumed he was the assistant or something. Now Nate was telling me he had his own department? You have got to be kidding me. He never spoke a word in interviews with the government. New York didn't even know he existed. It was probably for the best.

"Are you coming?" Nate held out his hand. He was standing outside of the cab with the bags at his feet. The driver was looking at me through the review mirror with an impatient look on his face. I grabbed Nate's hand, and he helped me out of the car. The driver sped away as soon as I closed the door. He was probably still mad at us for making him drive us all the way up here.

Nate picked up the bags, and we started walking. We walked in silence again. I felt Nate's gaze on me; I could see him looking from the corner of my eye. I tried not to look. We strode another few steps, but slowly came to a halt. Where could we go?

"Now what?" Nate asked, echoing my thoughts.

I shook my head. "I don't know," I muttered softly.

"Dammit." Nate threw down the bags. Dust floated up from the unsettled ground. "How many times do I have to tell you that I'm sorry?" Nate yelled in frustration. His sudden outburst made me flinch.

"I can't take this, Renn. I'm sorry, but you're just going to have to deal with it. I can't change anything. Don't you realize this is hard for me too?"

"Nate …" I started, but he ignored me.

He threw his arms up into the air. "Sure, say it's my fault, but I'm trying to come up with a solution. The only thing you're doing is staying quiet, probably hating me like crazy." His eyes flared but showed more sadness than anger.

Not knowing what to say, I said the first thing that popped into my mind. "Well, it is mostly your fault." I shrugged. *Bad idea, Renn.*

Nate stared at me. "Fine." He picked up the bags. "Forget it, Renn. Just forget it. Say what you want." He turned and started to pace forward. I followed behind.

Silence again. Time passed, but who knew how quickly or slowly? A gas station started to appear in the distance. I decided to speak up. "We should go …"

Nate cut me off. "Renn, I'm sorry. I'm sorry for everything. For bursting out, for putting you through this, for everything in the future … I really am sorry."

"Forget it, Nate. We're both stressed," I replied calmly.

It seemed to make Nate feel better. A slight smile appeared on his face. He moved his bag to his other shoulder and came to put an arm around me. "I guess we're off on some sort of adventure!"

I laughed. I could see the familiar sparkle return to Nate's eyes. He had humor; I'd give him that.

"Race you to the gas station!" He shouted. He gripped the bags tightly. I wanted to complain, but Nate was already off. I followed, chasing after him at full speed.

I ran behind Nate, my hair flying through the wind. Even though I was sprinting, Nate was still much faster. It must have been his werewolf genes. He hooted and started half-skipping half-running to fall back in line with me.

"Come on, Daniels. Make some speed!" He whooped with an amused look.

I glared at him. Then, for no apparent reason, Nate stopped running. He grabbed me from behind, and our forces colliding made me fall, taking Nate with me. We tumbled a bit, and I eventually landed on one of the bags. Nate rolled twice more and landed on all fours. Dust flew up around us from the path. Nate crawled over to me.

The instant we made eye contact, we both burst out laughing. I couldn't contain myself. My stomach ached, and my eyes teared up. When one of us stopped laughing, the other would just get us going again.

"That was fun." Nate grinned, exhaling loudly. He got to his feet and pulled me up. "You have got to work on your speed though.

"Well … I guess I'm not in good shape like you," I replied, putting my hands at my sides. I felt sweat drip on the back of my neck. The heat of the sun grazed my skin. It was warm for a fall day.

Nate chuckled. "You're in perfect shape." He picked up the bags and put them over his shoulders. He walked over to the gas station and opened the door. I ran to catch up.

A bell rang as the door closed behind me. At the end of the shop, I could barely see a figure that looked to have purple hair. Nate grabbed me from the side and pulled me along to the counter.

"I don't know what to ask," Nate muttered as we waited for the personnel to return. He shrugged. "I'm just going to ask for a motel or anything else they have here where we can spend a night."

I glanced at a clock that hung on the wall. It was already three o'clock. I had no idea how time had passed so quickly. I turned to Nate. "I thought you knew the place?" I asked with a laugh.

Nate rolled his eyes. "Sure, my parents moved to Brooklyn as soon as I was born, but I remember everything," he replied mockingly.

I laughed as the purple-haired figure came to stand behind the counter. She looked a little older than Colin. Maybe twenty-five.

"Can I help you?" she asked with a forced smile.

Nate read her name tag. The side of his mouth curved upward, and his mouth hung open before he spoke. "That's what I'm here for …"—he hesitated—"Hank."

The girl looked offended. "That is not my name, and you know it," she spit back at Nate. "I asked, can I help you?"

"Then what is your name?" Nate asked with a twinkle in his eye. He was teasing her.

"Well, for your information, my name is Zia, but that doesn't matter to you. You think you can just come in here and act like Prince Charming and get all the answers. Well, I'm not falling for that joke." She crossed her arms. "Now what do you want, Mannaro?"

Nate took a step back. "You know who I am?" A ghostly look appeared on his face.

"Your name is Nate, right? You look just like your father." She shrugged. "I used to be part of his pack, but I quit when Michael turned so idiotic." Zia hesitated for a moment. "The reason I got in his pack in the first place, though, is because we're kind of related." Her voice rose a pitch as she said the last few words.

Nate stayed silent, not replying to his newfound relative. I spoke up for him. "You're a Mannaro too?"

Zia shook her head, making her short, purple hair fall in front of her eyes. "No, I'm his second cousin, from his mom's side. I decided to move back to my roots when I quit my government job. Needed to get as far away from the city as possible."

Nate stared at Zia. "You really got upgraded, didn't you?" He hesitated. Zia glared at him. "If you'd gone in the other direction, you would've been able to go much farther away."

"And he acts like his father too." Zia looked annoyed. "You don't remember me, do you?"

Nate shook his head. "Well, I remember someone with blue hair."

"That was me."

Nate pushed his lips together, nodding his head. "Then I guess I do remember you."

"Good for you." Zia rolled her eyes. She nodded her head toward me. "So, why are you here?"

I didn't know what to tell her, so I looked at Nate expectantly. He was already talking.

"Because you're my cousin, I'm going to tell you things that you can't tell anyone else."

"Second cousin," I heard Zia mutter, but Nate continued. Zia nodded impatiently as he spoke.

"Renn here found out that I am a werewolf, so my dad, being with the government and all, went to tell Michael. Michael got mad and decided to come after us. So now, we're on a wild-goose chase."

Zia chuckled. "That's very inconvenient."

"Yes," Nate sighed. "So we need a place to stay."

Zia stayed silent. "I don't know what to tell you," she said, bending down and grabbing a map from under the counter. She unfolded it and placed it in front of us. Grabbing a pen she circled three places. "These two are motels, fairly cheap, but will become more expensive by the day," she said, pointing to two of the circles. "And this," she said, pointing to the last, "is an abandoned mansion."

Nate took the map and put it in his pocket. "Thank you."

"But I must warn you, all the places are worn-down, especially the mansion. There is a reason it's abandoned." She walked out from behind the counter and headed to the back of the store. "Good luck."

"I don't like her," Nate said as we walked out of the store. "There's something about her that doesn't sit right with me."

I grinned. "Of course not; she's your cousin. Families have feuds, right?"

Nate nodded slightly. "I guess you're right." He took out the map and started walking in a different direction.

"Where are we going?" I asked as I tried looking at the map over Nate's shoulder.

"The mansion," he replied simply.

I fell in line next to him. "I thought that place was worn-down."

"It is," Nate said, examining the map. "All of these places are worn-down, so if we have to choose between a place that's worn-down and a place that charges money and is also worn-down, I'd choose the one where you wouldn't have to pay."

"Why? The motels might have a cheap restaurant," I commented.

Nate laughed drily. "Because we shouldn't waste money. Who knows how long we'll have to hide. I'd rather pay for cheap gas station food for a few months than a good bed to sleep in for a few days."

I stayed silent. Nate shrugged. "We won't stay there too long; we probably have to find a better hiding spot soon."

We took a left, and the paved road turned to sand. Dust came up as I shuffled along the path. After a short while, the path started to curve upward. I looked up to find a big mansion. It stood at the top of a hill and overlooked a great deal of the town.

As we arrived at the porch, I noticed that Zia was right. The place was worn-down. Floorboards stood crooked, and the windows were covered with wooden planks. The wood creaked as Nate stepped onto the porch.

A crash sounded as the planks beneath Nate gave way and his leg went through.

"You okay?" I asked, stepping toward him.

"Yeah," Nate grunted when he pulled his leg out. A sharp piece of wood had ripped part of his jeans. He didn't seem to notice. "Follow me, but be careful where you step."

I followed Nate to the door. I watched his feet and made sure to step exactly where he stepped. He pushed the door open without any effort. At least we wouldn't have any trouble breaking the door down.

"The floor should be more stable in here," Nate said as he unzipped one of the bags. He took out a flashlight and switched it on. "Let's find a good room to sleep in."

We inspected the mansion. Well, the part of the mansion that was stable. When we entered the house, we came into a living room, which had couches that were turned upside down and tables covered in layers of dust. Besides that we found a rundown kitchen, two bathrooms, a bedroom, and a study. One of the two bathrooms had running water, and the bedroom was not an option because it was covered with bugs. The study was the cleanest of all the rooms, even though there were still layers of dust on everything.

"I guess we'll have to sleep here!" Nate said while dropping the bags on the floor. He knelt down and took out two sleeping bags.

I walked over and grabbed one of them. "What are we going to sleep on?"

"The floor," he replied simply. "Do you have a problem with that?" His eyes sparkled with amusement.

I frowned. "You mean the floor that creaks every time you make the slightest movement? Of course I don't have a problem with that. I won't go crazy at all!"

Nate shrugged. "It'll have to do. I'll try making my way upstairs in the morning to see if there's anything decent, but I can't promise anything." He winked. I rolled my eyes in response.

I spread my sleeping bag out on the floor and rolled up my hoodie to make a pillow. Nate did the same, placing his close to mine. He grabbed a packed-up sandwich and gave it to me. "Dinner," he said with a slight smile. "Not ideal either."

I shrugged and took a bite. It was one of those soggy store-bought sandwiches that taste gross. Mine had mushy tuna, so I couldn't help making a sour expression. Nate grinned, but we ate the rest of our meal in silence.

"When's full moon?" I asked while getting into my sleeping bag. I closed the material around me as tightly as I could. The temperature was starting to drop, and I was freezing.

Nate hesitated. I could tell that he was counting in his head.

"Tomorrow actually," he answered. "So you'll have to manage having me as a wolf for the night."

"Just the night? That's not so bad." I smiled. "As long as you don't snap your bracelet off and turn rabid."

"Don't worry; I've been doing this for a while. Everything will be fine." Nate looked at his watch. "How are you tired? You even slept on the way over here."

I shrugged in my sleeping bag, brushing against the material. I could hear the fleece rub against my clothes. "I don't know. I've had to process so much in my brain, I feel exhausted."

"I guess we do have to get enough sleep for tomorrow. If we want to find a better place, we'll have some hiking to do." Nate moved to get in his own sleeping bag. "Good night, Renn."

"Good night Nate," I said. I lay silent for who knows how long. By the sound of Nate's breathing, he was sound asleep. I sighed. I reached my arm backward and grabbed my phone out of my bag.

As soon as I opened my phone, the messages started blinking like crazy. I had dozens of missed calls and messages. I opened a text from Colin. *"Renn, I'm worried sick. Two men came to our house today and told us you were missing."* Of course, Michael had gone to our house. *"Where are you, Renn? I'm worried. Please just come back. We can work on Mom and Dad. I miss you like crazy. Please come back."*

A lump formed in my throat. Hot tears ran down my cheeks. Why couldn't it be that easy? Why couldn't I just go back? Why were they coming after Nate? What was so bad that we had to run away from?

I wiped some tears away. What would they do if they found us? I opened my phone and typed a quick message. *"I miss you too. I'll be back as soon as I can. Love you."* I clicked send. I owed my brother a message. Closing my phone I cupped my hand over my mouth to dull out the sound of my sobs. I tried to stop the tears, but they kept coming.

CHAPTER 12

I awoke to an incredible pain in my neck. I sat up and massaged my neck, trying to get the knot out of my muscle. I rubbed my eyes and realized that dried-up tears were stiffening my face. It made me laugh. I had been in a terrible mood.

I grabbed my phone, which was poking into my butt, and placed it back into my bag. Glancing next to me, I noticed that Nate was still dead to the world. The sound of his snores echoed through the room like a forest was being cut down. I quietly stood up and went to find a bathroom. As soon as I took a step, the floorboards groaned under my weight. Nate shot up out of his sleeping bag, his eyes wide.

"What's happening?" he muttered. His hair stood up in all directions, and I was pretty sure I could see a trail of dried-up drool on his chin.

I grinned. "Sleep does wonders to your hair, Nate."

Nate rolled his eyes. "Very funny, but you should also take a look at a mirror," he said, but not before running his hand through his hair and patting it down on the sides.

"Shut up," I retorted with a slight smile. I snatched my toiletries and headed to the nearest bathroom. Besides rust falling off the handle and having to use extreme strength to turn it on, the faucet seemed to be working. The running water appeared to be safe, as it wasn't yellow or filled with chunks. Grabbing my toothbrush I speedily brushed my teeth. Then I washed my face, scrubbing away the dried tears and sleep left in the corners of my eyes. I ran a brush through my hair and unknotted all the tangles. I examined the finished job in the mirror. I looked fine. Not amazing, but just fine.

Entering the study I saw that Nate had changed. He sat on his sleeping bag holding a square piece of paper. He was so focused on it that he didn't even look up when I entered the room. Behind him lay my bag, the zipper open and all of my things scattered over the floor.

"Nate!" I walked over and dropped my stuff on the sleeping bag. "Why'd you go through my bag?"

"What's this?" he asked softly, ignoring my question. He turned the small piece of paper around, showing me the front side. It was the picture I had taken from his room. "Where did you get this, Renn?"

I knelt down next to my bag and started to put all the things back into it. "Where'd you find it?"

"It fell out of your bag when I moved it. I didn't see it was open; I was only trying to clean up." Nate spoke softly. He was biting his lower lip, and it trembled slightly.

I couldn't say I wasn't surprised by Nate's reaction. He had the picture in his room; I hadn't expected him to get emotional about it. "I found it in your room when I was gathering my stuff. I decided to take it with me; I thought you might like it."

Nate gulped before he spoke. "I do. Thank you." He looked at me but quickly turned away when I caught his gaze. His eyes were rimmed red. He stared at the picture once more, running his thumb along the edge of it. Then Nate cleared his throat and stood, placing the picture back in his bag. "I'm going to wash up," he said, excusing himself.

I watched as Nate walked over to the door. He stood in the door opening, not moving a muscle. He glanced over his shoulder back at me and smiled awkwardly. I raised an eyebrow at him. Then without another word, Nate turned around and left the room, heading toward the bathroom.

What was he doing? My mind raced. Something was up with Nate. The situation we were in seemed to feed his sudden mood swings. Or was it his werewolf hormones? Was that even a thing?

I scooted off my sleeping bag and started to roll it up. I had placed most of my belongings in my bag already, so I started to search for some breakfast. I found a few granola bars, but other than that, we were out of food. I frowned to myself, and my stomach seemed to growl along with it.

"What in the world are you doing here?" a booming voice roared. I jumped, turning around rapidly to see if Nate had reentered the room—but there was no one there. The room was empty, no newcomer in sight.

"I said, what are you doing here?" the voice shouted again. The sound was strangely muffled.

I turned around again, trying to see where the sound was coming from. I felt my heart beat in my throat. "Who's there?" I shouted back, my voice shaking. Where was this person hiding?

The only furniture in the room was a wardrobe, a desk, and a few chairs. There wasn't a good hiding spot in sight.

Chills crept up my spine. "Where are you?" I asked, echoing my own thoughts. The person kept quiet.

"I asked who was there," I repeated, looking around the room once again, even though I knew I was alone.

"I asked *you* something first," the voice replied simply.

"Answer me!" My voice came out an octave higher. "Or else—"

"Or else what?" The voice seemed to grin. "You don't even know where I am. I don't know how you can hurt me, sweetheart."

"I, uh …" The words got caught in my throat. I clamped my hands to the side of my head. What if I was starting to imagine things? I probably looked like an idiot talking to an empty room. "Show yourself. I'll tell you why I'm here."

"Giving up so soon?" the voice sneered. I opened my mouth to call for Nate, but the voice spoke up again. "Don't even bother calling him; it won't help things."

"Please." I attempted to calm my breathing. "I'll tell you what you want to know."

The person snorted. "Making deals?" He laughed. "Whatever; you bore me anyway."

I jumped at the sound of a loud rumble. The dresser in front of me started to shake. I took a few steps back, tripping over one of the bags. I landed painfully on the ground, pain searing through my bottom.

Slowly, but loudly, the dresser started to move aside. I waited anxiously, my hands shaking at the thought. Someone was hiding inside the walls?

Peering behind the dresser, I saw that it was covering a hole in the wall. Some of the boards were broken right in half, and a piece was taken out. The floorboards creaked as the dresser moved the last few inches.

A small man came walking out of the hole. He fit through it perfectly, even though I would have to crawl in order not to hit my head. He was wearing a sort of purple suit, and it was covered in dirt. His face was wrinkly, giving him an old, wise look. The few gray strands of hair on his mostly bald head were caked in hardened soil. He seemed human, except something was off about his appearance. His ears were pointy, and his teeth were too spiky for human terms.

"No smart talk now, huh?" he said with a satisfied smile. Then he frowned. "Stop staring."

I tried to look away, but I couldn't. I couldn't help but stare. A bad feeling in my gut told me that this wasn't normal. Why was this person hiding in the walls? And where was Nate?

The man took a couple steps forward. "Got anything to tell me, sweetheart? Or are you going to threaten me again?" He seemed amused.

"Who … who are you?" I stuttered. I clenched my hands into fists to stop them from shaking.

The man frowned, even though his black eyes were filled with amusement. "I don't see how any of this is any of your business, but for your information … the name's Dale."

"Dale …" I repeated softly. I tried coming up with something smart to say, but my mind was blank. Dale seemed to notice.

"You don't have to be so scared, sweetheart. I'm not going to hurt you." Then in a sudden mood change, Dale's face turned red, and his eyes flared. He exhaled loudly. "I just want to know"—his voice filled with rage—"why *you* are near the entrance of *my tunnels!*" He shouted the last part, emphasizing the 'my tunnels' bit.

I cringed. I pushed myself off the ground and automatically took a step back. "What tunnels? I don't know about any tunnels."

"You're just saying that!" Dale shouted. Apparently he had a short temper. "Admit it! You work for the government, and you want me to give my tunnels up. Well, too bad! It's not going to happen. You can go running back to your boss and tell that to Michael."

I crossed my arms. "I don't work for the government."

"That's what they all say." He spat in disgust. "Too bad, sweetheart, you're just going to have to—"

Dale stopped talking at the sound of someone whistling. Relief flooded through me. Nate was coming. Glancing at Dale I saw that he had calmed down slightly; his face had returned back to normal color. However, his eyebrows were knit in concentration as he listened to the sound of Nate coming down the hallway. He didn't seem to be happy about the fact that I wasn't alone.

Nate walked in and closed the door behind him, not noticing the new company. He smiled at me and turned to look around. His things dropped to the floor with a loud *thunk* when he caught sight of Dale.

Nate stood frozen on the spot, staring at Dale. After a minute he turned to me. "So, Renn." He crossed his arms. Then he changed position and nervously scratched his head. "Where'd you find the goblin?"

My breath caught in my throat. Dale was a goblin? He looked like a small man with weird ears and a pointy nose. Nothing occult about that. Dale himself didn't seem so shocked. He pointed at me accusingly. "*You were lying.*" His voice was rising again. Then he pointed at Nate. "And *you*! What are you doing here, Mannaro? Did you follow your daddy to betray our world?"

I turned to Nate. "Why does he know you?" I whispered.

"I can hear you!" Dale shouted. "Everyone knows the Mannaros. Ben is Michael's right-hand man. You know he doesn't deserve it, doing all the dirty work."

Nate's nostrils flared. "Don't you dare speak about my father like that. And I am not betraying our world. As a matter of fact, we're running from the government." Nate picked up his stuff and threw it in his bag. "Now would you like to tell me what you're doing here, goblin?"

Dale rolled his eyes. "I have a name."

"I asked you a question."

"I told you that I have a name."

Nate took a step forward, his green eyes flooded in anger. Dale just looked amused. "Fine, what's your name, goblin?"

Dale's eyes twinkled. "Glad you asked. The name's Dale." He walked over to the dresser and hopped onto it. He crossed his legs and played with a book that was lying next to him. "I'm the boss around here. Keeper of the tunnels." He smiled.

"What tunnels?" I asked, taking a step toward Nate. I placed my hand on his shoulder to keep him back. He looked like he was about to launch at Dale.

Dale fingered a strand of hair. Dirt bits fell to the ground. "I am the keeper of the tunnels, sweetheart. I have tunnels, and I keep them." He cocked his head to the side.

"Goblins are stubborn, but also very loyal in nature," Nate started, as if that explained everything. "Most of them are employed by the government as leaders to keep track of different things. They are all in charge of something." He turned to Dale. "I've heard of you. My dad said something about you once. You're one of the only goblins in charge of something big that isn't owned by the government. Michael wanted your tunnels to become government property, but you fought to keep them."

Dale nodded. "So I did. I fought hard to keep my tunnels and still got most of them confiscated. Now, I'm not even allowed out of the East Coast." He spat in disgust. "As soon as I reach the border, alarms start blaring, and they come after me. Which they would probably only use to take the rest of my tunnels. And without my tunnels"—Dale hesitated—"I wouldn't have a purpose."

"Wait, your tunnels are big enough to lead out of the East Coast?" I asked. "How did you even manage to do all of that?"

Dale shrugged. "A little bit of digging, a little bit of magic; it's none of your concern. They lead everywhere, sweetheart. Up to Canada, across to California." Dale grinned. "I've worked on them since I moved here, which was a long time ago … By now I have a whole maze constructed under North America." He tilted his head up in pride.

An idea popped into my head. "So if you hate the government and Nate and I are running from them, you could take us to the border, right?"

Dale looked up, considering it. "I suppose so …" He spoke slowly.

I smiled. "Then it's settled. You're going to help us."

Dale looked blank. "Hold up, missy; I didn't agree to anything just yet."

"Yeah, hold up. I didn't either." Nate looked at Dale. "Is that even safe? And what if we get lost? You said yourself it was a maze. Most importantly, the border is really far from here."

Dale rolled his eyes. "Yes, it's safe; no, we won't get lost; and yes, Canada is far from here, but not in my tunnels."

"What is that supposed to mean?" Nate asked.

"That means"—Dale hopped off the dresser and went to stand in front of Nate—"that my tunnels are special. I had a warlock and a sorcerer combine some nifty spells, some basic, some ancestral, to make the distance between places much smaller. How else do you think I was in Boston two hours ago?"

I ran my hand through my hair. "Some what spells?"

Dale raised an eyebrow at Nate. "You haven't explained the different types of magic to her?"

Nate tapped his foot. "Haven't had the time," he muttered.

Dale chuckled. "Well, miss ...?"

"Renn," I answered.

"Miss Renn, there are different kinds of magic that exist. Warlocks only do basic spells. Sorcerers can practice either ancestral magic or dark magic. Most do ancestral; dark magic is the bad stuff. Things usually end up going catastrophically wrong."

"Huh." I shrugged. Even more new information to process. Apparently Nate had even more to tell me than he was letting on.

Nate stood silently, which amused Dale. He glanced behind him at the hole in the wall and shrugged. "Gather your belongings, and we'll be off."

"So where are you taking us?" I asked.

Dale considered this. "I'll take you up to the Canadian border, south of Montreal. I'll call a friend who knows Montreal and will take you there from the border. It'll take us a few days, three maybe."

"How do you know we can trust this friend of yours?" Nate asked, crossing his arms. He looked skeptical.

"He owes me a favor," Dale said simply.

Nate laughed. "So now we can trust him?"

"Look, Mannaro." Dale's voice came out harshly, and he slowly started to turn red. "He is the guy that lost me most of my tunnels. Since then he owes me a favor. If he doesn't do what

I ask, I tell Michael what he did that I took the blame for that resulted in the loss of my tunnels. And that would only mean trouble for him."

"And why would you want to be using that favor up on us?" Nate crossed his arms stubbornly.

Dale hesitated. "It appears that the three of us are all equally against Michael. I wouldn't want any one else to get caught under unreasonable pretenses. I heard about your little situation. There are rumors going around the occult world. I don't see any reason for the two of you to be caught. Plus, I feel like being nice for once."

Nate rolled his eyes. "Do you really?"

"As I said, I know your father Mannaro. I may have exaggerated before. Unlike Michael he fights for the right of the people. He stood up for my tunnels. Even though Michael won the fight in the end, it was due to Ben that I got to keep a section of the tunnels. I guess in a way I owe him a favor too. This could be my way to repay him.

"Fine," Nate considered this. His eyebrows knit together. "But why not take us to Toronto? Wouldn't that lessen the chance of Michael finding us since it's farther away?" I bumped Nate in the shoulder, and he gave me an angry look. I knew him too well; I could see through his cover. He was trying to find any excuse not to go.

"My dad often goes on business trips to Montreal, to talk to and do business with some of the occult. Michael will have connections there," Nate continued.

Dale glared at Nate. "Because I said so! For your information, my tunnels weren't the only things I lost. I'm not allowed back that way to Toronto; it's the only part of my tunnels on the East Coast that Michael has bugged! So, unless you want to get caught,

I wouldn't go that way," he shouted. Then, taking a deep breath, Dale straightened his suit, and his face slowly turned back to a normal color.

"I guess we'll pack?" I asked carefully.

Dale nodded, not meeting my gaze. "That might be a good idea."

Nate and I got to work. Not that there was much to pack. We put some of our loose items in the bags, and Nate rolled up the sleeping bags. Putting my backpack on my shoulder, I glanced at Dale. He stood next to the hole in the wall playing on a device. I could hear him muttering to himself. He seemed to be finding the direction that we needed to go in.

Nate put his bag on his shoulder and went to stand next to Dale. "We're ready to go," he declared.

"I'll take you to my home base first, to grab some necessary supplies." Dale's gray eyes sparkled as he looked at me, an amused smile appearing on his face. Then he pointed at the hole. "Ladies first."

CHAPTER 13

"I, um … okay," I stuttered. I looked at the hole in the wall. It was a void of darkness. I didn't want to go first. Who knew what lurked in there?

Dale snorted. "Go on, sweetheart; I don't have any vicious creatures hiding out in there." He smiled again, seeming to find amusement in everything I did. I glanced at Nate, who, probably still not convinced of the tunnels' safety, was drilling a hole in the wall with his gaze.

"Are you going to go or not? I don't have all day." Dale crossed his arms. "Actually, I do have all day, but I just don't have the patience." He smirked at his own comment, also finding himself rather amusing.

I nodded and took a step forward. The floorboards creaked under my feet. Securing my backpack over my shoulder, I knelt down to face the hole. I gripped the straps of my bag until my knuckles turned white. I glanced back at Nate and Dale once more. Dale nodded his head, encouraging me forward.

I looked at Nate, who still hadn't moved his gaze away from the wall. He stood with his backpack on his back and a duffel bag on either shoulder.

"Are you sure you don't need me to carry one of the bags?" I asked him.

"He'll be fine, sweetheart; he can manage," Dale said. Nate moved his gaze to me but still said nothing.

"The roof of the tunnel will get higher once you get to the intersection. Once there I'll take the lead. Tell me when you get there and watch your head. There are no turns; just continue straight forward.

I nodded my head in response. Getting on my hands and knees, I slowly crawled forward. Placing my hand in the tunnel, I immediately felt the dirt stick to my hands. A few stones pricked into my skin.

I crawled forward. Soon enough, the tunnel turned completely dark. I heard the last of the floorboards creak behind me, followed by a huge grunt from Dale. Something heavy scraped across the floor. He must have moved the dresser back in front of the hole. A strange click sounded, and the tunnel filled with a dim light. The light cast my shadow in front of me, making my figure seem like a giant blob. The light barely helped; there was nothing to see but dirt.

I continued to crawl forward, feeling a searing pain once in a while from a pebble poking into my hands and knees. I heard someone breathing behind me. The tunnel started to curve, and I ran my hand down the side of the tunnel to prevent myself from running into it headfirst. Dirt bits fell to the ground, and little pieces of gravel rolled down the sides.

The tunnel straightened out again, and I still couldn't see anything up ahead. I started to feel slightly claustrophobic. It was a cramped tunnel of endless darkness. Something hit my foot, and out of surprise I sat up straight. I grunted as my head smacked into the roof of the tunnel.

Dirt fell to the ground, covering me in a blanket of dust. My head throbbed from the impact.

"Sorry!" Nate's voice whispered from behind me.

"You don't have to whisper!" Dale hissed, his voice sounding farther away than Nate's.

"Then why are you whispering?" Nate spat back in reply. I could hear the hint of anger in his voice.

If I had been able to see Dale, I know that he would have been rolling his eyes. "I'm not, Mannaro. Now keep crawling!"

Silence. I made my way forward, farther into the darkness. Once in a while I bumped my head on the roof of the tunnel or slammed into the side when it decided to curve. My muscles started to ache. The skin on my hands was starting to break, and there was a hole in my pants, the gravel starting to stick to the skin on my knee.

After what seemed like hours of crawling, I began to see a light in the distance. I kept moving forward, and the light started to inch closer and closer. Dale noticed.

"That's the intersection. The roof of the tunnel should get higher soon."

I put my hand up, and soon enough I felt the roof of the tunnel start to curve upward. I slowly started to stand up, making sure not to hit my head. I walked forward, and once I could fully stand, I found myself in the middle of an intersection. There was a glow of light coming from a lantern hanging on the wall.

I stretched out my legs. It relieved the pain, but brought more at the same time. I dusted off my hands, scraping off the pebbles that were engraved into the skin. My skin stained red when I ran my hand over my knee; it stung, and I winced in response.

Nate came to stand next to me. "You okay?"

I nodded. Nate was covered in dust, giving him a faint brown glow. Dirt clung to his hair, and a trail of blood ran down the back of his arm. I grabbed his wrist, twisting his arm slightly. A scrape ran along his elbow.

"Are you okay is the better question."

Nate shrugged off my grasp. "I'm fine; don't worry about me."

We both watched as Dale emerged from the void of darkness. Besides some dirt, he was better off than the two of us. He fit exactly through the tunnel, so he hadn't had to crawl. Without looking up at us, he passed by and went to lean on the wall of the intersection.

"Now what?" Nate asked, echoing my exact thoughts.

Dale didn't seem to notice. He was busy pressing buttons on the device that he had used earlier. It looked like a more advanced version of a TV remote, with a small screen at the top. The device beeped a few times as Dale walked to the tunnel leading to the left. He pressed another button, and the tunnel lit up. Small lights lined the walls of the tunnel, each giving off a faint, luminous glow.

Putting the device in his pocket, Dale started to walk. Nate and I followed.

"The cave I was talking about earlier is about an hour plus, walk from here. I have supplies there, and I'll contact my friend there too," Dale said.

"So who is this friend of yours?" Nate asked. Out of the corner of my eye, I saw him rub his elbow.

Dale glanced back at us over his shoulder. He smirked. "Still don't trust me, Mannaro?"

Nate didn't respond. He slowly followed Dale and me down the tunnel. I could tell by the shaking of Dale's shoulders that he was laughing.

"I think you know," Dale continued. "I'm sure you must have heard some information from your father."

"I've heard a few things, yes." Nate sighed. "I have my suspicious about who you're talking about, but I'd rather not set myself up for humiliation by coming to the wrong conclusion."

Dale laughed. "Well, for your information, my friend has never agreed with the way the government has strict laws on keeping the occult and humans apart. He believes that with the right regulations and ideas, it's much better to live in harmony. He couldn't do anything about it without getting in huge trouble with Michael." Dale hesitated and looked at his device. We had reached another intersection. He clicked another button on his device, and the lights turned off in the tunnel we were in and turned on in the tunnel on our right.

"I was in Toronto one day and came across this young fellow," Dale continued while stuffing the device back in his purple pants pocket. "And he had just started a riot accidentally on purpose—"

"Accidentally on purpose?" Nate repeated with a hint of mockery in his voice.

Dale ignored him. "He was hanging with his usual group of friends, had a bit much to drink." Dale laughed. "More than a bit since he was underage, but anyway, while talking he ignited the fire about the subject that caused his friends to riot."

Nate's eyes widened. "So your so-called trustworthy friend is the person that started the infamous Toronto riots? It even appeared in human news due to the amount of casualties and wreckage."

"So you've heard?"

"Of course I've heard!" Nate's voice rose. "My dad spent a good six months going back and forth to Toronto to clean up the mess and make sure no humans figured it out!"

Dale scratched his head. "Anyways, my friend was scared; he didn't want to get in trouble with Michael so he made a deal with me. I would take the blame, and he owed me a favor. Stupidest thing I've ever done. Thanks to that, I lost most of my tunnels." Dale spat in disgust. "Now he owes me a favor; end of story. Lesson learned."

The conversation fell quiet. Dale started to pick up the pace, separating himself from Nate and me. I didn't dare speak up, knowing Dale would explode if I tried. So I kept my mouth shut.

When Dale was far enough ahead of us to be out of earshot, I turned to Nate. "Do you know who he's talking about?"

Nate shook his head. "My dad told me about the case, but he refused to tell me who had caused the incident. I tried to get it out of him, but he wouldn't budge. Like I said, I have my suspicions, but I'm not sure."

"Huh." I let my mind wonder about Dale's story. Who was this friend of his? Even Dale hadn't mentioned his name, just like Ben hadn't. Was there a reason for this?

I glanced at Nate. His dad had told him way more than he let on. He didn't seem surprised at all by the story. I wondered if he did actually know who Dale's mysterious friend was. He had been keeping so much from me lately that it wouldn't surprise me if this was something else he wouldn't tell. But why? Who was this person?

CHAPTER 14

Gravel crunched under the wheels of the car as it rolled to a stop. Michael looked out of the tinted SUV windows. After a good two hours of driving, they had finally reached their destination: an old gas station in Southampton.

Michael glanced in the review mirror. He caught sight of his son in the reflection, and he did not look happy. A permanent frown had been plastered to the boy's face for the past few hours. He hadn't spoken up once; he had been playing on his phone distractedly the whole time. However, it was more of an "I don't want to talk to you so I'm pretending to play on my phone" type of distracted.

Hector sat next to Michael, and the two unbuckled their seat belts to get out. A third click sounded, making Michael hesitate getting out of the car. He looked over his shoulder.

He narrowed his eyes when his son's gray eyes met his. "Stay in the car."

His son's eyes widened. "Seriously?"

Michael didn't even reply. He opened his door and slammed it closed behind him. He immediately clicked the lock button on his keys. At least it would hold his son up a little bit.

Michael looked up, squinting at the bright sunlight above him. The bulletproof windows of the car had dimmed the light more than he thought. He watched as Hector sprinted around the hood of the SUV. Even though it was only a few feet, the old investigator was panting by the time he caught up to his boss's side.

The two started to make their way toward the gas station. It looked a little abandoned, which came as no surprise. They had passed a much fancier station on the way over not even a mile away. That one had been alive and blooming, the customers lining up. This one just seemed dead compared to it. There were only a few people around, and they were all Michael's employees. Michael had already spotted Ben Mannaro standing off to the side, leaning against the side of his vibrant red car.

Hector cleared his throat. "Your son doesn't seem very happy."

Michael huffed, not at all surprised by Hector's statement. "Of course he's not happy. I forced him to come along. He wanted to stay with his friends, but I didn't want to risk it. Rather not have him causing trouble in the city."

"Couldn't he have stayed with your wife?" Hector asked.

The muscles in Michael's jaw tensed. "My wife is out of town. She went back to England, doing some of her own investigative work. She keeps saying she has leads on something. I'm not sure. However, she's also sorting out the occult government there and helping them with a warlock problem, which helps me out tremendously. Means I can keep my focus here."

"She went over there again?" Hector asked carefully.

Michael's eyes narrowed. "She never came back."

"Oh." Hector glanced at his boss. "She's never really here, is she?"

Michael shook his head, his expression blank. "Rarely."

The soft sound of a bell echoed through the air as Michael pushed open the door to the gas station. It creaked loudly and fell shut behind Hector with a loud bang. It made the shelves on the wall tremble. Something clanged to the floor off to the side.

Michael made his way over to the register through the small aisles. No matter how much he walked in the middle, he couldn't get through without banging into shelves on either side. He didn't really care. Hector, on the other hand, walked more carefully, trying to keep the supplies from falling to the floor.

A purple-haired figure was leaning on the counter. She smacked her gum displeasingly and didn't even look up at the sound of the incoming customers. She was too busy texting on her phone.

Michael squared himself in front of the register, placing both of his hands on the counter. He cleared his throat. "I was wondering if you could help me."

Zia smacked her gum. "What do you want?" she replied without looking up.

Michael said nothing. He only stared down at Zia's purple little head, waiting for her to look up. It didn't take long.

"What do you …" she started to repeat, but stopped as soon as she glanced up and caught sight of Michael. Her mouth fell open, making her gum roll out and drop to the floor. "Michael," she gasped.

The corner of Michael's lip curved upward. "Look who it is. Ms. Zia. I remember you." He laughed. "Your job didn't really improve much, did it? It seems you only went downhill from when you quit Mannaro's pack. I'm sure it paid more than this little dump."

Zia gulped. "How can I help you, Mr. Larson?"

Michael grabbed a pack of gum from a rack next to the register. He opened it and unpacked one of the gum pieces, popping the pink strip into his mouth. He chewed it a few times. "I'm looking for someone, Nate Mannaro."

Zia jumped as Michael spit out the ball of gum, aiming for the counter. It landed with a small *twack* right on the screen of Zia's phone. She frowned, a grossed-out look appearing on her face.

Michael crumpled up the gum wrapper. "I was wondering if you had seen him."

Zia started to shake her head. "No, I'm sorry, I haven't …"

"Please, girl. Don't lie. I don't have the time." Michael smashed his fist on the counter. The gum rack trembled. "I know he was here with Ms. Daniels. I watched the store's security footage and saw them talking to you. You showed them a map. Where did you send them?"

"I … I …" Zia stuttered.

"Tell me now." Michael narrowed his eyes. "Or I'll get you kicked out of this dump so fast that you won't even be able to finish the rest of your gum."

Michael glanced down at Zia's hands. They were starting to shake. A purple strand of hair fell in front of her eyes.

"I showed them three places. Two were motels and the third an abandoned mansion. I don't know which one they chose …"

"But?"

"But …"—Zia's voice shook—"I suspect they went to the …"

"Mansion?" Michael interrupted. A gleam appeared in his eyes.

Zia nodded, pulling some of her hair behind her ear. She looked down, avoiding Michael's gaze.

Michael smiled. "That'll be all. Thanks for your help. You've been a doll."

And with that Michael turned around and made his way back toward the exit. He ran into multiple racks, making things crash and fall onto the floor. Hector thought he saw Zia wince, but she didn't speak a word. He carefully followed Michael back outside.

Michael was making his way toward Ben. Before he entered the alpha's earshot, he glanced over his shoulder at Hector. A smile played on his lips. "Bingo," he muttered.

Ben looked up as the two men approached. He quickly pushed himself off the car and took a few strides to meet his boss. "And? What did you find?"

Michael hesitated. "Your son was here …"

Ben's eyes widened. "So he's okay? Do you know where he is?" He spoke so fast that he started to stumble over his own words. Michael could barely make them out, which made him automatically roll his eyes.

"We have an idea where he is, yes." Michael looked over to the side distractedly, his eye catching a gleam in the sun. Light reflected off the back door of his SUV. The door stood wide open.

"So we're going after him, right?" Ben's rapid voice interrupted Michael's thoughts.

"Yes, we're going after him." Michael frowned. "But I want you to stay here."

Ben's eyebrows knit together, and his jaw tensed; he could barely keep his mouth from falling open in surprise. "What for?"

"Look, Mannaro, we're going after this lead, and I don't want your attachment to your son getting in the way of your work. Sit this one out. I'll take some of your pack with me."

"But …"

"But nothing. I've made my decision." He waved his hand distractedly. "There won't be any consequences. I'll do this case on my own."

Ben's eyes narrowed. "You never do cases on your own."

"Well, I'm doing this one. I'll call you to keep you updated or if I need backup." Michael flinched as something vibrated in his pocket. Ben gazed down as his boss moved to pick up his phone.

"Just don't hurt him, Michael. Think of what you would do for your own son."

"You know as well as I do that I wouldn't do anything for my son, but I guess that's the difference between the two of us. Now if you'll excuse me …"

"Michael," Ben said sharply, "don't hurt him. If anyone lays so much as a finger on him or Renn, I'll quit."

Michael smirked. It amused him how Ben was the only one never afraid to speak up against him. It's why he had made him the alpha. Not just anyone had that much guts. And apparently the trait had carried over into his son.

"As you wish," Michael ended as he walked off. He flipped open his phone to receive the call. Michael's stomach churned a bit as he caught sight of who was calling. He took a breath.

"Michael Larson speaking," he answered into the cool metal of the phone.

A low voice grumbled on the other side. "Have you found it yet?"

Michael hesitated before speaking and scratched his head. "I'm working on it."

"Working on it?" the voice yelled at the other side. Michael couldn't tell if he was imagining things, but it seemed like power was vibrating through the phone. "You said that yesterday."

"And I am still working on it. I have a lead. We've almost caught up to the person who has it. Don't worry."

"I trusted you with this, Larson. I need it as quickly as possible. I thought you were better than this."

Michael shook his head, pinching the bridge of his nose. He tried to get the image of the caller out of his head. He could only imagine what his face would look like, his eyes glowing. "There were some complications, but we fixed it. I'll get it to you soon."

Michael turned and bumped into a figure standing behind him. He grabbed onto the person's shoulder to stabilize himself. He quickly composed himself, straightening his coat. He glared at his son.

He covered the receiver with his other hand. "What do you think you're doing?" he hissed. "Move."

He watched his son roll his gray eyes and return a similar glare. He walked off, grabbing a sort of device out of his pocket. Michael made sure that his son was gone before returning to the call.

"Who was that?" the voice spat on the other side.

Michael braced himself to prevent a flinch. "Just my son—nothing important. As you were saying?"

"I'm coming over."

Michael stopped in his tracks. "You're what?"

"I'm coming. It's apparent you need some help in the situation. I thank you for what you've done so far, but it isn't enough. It seems you need a little …"—the voice hesitated. It seemed to laugh as it spoke—"push."

"I've got it covered."

"That's what they all say, Larson. I'll be there soon. Await my men and I at your suspected location. Find me that marble."

Michael gulped as the phone fell silent. It started to crackle, and Michael closed it with a sigh. He looked around him. His men sat readied in their cars, and so did Ben, but the difference was that Ben's car wasn't on. The others were ready to take off. He looked around for his son, but his gelled head was nowhere to be seen.

Michael rolled his eyes. He would come back for his son later. He could manage for a bit on his own. He signaled to the cars, and they roared to life at his signal. He pointed at the road. "Let's move!"

CHAPTER 15

We arrived at Dale's cave after what felt like hours of walking. My limbs were in pain, and I desperately wanted to sit down so I could relieve my aching feet. Dale's cave was surprisingly like a typical cave. It was just like you would expect a cave to look, except maybe a few times bigger. It wouldn't surprise me if Dale had had to clear out bats before he moved in.

Light shone through some bushes at the end of the cave. I had never seen a wall of leaves that big. It covered the whole entrance of the cave, from left to right, top to bottom. Besides some light flares, it looked like nothing else could come through.

Dale came to stand next to me, following my gaze. "It's the entrance to the cave, so ultimately also my tunnels. It has to be well covered so that no one will enter. It's invisible from the outside. Can't say a warlock spell didn't have a hand in that."

I looked around the cave. There were supplies everywhere. Not only supplies, but also food, drinks, clothes, and other random things. I smiled to myself. Storage containers lined the walls, along with other furniture and clothing racks. Dale was a hoarder.

Standing on one side of the cave were two huge chests. I walked over to one and opened it carefully. The heavy lid creaked loudly as I lifted it. My jaw dropped as I saw the contents. The chest was filled with money. From coins to hundred-dollar bills, in currencies that I'd never seen before.

I jumped as Dale smacked my hand away. The chest closed with a loud *thunk*.

He gave me a strange look. "Don't touch my stuff."

Nate stood over on the other side of the cave. He was examining a rack full of strange-colored suits and neon ties. "You have an interesting sense of style," Nate muttered while holding up a blue and orange striped suit.

Dale hurried over to him. He stubbornly ripped the suit out of Nate's hands. "I said, don't touch my stuff."

Nate shrugged and went to sit on a couch that stood in the middle of the cave. Random pieces of furniture were strewn across the cave. Some were covered in knickknacks or turned upside down. I went to sit on the couch next to Nate. Pain seared through my butt when I landed on the hard cushions. It felt like there weren't any cushions at all; it was more like I was sitting on a piece of wood.

Dale strode over with a footstool. He placed it in front of us and stepped onto it. He cleared his throat. "I have a few rules for you. Number one, if it wasn't clear already, don't touch my stuff. You are welcome to take all the food and drinks you want, watch TV, I really don't care. Just don't touch any of the chests or anything else that looks valuable or like something I would own.

Nate snorted. "Don't you own all of this garbage?"

Dale's eyes narrowed at Nate. "Rule number two, do not leave this cave, under any circumstances. Do not move the bushes; do not touch them. They are there for the safety of all of us."

Nate opened his mouth to make another comment, but Dale continued before he could utter a word. "And rule number three: don't go back into the tunnels. You will get lost. I don't have the time and patience to go find you. That would be your own fault, and quite frankly, you won't make it out alive.

"I'll give you a zapper, and then you'll have a backup plan just in case Michael decides to show up. My friend has one, so then the three of you will have two among you, which should be enough …"

"Did you just say you'd give us a zapper?" I started, interrupting Dale. "Isn't that, like, something you electrify mosquitoes with?"

Dale rolled his eyes at me. "No, zapper as in remote. They're devices that I designed and made myself." He took the funny-looking remote out of his pocket. "The display shows you where you are, and you can type in where you want to go. It's like a GPS for my tunnels." Dale smiled. "It helps with the not getting lost factor."

He tossed me the remote. It had a keyboard on it and a small screen. It was slightly bigger than it had looked to be. It was wider and was more phone-like than a remote. At the bottom of the device was a small red button. I looked up at Dale. He had stepped down from the stool and was searching a big box. He emerged from it with another zapper in hand.

"What's the red button for?" I asked as Dale walked back toward us.

He grinned. "I was smart enough to install a feature that would let you find other zappers and message them. It is how I can contact certain people that I have given zappers to. The one

I have here is zapper D, for Dale, of course. The one you have is R because I changed it to Renn." Dale's eyes twinkled. "And this is how I'm going to find the person that owes me a favor. I will know for certain that he received the message, so I will be able to tell if he is avoiding us."

He pressed the red button on his device. It started to blink. A robotic voice spoke out of the zapper. "Which zapper would you like to locate?"

Dale held the remote up to his mouth. "J," He replied, a mischievous smile appearing on his face.

"Please hold on while we locate zapper J."

Dale tapped his foot. Nate and I watched Dale as he waited patiently. After a minute or so, the zapper voice spoke again.

"Zapper J has been located about thirty miles away from here. Taking the nearest tunnel, it would take him five to ten minutes to reach you. Would you like to send him a message? If yes, speak in the message after the tone." The zapper beeped loudly.

Dale's eyes sparkled as he spoke. "Dale needs a favor."

The red light stopped blinking. "Message has been sent."

Dale laughed, full of triumph. "Well, aren't we lucky?"

Nate crossed his arms next to me. "So he'll be here soon?"

"You heard the zapper." Dale took a seat on the stool. "The zapper is always right."

Nate sighed. "So that was it for the rules?"

"Pretty much, except for the fact that you aren't allowed in my secret chamber, but you wouldn't fit anyway."

"You have a room?"

Dale narrowed his eyes. "If that's the term you prefer."

Nate raised an eyebrow. "I see how it is; I annoy you. Well, if I do, why don't you go hide in your"—Nate air-quoted with his fingers—"secret chamber."

Dale squinted. "I never actually said that you annoy me, Mannaro. But if you want some alone time with your girlfriend, fine. I'll leave. I need some alone time anyway. You talk too much."

"I'm not his girlfriend," I retorted quickly. Dale shrugged and walked over to a wardrobe on the side of the cave. He opened the door, revealing a small hole carved in the back. I could just make out some stairs. Dale looked at me before stepping inside and slamming the door closed behind him.

We sat silently as Dale's feet tapped up the stairs. Then the sounds were gone. Who knew where his secret bedroom was? I turned and sat cross-legged facing Nate. He didn't meet my gaze and stared straight ahead.

"You don't have to be so mean to him, you know."

Nate's eyes narrowed, but he didn't move his gaze. "I don't trust goblins."

"You said yourself that they were loyal." I twisted a piece of hair around my finger.

"Yes, I did. But I also said that they are self-centered and work in their own behalf. They're difficult creatures. You have to be careful. They are loyal, but it's hard to figure out where the loyalty lies."

"Huh." I sighed, gazing around the cave. Dale seemed nice enough and willing to help. Nate needed to start seeing the good in people's intentions. "Why is he such a hoarder?" I asked, changing the subject.

Nate burst out into laughter, finally turning his gaze on me. "Because he's a goblin." He grinned. "All goblins are that way. They're stubborn creatures that love gathering stuff. They see the strangest value in everything. Yet their only great love lies in money. That's why he has those huge chests full."

My eyes widened. "He stole all of that? He has thousands of dollars!"

Nate shook his head, still smiling. "He probably didn't steal it; I bet it's all his. Goblins live for a long time. He's old. He's been collecting forever. It's probably not his only money he has either. Goblins are smart. He probably has a bunch of these caves with chests full of valuables. The worth of it all could end up in a million at the very least." Nate looked at me. "He collects all of this stuff; it's in his nature."

I smiled. Dale was an interesting creature. He was a waist-high, old, stubborn hoarder. But that didn't mean he couldn't be trusted. "Why are you so skeptical of him though?"

Nate rolled his eyes. "You asked this like a minute ago."

"Yeah, I know." I hesitated. "But you didn't give me a straight answer. You only told me about goblins in general. What's so bad about Dale? You'd be blind if you can't see his good intentions."

Nate frowned. "I don't know, Renn. I guess Dale is okay, but like I said, there are worse goblins out there. That's not even their real appearance. Their true form is like a little monster, only some of it shows through the illusion. The small piece of magic that they do have allows them to deceive and hide their looks to look like small humans." Nate sighed. "And they're stubborn, which doesn't help if you're trying to hide and do the best thing."

"But Dale is fine though," I commented.

Nate nodded slowly. "Yes, but I don't trust this friend of his. My dad told me some stuff about the riot and what happened in Toronto. It didn't sound good. And it doesn't give me a good feeling that no one will mention his name. Something's up, and it's on the tip of my tongue, but I can't put my finger on it."

"It'll be fine." I looked at a clock that hung on one of the clothing racks. Five minutes had passed a long time ago. Was Dale's friend even going to show up? I didn't know if I would.

Nate and I both jumped at the sound of a loud crash. The sound had come from the entrance of the tunnel. I rapidly turned my head to see some clothing racks fall over. Nate stood and tilted his head up to try to gaze over the wreckage.

"Dammit," a voice said. It was a male voice, but definitely not Dale. "Dale really needs to get rid of all this garbage."

I couldn't help but laugh. But my hands were shaking, and my heart beat in my throat. Nate had said the same thing. But that didn't matter. My smile disappeared as the sound of footsteps came closer.

I stood up to join Nate. I slowly turned around to face the newcomer.

A guy about our age was walking our way. He was holding a zapper. He laughed at the sight of us. "Look who we have here! Two refugees." His eyes danced with laughter. "How great is that?"

CHAPTER 16

Before my brain could properly process what was happening, Nate leaped over the couch and charged at the newcomer. The bottom of the couch cracked loudly and split in two when he pushed off of it with his foot. He collided with the guy, grabbed his shoulders, and pushed him backward.

"*What are you doing here?*" Nate spat out each of his words individually.

I stood in shock as the guy hooked Nate's arm and flipped him over onto the ground in one swift movement. Nate landed with a smack.

"What am I doing here? Shouldn't I ask you the same question, Mannaro?" the guy spat back in return. One strand of his dark hair stuck out of his otherwise gelled-up style.

Nate lurched up and grabbed him around the throat, pushing him backward into the couch. I jumped as the couch scooted toward me, loudly scraping the floor. "Dale!" I yelled shakily.

"Aren't you the one that needed Dale's help to not get in trouble with your daddy?" Nate mocked. He ducked as a punch came his way. His grin disappeared as a second blow hit him in the jaw. I cringed at the ugly sound it made.

Nate's first punch hit the floor. His second hit the newcomer right in the eye. He was thrown back as the guy leaped toward him and smashed into his stomach.

"Dale!" I shouted again. I tripped over something as I backed up toward the wardrobe.

Nate scooted backward on his bottom as the newcomer stalked over to him. "I think you're the one with daddy issues. You're the one that ran away!"

Nate hooked the guy's ankle, making him fall backward. An ugly bang sounded as his head hit the floor Apparently unharmed, the guy got onto his hands and knees and launched himself onto Nate. The two rolled around, bumping into pieces of furniture in their way. I cringed as another few punches hit home. I turned toward the wardrobe.

"Dale!" I shouted. I knocked on the door as loudly as I could. Rapid feet clattered down the hollow stairs inside. I stepped back as Dale pushed the door open. He glared at me. He opened his mouth to say something, but stopped to turn toward the sound of Nate and the new guy crashing into the wall. Dale's face turned bright red.

He strode over to the two guys. They were both on their knees, attempting to push each other over. Dale grabbed each one by the collar and pulled them apart. Then he hooked his arms around each of their necks. Nate and the guy both struggled against Dale's grasp, but he was surprisingly strong. He pulled them along to the couch and pushed them onto either side. The broken plank of the bottom ripped the seam of the fabric and stuck upward as their weights dropped on either side.

"Now I know the two of you have your differences, but to have a brawl in the middle of my cave? That is unacceptable. Act like you get along for goodness' sake. I'll add that to the rule list. No fights in my cave. Understood?"

The new guy nodded his head reluctantly. Nate rolled his eyes. Dale glared at them once more before walking over to some refrigerators in the corner. Nate crossed his arms, an annoyed and stubborn look on his face. A bruise was starting to form on his jaw.

I felt the newcomer's eyes on me before I looked over. I averted my gaze when we made eye contact, but I could see that his eye was also starting to swell. Aside from the purple bruise, he was actually quite handsome. He seemed to have a permanent smirk tattooed on his face, which created a dimple in his cheek. His gray eyes were still on me.

Catching my gaze again, he stood and walked over to me. He grabbed my hand in one swift movement and kissed it. "Josh Larson, at your service." He winked. I opened my mouth to reply, but no sound came out.

Before I could figure out how to form words, Nate had bumped Josh out of the way. "This is Renn," he said simply, folding his arms over each other.

Josh cocked his head. "I know," he said, the smirk still present.

"Sit down, you three!" Dale said from behind us. Nate and Josh trudged back to their seats on the couch. My shoulder tingled from where Josh brushed it as he passed. Because the couch was broken in half, I opted for the floor. I sat between the two boys, leaning against the broken couch behind me. It was extremely uncomfortable and awkward, to say the least.

Dale threw Nate and Josh ice packs, which they both held up to their bruises. I couldn't help but laugh as they cringed behind me while attempting to hide their pain.

Dale grabbed his footstool and took a seat on it. He turned to Josh. "Mind telling me how you got here so fast?"

Josh shrugged. "I was in the area."

Dale's eyes narrowed. "And why were you in the area?"

Josh laughed a fake laugh. "Oh, right. Well, my dad is in the area searching for these two." He pointed at Nate and me. "He's quite hot on their trail actually, except for the fact that he doesn't know how to get into the remaining tunnels that you have under control. My dad made me come along because he didn't trust me to be alone back in the city. And besides, I wouldn't pass up the opportunity to see Nathaniel here get busted …"

It was then that I noticed Josh had an accent. It was slightly off, almost British, but too American to be so. Josh Larson. Where had I heard that name before? Larson. Realization dawned on me. "Hold up. You're Michael's son, aren't you?"

Josh raised an eyebrow. "Bingo."

"Why else did you think I jumped him? Have you not been paying attention? He's mentioned it like three times now," Nate commented from beside me. His voice was muffled from the ice pack he held to his jaw. "It's why I didn't trust Dale. I had my suspicions it would be Joshua here …"

"Don't call me that!" Josh snapped from my other side.

Nate glared at him. "Then don't call me Nathaniel either."

Dale rolled his eyes. "Calm down, you two."

I turned myself around so that I sat facing them. "How do you two even know each other?"

Dale burst into laughter when the question had left my mouth. I glanced back at him over my shoulder. He just gave me an amused look.

“We met a long time ago,” Josh said, looking up at the ceiling distractedly.

Nate shifted his ice pack. “Our dads work together, so we went to parties and stuff.”

Dale jumped off his stool and clapped his hands together. “And the first time they met, they got into a fight! History repeats itself, doesn’t it?”

I rapidly turned to face Dale. “You knew this?” I could feel the heat rising to my cheeks. “You knew this and brought them together anyway?”

Dale waved away my comment. “It was the only way I could think of. I thought they could just get over it and get along.” He scowled at them. “Apparently not.”

“Well, if we can’t get along, I might as well leave. There’s no point to me being here.” Josh stood and started to walk toward the tunnel entrance. He grabbed a bag off the floor that I hadn’t even realized he had brought with him. “I’m no help to you anyway.”

Dale crossed his arms impatiently. He stepped onto the stool to get a better view. “If you leave, I’ll tell Michael about Toronto.”

Josh stopped in his tracks. I watched as his hands balled up into fists.

“You owe me a favor.” Dale raised an eyebrow. “It said so in my message, Josh. You wanted to come even though you won’t admit it. You’re as against your dad as much as anyone else. Maybe even more.”

Josh looked back over his shoulder. “So, you’re blackmailing me?”

“Not so much blackmailing; more of a warning.”

Josh shook his head. "Making me stay or else you'll ruin my life by telling my dad one of my greatest mistakes? I would call it a threat."

"If you put it that way ..." Dale smirked. "Yes."

Josh rocked on the balls of his feet. Then he turned around and came to take his seat on the couch again, dropping his bag along the way. "So, what's our plan then?"

Dale smiled. "I'll take the three of you up to the border as far as I can go through the tunnels. Then you have to take Nate and Renn up to Montreal. Use the tunnels, and then try traveling at night until you get to the city. Michael has people around the border, but not into the city."

"When do we leave?" Nate asked. He had an uncomfortable look on his face, like something was bothering him. He tried to hide it as soon as he caught my gaze.

"We can leave tomorrow?" Dale asked.

"No, that won't work," Josh said, interrupting. "We have to leave now. This cave is really easy to find if you know where it's at. My dad knows the cave exists. It's the way the tunnels work. They'll somehow manage to direct you to the place you want to go."

Dale rolled his eyes. "So?"

"It's only a matter of time before my dad finds the entrance of the tunnels. When I left he was already on his way to the mansion. We can sleep in the tunnels. The first place my dad will look is here."

My mind was buzzing. "What is that supposed to mean?"

Josh's gray eyes studied me. "What is what supposed to mean?"

"That the tunnels direct you to places? That makes no sense."

Dale sighed. "Enchantments, sweetheart. Remember when I said the spells put on the tunnels make the distance between places much smaller?"

I nodded.

"Well, it's because the spells allow the tunnels to move. They direct you to the place you have in your mind. It's part of the reason why you need a zapper to get through them. If you get lost and don't know where to go, the tunnels will reflect that and only lead you astray."

Josh smirked. "It's one big death trap."

"But how did your dad find out about the mansion so fast?"

Nate slammed his fist on the couch. "It means that Zia can't keep her trap shut."

Josh grinned out of amusement. "Exactly. That purple-haired chick spilled her info as soon as my dad showed up. My dad is pretty persuasive in that way. Good at getting people to talk." He frowned. "Which doesn't help our case."

Dale stood. "Then it's settled. We'll leave in half an hour. We can gather supplies, and we'll be off."

We searched through Dale's cave to find the necessary supplies. Dale gave us all traveling backpacks that he had lying around, so that we could transfer our items from the duffel bags. Mine was an ugly shade of yellow and was caked with dried mud. I opened my mouth to comment but shut it as soon as I noticed Dale's sour expression.

We all gathered the things that we needed and filled an extra bag full of food. Not even fifteen minutes later, we stood at the back of the cave.

Nate took out the zapper Dale had given him. He clicked a small button, and the lights turned on. "I guess we're off . . ." His voice trailed off.

"Don't worry," Dale said, coming up from behind us. "I'll know when someone enters the cave. I'll be able to see who. We'll know as soon as Michael is close."

Dale stepped into his tunnel. He looked back over his shoulder with an amused look. "Follow me, runaways."

CHAPTER 17

We followed Dale back through the tunnels. Everything looked the same. Dirt wall after dirt wall. I couldn't tell if we had gone back through the same tunnel or taken a turn. We passed a few intersections, but Dale took a turn without hesitating. He would take out his zapper, turn on the light, and continue on. Josh, Nate, and I followed quietly.

Every once in a while, Josh would glance back at me, as if to see that I hadn't escaped. He quickly averted his gaze when our eyes met.

I heard Nate flare his nostrils behind me after what seemed like the twentieth time that it happened. I looked over my shoulder at him, but his expression was blank. He looked down at the zapper he was playing with, but that was it. He didn't bother to look up when I did, but I knew that when I turned to look at Josh, Nate's eyes would be on me.

After another few minutes of silence, I cleared my throat. “So, Josh,” I said, trying to start a conversation, “what’s up with your accent?”

Nate snickered from behind me. Josh ignored him. “My dad is from California; I moved to New York at a very young age. My mom is British, so I guess that’s the accent you hear.” He said the last part bitterly, like he was mad at something.

“Why is that so bad?”

Josh shook his head, making some of his dark hair fall out of place. “It’s not bad; it’s just that my accent used to be pretty strong because my mom was always home to take care of me. But that went away as soon as my mom stopped coming home. My dad took care of me for a while, so I ended up with this half New York, half Californian accent mixed in with the British. But as soon as my dad become occult prime minister, I was left alone.

“I was very young, became rebellious, switched babysitters, that type of thing. Once I figured out that that didn’t get my parents’ attention either, I learned to cope with doing everything on my own. I made my own friends, did my own thing, and ended up with this accent.” He sighed. “Now it just reminds me of my lack of childhood.

He glanced over his shoulder at me. “Make sense?”

I nodded. He turned his head back and continued to walk. I studied the back of his head. Apparently Josh wasn’t one to have an easy childhood either. It seemed to be the theme of our little group.

“So why don’t you tell us how Dale fits into all of this?” Nate asked from behind me. I heard Dale snort from up ahead. He clicked a button on his zapper and switched the light on in a tunnel on our left. The tunnel we were in darkened.

"Well," Josh started while rounding the corner, "I know a lot of people; I tend to know things or be able to find out everything. It helps because it always gives you a backup plan. Or leverage."

"A backup plan for what?" Nate asked. There was a vindictive tone to his voice. *What a douche.*

Josh shifted his shoulders. "I'm the opposite of my dad. I don't agree with his plans of the government. I believe that the human world and the occult world can live together without people ruling and overpowering each other. Times have changed. It's not like the olden times anymore.

"One day I was with a group of friends in Toronto, and they were all against my dad. They wanted to kick me out because I was related to him, but I told them that I was also against him. I got mad and gave a speech with evidence that I had found and didn't agree with. The people took it as a call for protest, so that's what started."

"And who came to save your sorry butt?" Dale said from the front.

Josh sighed. "I came across Dale and begged him to cover for me. He did that, and Michael got his tunnels." He cocked his head. "If you ask me, I think he was happier about getting the tunnels than stopping the protest."

"Something's up with your dad, Josh, and I'm going to find out what," Dale said as he exited the current tunnel we were in. I heard him press a button on his zapper. The lights turned off, and it was completely dark. Then the sound of a generator turning on buzzed and zoomed. Slowly the lights blinked on. We stood at the entrance of a huge cave. My jaw dropped.

A faint bluish light glowed through the cavern. Water dripped down from the roof of the cave, and rock formations surrounded us. Marble-like crystals stuck to the walls on either side of us. They reflected a sea of color onto our skin.

Nate walked past me to a group of the crystals. He touched one where the light reflected off of it. He recoiled when it fell to the ground and shattered with a loud chink.

"They're soft crystals," Dale commented walking past us. He pulled one of the crystals off the wall. "Quite beautiful. They reflect the light like no other stone; it's magical."

Josh examined the cave from where he stood. "Don't they form wherever strong magic occurs?"

Dale nodded. "They're called divine crystals, because the sorcerer that found them was into foretelling and divinity. Ironically he named them wrong. They do the exact opposite. They form after a major magical event has occurred in the area. No one knows why. It has to do with the amount of magic and the balance of things being restored."

Nate pulled one of the crystals off of the wall and held it up to the light. The reflections of color made it look like mist was moving inside of it. It was almost completely round, aside from some misformed bumps.

That's when I noticed the noise. It wasn't very loud, but it was definitely there and prominent. It sounded like rushing water. I cast my gaze over the cave. Opposite us I spotted an opening just like the one we were coming out of. Except there was one problem. The canyon.

Between this side and the other, there was a huge canyon. I slowly passed the guys and walked over toward the edge. I peeked over the side, and the sound of rushing water overwhelmed me. There was a vast river streaming through the bottom of the canyon.

I jumped as someone grabbed my wrists. I looked down at Dale.

"Careful," he said. "If you fall in, you're not coming out."

I took a few steps back to where Josh and Nate now stood.

"How do you expect us to cross this?" Nate said, gesturing toward the canyon in disbelief.

Josh crossed his arms. "I agree with Mannaro. A boat doesn't work; the water is too low."

"Yeah, the water is like fifteen feet down; it's too far."

Josh turned to Nate. "Wow, you agree with me for once?"

Nate glared at Josh. "You agreed with me first."

"Shush." Dale held his finger up, quieting the two boys. "Calm down before you explode into another fight. See that over there?" He pointed behind him. "That'll help us."

I looked past Dale. A tattered, termite-eaten bridge hung loosely from one side of the canyon to the other.

Nate, Josh, and I all spoke up at the same time. "That is not going to hold us!" "It gives us a bigger chance of getting killed than the boat." "Are you out of your mind?"

Dale held up his hands. "Shut up. All of you."

I clamped my mouth shut, and Nate and Josh did the same. We stood quietly, staring at the bridge. Dale walked over to it and leaned against one of the poles that was holding the bridge up by ropes.

"The bridge is designed to look like a wreck. If it looked like a sturdy metal bridge, people would cross it without a doubt, giving them a clear entrance to the rest of my tunnels. By making it look like it's about to break, people will hesitate to cross it." He grinned. "Who's first?"

"I'll go." Nate stepped forward. He walked up to the bridge and placed a foot on the first plank. It creaked slightly. Putting his other foot on, the bridge groaned under his weight. "Designed to look weak or be weak?" Nate mocked as he carefully started to make his way to the other side.

Dale rolled his eyes. "Designed, Mannaro." He turned to us. "I'll go next, then Renn, and then Josh, understood?"

Josh and I nodded. We watched as Dale stepped onto the bridge and started to cross with ease. He grabbed the ropes and started to swing back and forth.

Nate ducked in response, grabbing the ropes tightly. "Stop it," he snapped.

Josh laughed quietly. "What a wimp."

Dale stopped swinging, and Nate crossed over to the other side. Dale followed close behind. Then it was just Josh and I.

"You first," Josh said with a smile. I walked over to the bridge. By being closer, now I could see the holes in the wood and the thinned-out pieces in the rope. I shuffled forward. Staring over the edge again, I saw the river racing past. Leaves passed from my right to my left in seconds.

"You'll be fine, sweetheart." Dale's voice echoed through the cave. His voice had a reassuring hint to it. I took a deep breath. I could do this. Step after step.

I put my first foot on the bridge. It creaked loudly. Then I placed my second foot. A louder groan followed. I would be okay. If Dale and Nate could make it across, so could I.

My heart beat in my throat as I slowly walked across the bridge. Ten more planks to go. Halfway. Now eight. I was doing fine. I would make it. The bridge creaked behind me as Josh stepped on. I heard the bridge groan after each step he took. I only had five planks left. Almost there.

The sound of a snapping rope rang through the tunnel. I froze. The creaking stopped, meaning Josh had also stopped moving. I looked up at Dale. His face was reassuring, but his eyes said differently.

A few strands of hair fell in front of his eyes. I could see the dirt attached to it.

"You're doing great, sweetheart," he said. I could tell he was trying to hide something. He took a crisp breath. "Keep moving; you're almost there."

Nate's eyes widened as another rope snapped. "Renn, slowly come forward. Don't put too much weight on one foot.

"Guys, what's going on?" Josh yelped behind me.

A third rope snapped. Nate's and Dale's eyes flew to the side. They stared at something behind us.

"Start walking, Renn," Dale said carefully. He looked me straight in the eye. "*Now.*"

I stepped forward onto the next plank. It shook under my weight. I took a deep breath. It was going to be okay. As soon as I took my second step, I felt the bridge start to tilt. The ropes in front of me started to twist, making the bridge start to turn.

When the fourth rope snapped, everything seemed to happen at once. It was the last rope holding the bridge up on one side. The left corner behind me fell down, plummeting toward the ravine. I heard Josh shout something behind me, but I couldn't make out what. My heart beat loudly in my throat, seeming to tune out all the noise. I couldn't focus on anything.

I could faintly hear another rope snap. The bridge shook and twisted. It creaked as if yet another rope was starting to come loose. Nate held out his hand in front of me. I could see his mouth moving, but I couldn't make out what he was saying.

The river splashed as a few planks fell into the water. Then a force ran into my back. I was thrown forward as the last rope snapped. The wind was knocked out of me as I smashed into the rock wall on the other side. I held onto the side of the canyon for dear life. I couldn't fall. I could hold on.

Something heavy yanked on my leg. My hand shot from the crevice I was holding onto as a force pulled me down. Nate held out his hand from above. He was shouting. He was telling me to grab his hand. I could do that. I tried to reach my hand up, but pain seared through my ankle. I looked down.

Josh was hanging from my leg, his hands wrapped around my ankle. His feet stood on a small ledge, but I could tell they were slipping. Water from the ravine crashed into him. His expression was saying something. All sound came rushing back to me.

"Grab Nate's hand!" Josh yelled as another wave crashed into him.

I looked up at Nate. He was lying on the cave floor and reached his hand down. I tried putting my hand up, but I felt myself slipping.

"It's too high!" I yelled. My voice was drowned out by the sound of roaring water.

I shook as another wave of water crashed beneath me. I looked down at Josh. He was drenched to the bone. His hair clung to the sides of his head and his clothes to his skin. Only his toes were on the ledge. He didn't have long.

"I'm going to push you up, okay?" he said. He spat out water as another wave hit. "As soon as I do, grab Nate's hand. It's your only chance."

I nodded. "What about you?"

I watched as Josh let my ankle go with one hand and grabbed a crevice in the rock to stabilize himself. Then he stepped up onto another ledge. He put his other hand underneath my foot. "I'll sort that out myself," he said with a fake grin. The fear showed in his eyes.

Josh grunted loudly as he pushed me up. I jumped up, pushing myself off his hand. I reached up, but soon felt the momentum take over, rushing me back down. I was falling. Then a force yanked me up. I looked into Nate's eyes. He had grabbed my arm. He pulled me up over the edge and onto the cave floor.

I trembled as Nate pulled me into a quick hug. "You're okay; you made it," he whispered in my ear.

Josh yelped from the canyon. Nate and I turned around and crawled over to the edge. Dale was busy lowering a rope down into the ravine. He had tied the other end of it around one of the huge stalagmites.

The rope went tight as Josh grabbed it from the canyon. He would make it. He grunted as he started to climb up the rock wall. Sweat and water dripped down his face. My heart seemed to stop beating every time his foot slipped. I held my breath, watching Josh struggle up the rocky side. Then the top of his head appeared over the edge. With one last heave and help from Dale and Nate, Josh pulled himself over the edge. He rolled over onto his back and closed his eyes. Water dripped from his clothes, creating a dark ring in the dirt around him. He ran his hand through his soaked hair.

"I thought you said the bridge was designed to look weak," he said with his eyes still closed.

Dale sat down next to us. "I only said that to get you to cross. I lied. It holds my weight, but I'm much lighter than you."

Josh didn't reply. We sat in silence. I watched as Josh's breathing became even. He had fallen asleep.

I lay down on my back too, exhaustion flooding over me. I didn't even know what time it was. Probably in the middle of the day? I didn't even care.

My ankle throbbed, but I ignored it. I let myself doze off.

I could faintly hear Nate and Dale talking. Dale said something about ordering some fairies to get the bridge fixed. I didn't even bother making a remark. Nothing surprised me anymore at this point.

CHAPTER 18

I awoke to a searing pain in my ankle. My eyes flew open, and I jerked upward, off of the cold dirt ground. I looked around. Nate was snoring loudly next to me, his chest heaving and falling. Dale leaned against one of the rocks, also sleeping. Josh was nowhere in sight.

I turned my gaze back and ran my hand over my ankle. It was slightly swollen, but seemed fine otherwise. I tried twisting my foot around. I felt the bruise, but there was no intense pain. I let out a sigh of relief. Josh hadn't done too much damage.

I stood carefully and walked over to where Josh had been lying earlier. Small spots of red liquid were spattered around. I bent down to touch a drop, and my finger stained red. I smelled it. The thick scent of fresh blood spread through my nostrils.

I let my eyes follow the small trail of blood. From what I could see, it rounded a corner and disappeared from sight. I turned back to Nate and Dale. They were still dead to the world.

I followed the drops of blood, limping slightly to avoid putting too much pressure on my injured ankle. The trail rounded around one of the stalagmites. On the other side, leaning against the rock, was Josh. He held a cotton ball up to the front of his bare shoulder. His shirt lay in a heap on the ground next to him. The left sleeve was soaked in blood.

I walked over to him and kneeled down. I grabbed the cotton ball from him and held it up to his wound. There was a deep cut on his shoulder that was giving off most of the blood. A slightly smaller scratch ran down the side of his chest to his midriff.

I put down the cotton ball and grabbed a new one. I put some of the ointment on it that Josh had standing next to him. The alcoholic scent burned in my nose. He winced as soon as the cotton came in contact with his cut.

"What are you doing?" he asked. His gray eyes were watching me closely.

I cleared away the last of the dried blood, being careful not to reopen the wound. Then I grabbed a bandage and started to wrap it around his shoulder. "Cleaning you up."

Josh laughed. His eyes sparkled. Then he winced as I wrapped the last bit of bandage around his shoulder and pulled it tight.

"I must have banged it up climbing up the rocks yesterday. I didn't notice last night, but it hurt like crazy this morning." He examined me. "Are you okay? I know it must not be the easiest thing to have me hanging on your leg."

I waved the subject off. Grabbing another piece of cotton, I dabbed his chest clean. I silently let my fingers trail down his toned chest in the process. I put on more ointment and started to look for another bandage.

"You seem to be handling this magical stuff really well," he continued. "You're different than a lot of the other people I've met. I like you."

He met my gaze. "Thanks, I guess." I tried to smile, but I'm sure it came across as fake. I grabbed a clean shirt that was lying next to him and handed it over. He took it and put it on.

"I mean it. There's something about you that's …" He hesitated. Then he leaned toward me. "Strong." His eyes seemed to smile for him. He grabbed my hand and pulled me up with him.

We walked back over to the edge of the canyon, not speaking another word. Dale was awake and going through one of the bags, presumably in search of some food.

Josh glanced at his watch next to me. "It's almost ten at night?"

Dale nodded, his focus still on the bags. "You guys fell asleep around three. Nate and I stayed awake for a bit, but we got bored and ended up dozing off around …"

Dale was interrupted by Nate, who jumped up out of his sleep. He started to cough, wheezing for breath. I could see him shake from here.

"Nate?" I asked cautiously, sprinting over toward him.

Before I made it over to him, Nate scooted himself backward, recoiling away from me. "Don't …" was he could muster before his whole body went rigid. He yelled out in pain.

"Nate!" My voice came out in a scream. Dale had looked up from his bag; a worried look crossed his face. I glanced back at Josh, but he only shook his head. He didn't look worried at all.

Nate gasped as his body stopped spasming momentarily. He pushed himself off the ground and ran away from the clearing we were in. He fell on the way, collapsing onto the ground. He pushed himself up again and continued until he was out of sight.

Before I had even fully processed what had happened, my legs started to move me forward.

"Renn," I faintly heard Josh say after me. I felt his grasp around my wrist, but I yanked myself free. I continued after Nate, sprinting around some of the rocks. His stumbling footprints had unsettled the dust on the ground, and stones had crumpled where he had crashed into one of the stalagmites. I found him collapsed onto the ground, his head in his fists. The tensed muscles in his back showed through his thin T-shirt.

"Nate, what's happening?" I rushed to his side. I attempted to place my hand on his back, but he flinched away from me.

"Don't touch me," he growled, his voice coming out lower than usual. He glanced at me, an apologetic look momentarily on his face. Then he squeezed his eyes shut and clenched his teeth.

"Nate, talk to me!" I tried to look at his face, but he turned away. "You're in pain!" I grabbed his face in my hands, forcefully turning it toward me. Nate didn't fight it. He opened his eyes. His pupils had gone yellow.

"You're changing?" I gasped as blood welled up on his lip. I forced his lips apart with my thumb. Canines were slowly producing themselves into his skin.

"Don't fight it, Nate."

"How would you know?" He groaned in pain.

I tried to say something, but the words got caught in my throat.

"I don't want to hurt you," Nate interrupted, spitting through clenched teeth. He pulled himself away from me and crashed into one of the rocks, where he sank to the ground.

I crawled over. "You said it yourself. With the bracelet on, you'll be in control. The full moon will force you to change anyway. Don't cause yourself this pain."

Nate grabbed his face in his hands, running his fingers in the ends of his hair. "What if I lose control?"

"You won't. You never have before." My heart ached as he rocked back and forth. Dark hairs were starting to produce on his skin. "Nate, seeing you in pain is hurting me more!"

I forced his chin up, making him look straight at me. An emotion changed in his eyes, his yellow pupils dilating.

"Let go," I heard myself whisper.

Nate pushed himself away again, crawling to the other side of the rock. But I could see the muscles in his shoulders relax. Slowly he started to change.

The opposite of what I had watched two nights ago started to occur. He got into a crouched position, his limbs becoming thin and strong. Hair produced through his clothes, covering him completely. His face started to change, becoming a muzzle. Only his eyes stayed the same. Even though the color had changed, I could see a hint of Nate left in the feature.

I carefully walked over, leaning in front of my best friend. I put my hand up, and Nate nudged it with his muzzle. I scratched between his ears, and his tongue rolled out of his mouth. I couldn't help but laugh. I pulled the creature into a hug, cradling my arms around his strong shoulders. Wolf Nate whimpered.

We walked back over to the edge of the canyon, Nate's paws pattering softly on the ground. Dale had set up plastic plates and had built a small fire with some rocks and twigs. The small fire crackled loudly. He had some eggs cooking on it.

I winced as I sat down, pain shooting through my ankle again. Wolf Nate shot me a concerned look.

"You should ice that," a voice said. I looked around. No one had said a word. Josh and Dale didn't bat an eye. Wolf Nate had lain down, but his head was raised. No one looked like they had heard anything.

"Calm down," the voice said. "It's just me."

I clamped my hand over my ears. Voices were spinning around in my head. That wasn't supposed to be a good thing.

Josh looked at me. "Are you okay?"

I shook my head. Looking over at Dale, I saw that he was busy serving up the plates. It wasn't his voice either. Wolf Nate shuddered in front of me, as if he was shaking with laughter.

"Renn, calm down. It's just me," the voice said again.

Josh looked at me and then at Nate. Then he burst out into laughter. "This is so sad, Nate!" He barely got his words out through his laughter. His eyes started to water. "She doesn't even recognize your voice!"

I stared at the wolf. I was still trying to come to terms with Nate being a wolf, but now that Josh mentioned it, the voice in my head did sound like Nate's.

"Was that you?" I asked.

The wolf cocked his head to the side. He held up his paw, where a familiar rope bracelet hung. Then Nate's voice spoke again. "This is how I communicate when I'm a wolf. The bracelet allows me to." There was a hint of irritation to his voice. "It's just something we'll have to work around for today."

Josh grinned next to me. "Or it might give you an excuse to be quiet for the day."

Wolf Nate glared at Josh. "Or I'll just talk in your mind for the whole day."

I turned to Josh. "So you can hear him too?"

He nodded in reply. "I can hear it if he wants me to. He can choose who he talks to. You won't be able to tell, but he can."

Wolf Nate put his head up in pride. Out of the corner of my eye, I could see Dale roll his eyes.

"Breakfast!" he exclaimed, changing the subject.

Josh, Wolf Nate, and I came to sit around the blazing fire. We all ate our toast in silence. It was stale and took my teeth an incredible amount of strength to pull a bite off. The eggs were okay, but lacked salt. They tasted like nothing.

Nate was putting the food on his tongue and gulping it down in one bite. It made me laugh. He tried to smile in whatever way a wolf could smile, but his tongue rolled out of his mouth. He looked like a dog. He was a dog. It made me laugh even more, and Wolf Nate closed his mouth stubbornly.

When we had all eaten and Dale had cleared away the supplies, we gathered our bags and continued into one of the tunnels. There were three entrances, and Dale seemed to pick a random one, not even looking at his zapper on the way. I only hoped it was the right direction.

Soon enough the tunnel engulfed us in darkness. I heard Dale click a button on his zapper, and a dim light filled the cavern. We walked like this for two hours.

After a while of who knows how long, the tunnel started to shake. Rocks and dirt rained down on us, getting caught in my tangled hair. We stopped moving until the shaking had stopped and the dust had settled. Dale looked back at me. "Train."

I had no idea where we were. I tried to think of places where we could be walking under what seconds before had obviously been train tracks. We could be anywhere. Multiple mazes of trains ran around New York. Dale had also said that the tunnels made traveling distance smaller. Something about a warlock spell that had been put on them. Whatever Dale said, he was probably right.

We walked for another half hour and sat down for lunch. I guessed we had been walking for about three hours now. Dale nodded when I asked, glancing at his watch.

"Approximately. It's 2:37 a.m." He handed me a packed sandwich. It was the same type as the one that Nate and I had eaten in the mansion. "Here," he muttered.

I laughed to myself. Our sleeping schedule had been completely distorted. I guess that's what happens when you're a fugitive.

Josh flopped down next to me. "Who's up for some storytelling?" He rubbed his hands together excitedly.

"Don't." Nate's voice echoed through my head as if he knew what story Josh was going to tell.

Josh rolled his eyes at Wolf Nate. "Come on, Nate! It's about time she heard some occult myths and stories! It's not like you've been telling her any."

I crossed my arms. "Myths? As in myths that turned out to be real?"

Josh considered this. His gray eyes met my gaze. "Yes."

"Which story are you going to tell? Are you going to take her in?" Dale said in between bites of his sandwich.

Josh's eyes sparkled. "The one that everyone knows. The one that they should know if they're related to the occult in any way."

Wolf Nate growled, but Josh ignored it. "Everyone must have heard of this story at one point in their occult life. It's the greatest myth there is. Or is it the truth?" Josh shrugged.

My eyebrows knit together. "What do you mean by taking me in?"

Wolf Nate laughed, which Josh ignored along with my question..."I haven't been completely honest. I am about 99 percent human, 1 percent occult," Josh started.

I narrowed my eyes at him. "What occult?"

"I'm the most human occult you can find. Most of my kind don't even realize that they are occult," he said mysteriously. "I'm an illusionist."

Wolf Nate snickered. "You say that as if it's a good thing."

Josh glared at him. "It's better than being a wolf." He cleared his throat. "You may think that an illusionist is like a magician, but it's not. Magicians are humans that pretend to be able to do magic tricks. An illusionist in the occult world is like a storyteller. Most of the time we are considered human, but the law does say we are only allowed to take people that know of the occult into our stories."

I frowned. "That doesn't answer my question. How do you take people into stories?"

Josh smiled; his eyes twinkled in the dim light of the tunnel. "I'll show you with my first story." He snapped his fingers, and my eyes began to droop. "Ever heard of a guy named Ker Moros?"

CHAPTER 19

When I opened my eyes, I wasn't in the tunnels anymore. I was in a dark, chamber-like room. It reminded me of an old police station. Cells lined one of the walls, and a heavy metal door was on the other. Nothing else was in the room except for a table that stood in the middle, with two chairs on either side and a lamp in the middle of it. I walked over. Papers were strewn all over the table. There were pictures of people that looked like mug shots. I turned to look at a huge map on the wall. It looked like a detective board, with red strings pinned and strung from side to side.

Seven locations were circled in thick red marker. I took a step forward to examine one spot in particular. New York was circled. I followed the string that was pinned there to the side of the board. Different pictures and photographs hung around the pin. They were scribbly annotated; it reminded me of a doctor's handwriting. A photo of a marble ring hung on the side. The ring had a bluish glow to it, and a symbol was etched into the top. It was a crescent-like shape. I put my hand up to run my hand over the symbol.

That's when I noticed my hand was a strange color. I looked down. I was a strange tint of gray, like the people in one of those movies from the fifties. Everything in the room had color but me. Like I was a projection into this strange place.

Before I was able to wrap my head around the weirdness of it all, something creaked behind me. I turned to look as a figure sat down in the chair. He flicked on the lamp. He turned it so that it shone directly onto the chair on the opposite side. Then he sat back and waited.

He tapped his fingers on the arm of the chair. He was a tall man, with a fierce look to him. Almost like you had to be afraid of him. Then he looked straight at me. I tripped backward into the wall. His eyes were red. Red and powerful. His eyes shifted slightly to the side.

"He can't see you, you know," a voice said coming up to me. "He's just looking at the map. Looking straight through you."

I looked at Josh, still rubbing my head from where I had hit the wall. Even though this place was an illusion, I could still feel everything around me. My head throbbed. Josh was also a gray shade. Just like me. A projection.

"What is this?"

"This," Josh said, signaling around the room, "is an illusion. It's playing off in your head. Telling you the story. Everything that happens, I control it."

I looked at the strange man sitting in the chair. He was frozen still, like a movie put on pause. "Who is he?"

Josh smiled. "That is Ker Moros. He is a sorcerer. His story is one of the stories that parents tell their children to scare them. Like some scary Halloween stories.

"Ker Moros is not his actual name, but it's his most common and feared name. No one knows his actual name. He tried to take over occult and human power a long time ago. He practiced dark magic, through which spirits got into his head and turned him insane. Sorcerers tell the story often as a warning to be careful with power and that ancestral magic is the safest. The ones that practice dark magic have to be carefully moderated. Especially after Moros caused all that chaos." Josh laughed at my expression.

"He seems like a nice guy," I muttered.

"Everyone fears him. His red eyes are said to be able to kill someone on the spot. Apparently they're only red when he uses his power, but I thought it would be nice to add the fact in." Josh shrugged. "A lot of people don't believe his story. They'll do anything to deny his existence. He has risen up in the past and been destroyed. Many, many years ago. I saw the records, the pictures; it's all true.

"However, people don't believe it because there is a bit of magic involved. It is said Moros is gathering the original power of all the races to become leader of the world, or so you could call it."

I held up my hand. "Races?"

Josh nodded slowly. "Did Nate not tell you? He couldn't have told you about the occult without telling you about the races."

I shook my head. "He mentioned something about sections, but that's it."

Josh frowned. "Well, long ago the occult were split into races. I'll tell you more about it in my next story. For now, all you need to know is that there are seven occult races. It is said that each race stored its power into a token and this power can be utilized under the right circumstances. Like any power, it can be used for good or evil.

"Most people don't believe this story. They don't believe in tokens that can possess power. But Moros did. He has risen up in the past trying to gain this power, but he failed. He was killed.

"Lately things have been stirring in the occult world. Power is being distorted. Now I'm a curious guy. I went into my dad's records and found out more about Moros's past. They are saying he somehow survived and is trying to regain this power and this time use it for the worst. I also heard this story." Josh gestured around the room. "And this is my interpretation of how it happened. Now I'm showing you. This happened a long time ago, before Moros's first uprising."

Josh snapped his fingers. Instantly Ker Moros started moving again, his chest heaving and falling. He blinked slowly. A heavy knock echoed through the room.

"Come in." Moros's deep voice boomed through the chamber.

A lean man came in. His skin was tanned, and his styled-back hair was yet black. "Yes, sir?"

"What have you found out so far?"

The man sat down in the other chair. He squinted his eyes at the bright light. Then the light moved. It swung back and forth, creaking loudly. The bulb now hung down. I blinked. Almost like it had been done by magic, but it was too natural. Like the tanned man had moved really fast and my eyes couldn't quite catch the movement.

"Vampire," Josh whispered next to me.

"I found that there are seven marbles in total, one for each race. They exist. Different people own them; some came across them by accident, others by inheritance. I don't know who has them exactly, but I'm working on that ..."

"Stop!" Moros interrupted. "I don't care who has them at the moment. I want to know what power they possess."

"They?" I asked Josh. He shushed me and nodded toward the scene.

The tanned man cleared his throat. "As I said, there are seven. They're usually hidden in some sort of accessory or object so they are easier to keep track of. There is one for each of the occult races: the werewolves, the vampires, the gifted, the sorcerers, the goblins, the humans, and the creatures." He leaned back calmly, as if Moros didn't threaten him at all.

Moros raised an eyebrow. "Creatures? And what about the humans? They're not occult." He spat his last words in disgust.

"The humans have one so that the power is balanced. Creatures as in pixies, fairies, harpies—those types of things."

I turned to Josh. "What do you fall under?"

"I fall under the gifted," he whispered. "Occult like illusionists and healers are considered gifted because they have some sort of power that can do something. Creatures are minor magical occult that don't have a specific power."

I turned back to Moros. He was looking at the map again. "Are these the correct locations?"

"I believe some of them are. There is one in the New York area, another in the south, and another in the west. Those are definite. I'm not sure about the rest yet," the tanned man answered.

Moros nodded slowly. "Research more. I want to know who. And get me in contact with whoever has the human marble. I definitely want that one."

The tanned man stood up and headed back into the shadows. "Will do, sir."

Ker Moros smiled wickedly. "Perfect."

The scene paused again. Everything stood still. Then it all started to shift slowly, turning around and around in my vision, making me dizzy. Then everything turned pitch-black. I opened my eyes.

I was lying on my back in the tunnel, my head resting on one of the bags. I sat up. Wolf Nate and Dale were watching me. Josh sat with a wide grin on his face. "Well, there you have it."

I rubbed my eyes. "So the legend says that this Ker Moros guy possesses power?"

Josh's eyes sparkled. "It's not a legend, it's a fact. It's happening again right now. People just don't want to believe it. When Moros failed the first time, everyone erased it from their minds. Which is why I have taken the liberty to watch my dad—just in case Moros strikes."

Dale rolled his eyes. "It's a myth, Josh. Nobody can prove it. It's superstition. People just want to scare each other."

"It's a fact." Josh glared at the goblin. "I have done much research, and there are dozens of files on him. How he was jailed, how he tried to gain power—all of that. Years ago he failed due to complications and couldn't receive the power. If he has risen again, there is no doubt that he will try again. If you have all the marbles of the races, you have control over all the races."

"Really, Josh?" Dale's eyes widened, his cheeks turning red. "Then how come I don't remember, huh? I'm older than you think; I was there in the 1900s. There is no way I could have missed a revolution like this."

Josh shrugged. "I looked into this too. People had their minds erased if they couldn't handle the truth or if it was too painful. Either you were too busy with your tunnels or you had a reason to forget."

Dale shook his head. "I would never do that, Josh."

Josh narrowed his eyes. "Well, you wouldn't remember now, would you?"

"Even if I did, those marbles are also fake."

Josh crossed his arms. "No, they're not. They're from the beginning of time. When the leaders decided to split the occult into races, they created the marbles." Josh rubbed his hands together. His eyes gleamed mysteriously. "Which brings me to my next story."

Before I could utter a word, Josh snapped his fingers. My eyes drooped, and everything turned black.

When I opened my eyes, I was standing on a hillside. The clouds were dark, and rain dripped onto my skin. I shivered. The wind howled around me, chilling me to the bone. I felt a hand on my back. I glanced over my shoulder to see Josh was starting to steer me forward.

We headed to a small stone building. My feet made squishing sounds in the wet grass, and mud caked my shoes dirty. Thunder crackled in the distance as we entered the building.

There was no door, only an opening in the wall. The ground and walls were all the same shade of gray concrete. Inside stood a round table. It was made out of wood and looked like it was as close to falling apart as Dale's bridge had been.

Seven people were seated around the table. On the side stood a woman, her blond hair ragged and dirty. A small braid held it out of her eyes. She wore a piece of cloth clothing, and a string waistband hung on her hips. The color in her tunic was faded, as if it had gone through harsh conditions. With a quick glance around the room, I saw that everyone wore the same thing, and they were all in the same condition as her—dirty, beaten-up.

The woman held a straw basket with marbles inside. They were each a different glowing color, and a symbol was etched into them. I couldn't make the symbols out from where I stood. I quickly counted in my head. There were seven marbles.

"We have gathered here today to discuss the solution to our recent problems." One of the men stood from his seat. His brown hair hung to his ears. He came across as the self-nominated leader, but yet he didn't tower over everyone. He looked as their equal.

"The powerful dark magic that had stricken our land has finally been defeated. We couldn't have done it without each other." He gestured around the room. "Without each other's contributions, our individual power would not have been strong enough to defeat the dark forces. By coming together we were stronger. I think you would all agree?"

A silent nod went around the room. Another man stood as the previous one took a seat. His skin was pale, and when he started to talk, I could see fangs coming over his bottom lip. "With much discussion we have decided that we will split the occult into races. Each race has its own power, which will be placed into a token. This way we can live separately and be responsible for our own, but yet we will be connected." He gestured at the woman standing in the corner. "Elise will explain."

The woman nodded. "Thank you, Louis." She stepped forward and started to pass out the marbles. She checked the symbol on each before giving it to the correct representative.

"Each of these marbles contains the essence of your race. Alone, they have no power. But when brought together, all the power that was harnessed here will come out and be able to defeat a great evil if one so reappears. This will remind our people that great evil can only be defeated by greater good.

"Because we don't want the power falling into the wrong hands, there is a fail-safe. This fail-safe lies with the human race." She gave a marble to a dark-haired girl. She looked younger than the rest of the group. Her blue eyes shone as she looked down at the light green marble. Elise rested her hand on the girl's shoulder.

"I will create a doppelgänger line from your blood. Another doppelgänger will be born once the previous has passed on. Only the doppelgänger will be able to activate the power of the marbles with the help of a powerful sorcerer. All other races need to be present to feed the power that will then be able to be collected through that sorcerer." Elise smiled. She had passed around all the marbles and went to stand in the corner again. "Pass the marbles down through your family. Tell no one of its power, but make sure your heir knows of this legend we're creating."

Louis smiled. He twisted his own marble around between his fingers. "Then it's settled. The races are as follow: the werewolves, the vampires, the warlocks, the humans, the sorcerers …" Louis hesitated as thunder crackled outside. The stone chamber lit up momentarily.

"The gifted, for creatures or people with magical ability," Louis continued. "And lastly the creatures, for any occult creature that isn't able to harness power."

The man from before stood as Louis took a seat. "Any concerns?"

One frail hand raised in the air. It was the human girl. "As the human representative, I would like to request that the human race be withdrawn from the occult world. The pressure is too much for most to handle. It drives our race insane to know that there is someone stronger that they can't fight. I will keep the legend alive in my family and pass down the marble. Other than that I would like to have the memory of the others erased."

The man considered this. He scratched his chin. "It's not a bad idea." He turned to Elise. "What do you think? Is this possible?"

Elise nodded. "Definitely. The only issue is that the new doppelgänger won't know what she is, but that might not be that bad. It would help keep her secure and safe. I will erase the memories of the humans."

Louis smiled from where he sat. "So it's been decided?"

Again silent nods went around the room. Everyone was quiet, examining his or her own marbles. The human girl stood and left with Elise. Thunder crackled as they disappeared into the rain.

The colors in my vision started to blur. Everything started to spin, making my stomach churn. I looked down at my gray projected hands. They were starting to fade.

Instead of my sight turning black like last time, the scenery shifted. I looked around. Josh stood next to me, still in his gray shade. The sky was still dark, but it was night instead of a storm. We stood on a paved street, with old Fords lining the sidewalk. Except the old Fords were brand-new.

Josh smiled next to me. "Welcome to the fifties." I quickly followed Josh as he started toward one of the buildings.

CHAPTER 20

I followed Josh into one of the houses on the side of the street. The door was unlocked, and we made our way inside. It was completely isolated. There was no furniture in the house; it was one big empty room. The only light was coming from a bulb on the ceiling, and it seemed to be the only appliance present inside the house.

Inside stood three men. Ker Moros was one of them. He looked slightly younger, but the evilness still radiated off of him. The tanned man was also in the room. He leaned against the windowsill, his gaze focused on something outside. The third man looked familiar to me, but I couldn't recognize from where.

"Louis," Josh explained as he walked into the room. I carefully followed him. It didn't seem like the safest thing to be around two vampires and an evil sorcerer.

"Don't worry," Josh said, grabbing my hand and pulling me inside the room. "They're frozen. Plus, I wouldn't let them hurt you. They're my illusion, remember?"

I followed Josh's gaze. He was right. The men stood unmoving, not even blinking or breathing. I didn't actually know if vampires needed to breathe, but still. I had forgotten we were in Josh's illusion. Everything seemed so real.

Slowly the men started to move. Moros held up a bag filled with red liquid. I tried not to gag as the smell hit my nostrils. It was blood.

"Here you have it—doppelgänger blood." Moros threw the bag to Louis. He caught it in one swift movement. He didn't seem too bothered by the blood. The tanned man, on the other hand, turned his gaze away from the window. A hungry look appeared in his eyes. Moros noticed.

"Calm down, Vasco. Keep it under control."

Vasco shook his head, returning his gaze out the window. "Sorry," he muttered. "Haven't fed in days."

Moros clapped his hands together. Louis hadn't moved his gaze from the blood bag.

"Tell me what to do, Louis. I have the doppelgänger blood, and I am a sorcerer. Tell me what I need to complete the spell."

Louis shrugged, placing the blood bag in his coat pocket. "I'm surprised, Moros. I thought you were smarter."

Moros frowned. He waved the subject off with his hand. "Yes, I know I don't have all the marbles yet, but Vasco's army is out looking for the remaining few. I know where they are, and I already have some in my possession. They are well-hidden. Now, tell me what I need to do with the blood."

Louis shook his head. "That's not what I meant. I said the doppelgänger was dangerous but important. I never said you had to kill the innocent girl."

"You need to kill someone in order to take their blood."

Louis started to pace. "Not necessarily, but that's not the point either. I said you needed the blood of the doppelgänger. As in the original doppelgänger's blood that runs through this girl's veins. It needs to be present. I never said you needed a bag of her blood. You need her alive, not dead."

Moros strode forward. He wrapped his hands around Louis's throat, stopping him mid-pace. He smashed the vampire into the wall. It didn't seem like Moros was stronger, but the sorcerer caught Louis off guard. I saw Moros's fingers tightening around Louis's neck.

"It's okay," Josh whispered from beside me. He loosened my fingers from his. I hadn't realized I was grabbing him so tightly—or that I was holding him at all. His skin had paled where my fingers were. He moved my grasp to his palm and squeezed tightly. "It'll be okay. Just watch."

Louis reached up and grabbed Moros's fingers. "You can't hurt me, Moros."

"Watch me." I saw Moros's eyes start to go red. Veins popped out of his skin in a strange black color. As if his blood was poisoned. He squeezed tighter.

"We have a blood oath." Louis's voice sounded raspy, as if he was not getting enough air. "If you hurt me, you know what will happen to you."

Moros's eyes filled with anger, but he did nothing. His muscles relaxed slightly. Louis saw his opportunity and pulled away. He straightened his collar as he walked around the sorcerer. He nodded at Vasco. Vasco caught the movement and signaled at something out the window.

Moros turned. "What are you doing?"

Vasco stood. "Just signaling at my army."

"Your army?" Moros's eyes narrowed. "You mean the army that I helped you create? The vampires I helped you turn so that you could help me?"

"Well, Louis and I have been talking, and you know I have been saying that this dark magic is doing you no good. So we decided to help the government out."

"You what?" Moros screamed. His voice boomed through the room, making the lightbulb shake on the ceiling.

"This power will never do you or the world any good. I'm sorry, but it's for the best." Vasco looked sad. Then he glanced out the window. "They won't kill you, but you'll be taken care of. Good-bye, Moros."

Vasco turned and jumped out the window. The glass fell to the ground in shatters. Louis followed quickly behind. In an instant people sprang in from outside through the broken window. They leaped inside, landing in a stance. Fangs produced over their lips.

Vampires raced in through the door and from another window behind Josh and me. In an instant the room was flooded with vampires. Some fell dead to the ground as Moros's magic killed them on the spot. But there were too many. Vampires raced around, breaking my grasp from Josh. I screamed his name, but no sound came out. Vampires lurched at me.

My eyes flew open. Sweat dripped down my forehead. I looked around and noticed I was back in the tunnels. I inhaled deeply, staring at Josh.

"That's what happened?"

Josh nodded. "I assume. I made the dialogue up, but the facts are from my dad's records. Moros had created a vampire army with Vasco to help him. But he didn't agree, and neither did Louis. Like the illusion showed, they tricked him into killing the doppelgänger, which was necessary to complete the spell in the end. They captured him with the vampires and brought him in."

Dale smirked. "The vampire epidemic of the fifties. I remember that."

"See." Josh narrowed his eyes at the goblin.

I shook my head rapidly. Hair fell in front of my face. "You need to show me another illusion. You have to tell me what happened after he got captured and how he survived to rise up again."

Nate growled. Waves danced in his fur as he shook his head. "Too many illusions aren't good for you."

Josh nodded. "As much as I would like to disagree with Mannaro, he's right. Too many illusions will mess with your brain and make it hard for you to tell the stories from reality. It's dangerous."

I gasped before I could stop myself. Josh looked at me, but no emotion showed in his face. I spoke carefully. "So illusionists can be used to torture people then? To confuse them? That's horrible."

Josh looked grim. "Yeah. That's why I have to be careful. Sometimes it's hard for me to tell when I go too far, because I can tell the difference due to me controlling it. Others, I'm not so sure."

"That's how they tortured him, right? Moros." Dale looked at Josh. He frowned when Michael's son smiled.

"That's right." Josh turned to me. "According to my dad's files, they captured Moros with the help of the vampires and were able to suppress his magic with some strong ancestral magic. Like a very strong good magic to balance out the dark evil magic. It worked, and they put him in jail.

"At first they didn't want to kill him, because he had been good once. They believed that the dark magic had just taken over.

The government brought in illusionists to wipe his memories of the marbles and make him forget. However, it didn't work. He forgot some small details, but the big facts still remained.

"So they sentenced him to death. They killed him with magic and whatnot. I don't even know how. It must have been horrible enough for the government not to take any notes on it."

Dale rolled his eyes. "It still doesn't explain anything. How would he have risen again? And there's still no proof of the marbles actually existing."

"Like I said, Dale, I did research. It's true. Apparently the dark magic was rooted so deep that over time it brought him back to life. There are multiple articles on that big jail escape break a year or two ago. It's happening."

Nate growled again. "So what does this have to do with us?"

"That's the thing, Mannaro. I have a theory. I think my dad goes after things with an excuse. That's what it seems like anyway. Take the riot and my case. I looked into it. My dad knew Dale had tunnels there. He always talked about how much he wanted them. He sent me to Toronto that week and put me in a hotel near those people. As if he expected them to riot. He knew Dale would cover for me."

Josh laughed bitterly. "It's that simple. My dad finds something to go after to pretend that that is what he wants, but he gets the thing he wants instead. What if he wants the marbles himself so he can be in control or for some other sick twisted plan?"

I shook my head. "I'm sorry, Josh," I said softly. "These are all different points. They aren't connected."

Josh laughed loudly. "Oh, but that's the thing. They are. I did some sneaking, and the reason my dad has Moros's files lying around is because he's looking into it. I found out that one of the leads they have is the marble one."

"So?"

"So, my dad must think Mannaro has it! He doesn't care about the human knowing about the occult. He wants to see if Nate has the marble. Do you really think my dad cares about Renn knowing? It's just one person." Josh winked at me. "See the connection?"

Nate shifted uncomfortably. He let out a soft growl, but spoke nothing in my head.

Dale stared at Josh. "Is that your theory?"

"That's my theory."

Dale's face turned red. "Is that why you're here? To prove your theory? The marbles don't exist! Josh, they're a myth. People come up with stories like this …"

I tuned out Dale's ranting. Josh's idea was interesting. It made sense, but it was like a random connect the dots. Like someone hadn't followed the numbers and opted to connect the dots randomly instead. I looked at Nate. He was lying on the ground, his paw twitching. Even though he was a wolf, I could still tell if something was up.

"You okay?" I asked. I heard Dale and Josh stop arguing. They both looked at Nate.

Wolf Nate shook his head. Waves danced in his fur. "Not exactly. I just want them to stop fighting about that theory."

Dale narrowed his eyes. "And why is that?"

Nate shifted again. He looked at me and then back at Dale. "Because his theory is correct."

Josh smirked. "And why is that, Mannaro? Are you on my side for once?"

Nate looked at me. "Grab my bag and open the front pocket. Take out what's inside."

I did as he said. I unzipped the pocket and took out two objects. One was the picture I had taken from Nate's house. The one with him and his mom. The other was a small box. I opened it. Inside was a ring. A marble ring.

"So, it's just a marble ring," I said. I could hear my own voice shake. I carefully placed the box on the ground.

Josh cleared his throat uncomfortably. "Yeah, Renn's right. There are millions of marble rings in the world. This doesn't have to be that marble ring, right?"

Everyone stayed quiet, staring at the small aqua-colored sphere.

"Right?" Josh repeated in a whisper. Nobody answered him.

Dale spoke up first. "Let me get this straight," he said. "Michael is after us. We know that. And we're assuming he is also after the marble. Why?"

"That we don't know. He has a reason, I'm sure of it, but I don't know what," Josh said while he examined the ring. I hadn't even noticed him pick it up out of the box. He carefully placed it back on the ground.

"Right," Dale continued. "But that's not necessarily important for us. We don't need to know why Michael needs the ring; we just need to know if this is *the* marble."

"It is." Nate's voice echoed in all of our heads.

"Let's not try to come up with a conclusion. It might not be," Dale replied.

"But that's the thing. I know it is," Nate snapped back. He closed his eyes and continued calmly, "I have the ring, which I inherited from my mother. She's wearing it in that picture. I'd always thought that the ring was hers, but apparently my dad had given it to her when they married. My dad always used to tell stories about it being passed down for generations; it goes all the way back to the supposed founding leader Josh showed in his illusion. My family comes from a strong line of werewolves; I told Renn that when I explained about my dad being the pack leader. It's the original marble that has been around since the beginning of the races."

"Okay," Dale said slowly. "So it's the original werewolf marble, passed down from ancient times. It's the marble from the myths. The myths in which Moros nearly destroyed everyone in his path to gain the power. Michael wants this marble. Moros wants this marble. It possesses the power to unite all races and ..."—he hesitated and stared down at the ring—"it could get us all killed."

CHAPTER 21

The tunnel was silent. Nobody said a word. I could hear my own heart beating silently in my chest. Nate lay with his head in his paws, a relaxed look over him. But his eyes said differently. His yellow pupils were flooded in worry. He knew he had brought all of us into danger. He had heard Moros's story even though he hadn't admitted it. He knew that Moros was after the marbles and that he had one. He had known all along.

Josh was the first to speak. "I was right!" he exclaimed. He pointed at Dale. "My theory was correct. My dad is after the marbles. Told you."

"I don't think that is the most important matter right now," Dale replied quietly. He looked from Nate to the marble and back. "How do we know this is the same marble?"

I turned the ring over in my hands. The marble had a strange glow to it. "Dale is right," I said. I felt my voice shake. "It could be a totally different marble."

"It's not. It's the marble Josh was talking about." Nate's voice echoed in my head. I could tell by the others' reactions that they had heard it too.

"You have no proof," I said as I touched the marble. It spun loosely in its clasp.

Nate tilted his head sideways. "Take it out of the clasp."

I frowned. "I'll break it."

"No, you won't. It's designed that way so that the marble can be used. Just click it out."

I grabbed the marble and pulled it slightly. It came out without any effort. As I held the marble, it started to vibrate. The mist swirled inside. As I turned it over, something scratched my hand. I looked at the bottom of the token. A familiar symbol was engraved into it. A silver crescent was etched into the blue outside of the marble.

I jumped as some sort of power exerted off of it. It fell to the floor, where it rolled to a stop.

"That's your proof. It's exerting power in an attempt to find the other marbles." Nate sighed. His wolf chest heaved and fell. Then he laid his muzzle on his paws.

Josh leaned forward and picked up the marble. "This is amazing," I heard him mutter. He ran his thumb over the crescent mark. "I was …" His voice faltered. Josh placed the marble down on the floor and put his face in his hands.

Dale frowned. "Are you okay?"

Josh looked up and glared at the goblin. "Am I okay? Do I look okay?" He pointed at the marble. "I thought I wanted to be right. But I don't. You know what that means?" The sparkle disappeared from Josh's eyes. "It means that my dad is a liar."

"We knew that already," Dale commented lightly.

"You don't get it, do you?" Josh stood. "Don't you understand what it means? This means that my dad is coming after us for that marble, not for Renn. It also means that he used me to get to your tunnels." He turned and started walking down the tunnel. He kicked at some of the gravel. When he spoke again, his voice shook. "I knew he did some horrible things, but I didn't know that he used people. He used me. His own son."

Josh cleared his throat. "I know how he is, but he's still my dad. Now it just doesn't feel that way anymore."

We all watched as Josh disappeared into the shadows.

"Did he just leave us?" Nate's voice spoke in my head.

Dale silently shook his head. "He just needs some time."

I picked up the marble and clicked it back in the clasp. As soon as it fell into place, it spun around in the accessory. I placed it on Nate's overturned paw. It didn't help anything—he couldn't pick it up—but he left it there.

"Stop being so hard on him," I said.

Nate's wolf eyes widened, his yellow pupils vibrant. "I don't think he likes me any more than I like him."

"So? He just found out that his dad's been using him!"

Nate glared at me. "The only reason I have that ring is because my mom died, remember? I killed her!"

I stood up. "Please, Nate, don't play the sympathy card. It's pathetic."

"I'm not playing any sympathy card!" Nate's voice roared in my head.

I turned around and started to walk in the direction Josh went in. I heard Nate take a breath as if he was about to say something. No sound followed.

"Just let her go," I heard Dale tell him. "It's been a rough few days for all of us, especially her. She needs some time. She'll come back."

Their voices started to fade in the distance. I heard Nate say something, but I couldn't quite make the voice out in my head. As if the farther I got away, the weaker the connection between us got. Soon enough, I couldn't hear him speaking anymore. The dirt cracked under my feet as I continued down the tunnel.

Soon the tunnel turned pitch-black. The lights were off. I tried to feel the sides of the tunnel, running my hand along the wall in case a turn came. Then the walls disappeared on both sides, my hands being left in the air. I had come across an intersection.

I groaned to myself. I hadn't exactly thought my plan through. Josh could have wandered off somewhere, and he had a zapper. I didn't even have light. I turned around. I didn't actually know for sure, but that's what it felt like. I couldn't place myself as to where I was. Everything was black. For all I knew, I could have been lying on the ground.

I tried to feel around for a wall, but my hands met no sides. I shrieked as I felt something run across my foot. Or did I imagine it? I couldn't tell anymore. What was up, and what was down? It felt like I was drowning. Drowning in a pitch-black tunnel.

I gasped as something flickered behind me.

"Renn?" It was Josh.

I turned around and jumped into his arms. I hugged him tight.

"Hey, it's okay," he said softly.

I pulled away and sat down, leaning my head on the tunnel wall. Josh knelt down and sat next to me.

"Guess you learned the hard way not to go into Dale's tunnels without a zapper." He smirked.

I swallowed. "I didn't really think my plan through."

Josh twisted his zapper around in his hand. The built-in light gave off a faint flow, just enough to illuminate our faces. "Were you planning on running away?"

"No." I shook my head. "I came to find you."

Josh looked at me blankly. Then the corners of his mouth started to curve upward. "You came to find me?"

I nodded. "I thought you might want someone to talk to."

"Well, I appreciate that," he said with an idiotic grin on his face. "For a second there, I thought you liked Nate a little too much."

I frowned. "What is that supposed to mean?"

"Well," Josh shrugged, "he's very protective of you. I think that's part of the reason why he doesn't like me very much. He sees me as a threat, like I'm stealing you away from him."

I rolled my eyes. "That is not true."

"It is."

"No, it's not."

Josh grinned. "I can't say I'm not glad that you think that way. But it's true. He likes you a little too much. It's really obvious.

"But it's Nate."

"It's Nate, the guy you've known since kindergarten. I know. But that doesn't mean it's not true."

I sat back. Was Josh telling the truth? Had I really missed all the signs? He couldn't like me. Especially since he'd been really mad at me minutes ago. I turned to Josh. "And why are you glad that I think that way?"

Josh gazed straight ahead. After a moment he grabbed my hand in his. His palms were warm. "I already told you that I liked you."

I felt my eyebrows knit together. "No, you didn't."

"Yes, I did," Josh said. He held my hand and started to trail the lines of my palm with his finger. "I told you that you were different than a lot of the other people that I met. Then I told you that I liked you."

Then I remembered. The memory popped into my head. It was when we were in the cave when I had been putting a bandage on his wounds. I had waved the comment off, thinking he had just been trying to be nice. But he had meant it. So did that mean Nate and Josh were jealous of each other because of me? There was already bad blood between them; did that mean I was the match that reignited the old flame?

"Both of you have been acting so horrible toward each other …" My voice faltered. I didn't know what I should say next.

Josh considered this. "We have our issues …" He shrugged. "I have the tendency to try to be the smart one. I grew up without parents—not my fault. Some things change you, that being something that changed me. I try to control myself, but sometimes I let it slip."

He sighed. "And then there's Nate. Pretty perfect life. Then he killed his mom—again, not his fault. It changed him. It's why he's so defensive. He knows what it's like to lose someone close to you when it's entirely your own fault.

"He's had that stupid ring all along. He knew what power it possessed, and I bet he had his suspicions about my dad. The reason he didn't say anything was because he didn't want to lose you."

We both sat quietly. Then Josh shifted closer to me. He was still holding my hand. I liked this side of Josh. More down-to-earth and not as cocky. Not trying to compete all the time.

I felt his gaze on me. I turned my head and looked back at him. His gray eyes sparkled in the dim zapper light.

"I don't think you're a bad person," I said quietly.

Josh looked at me. "I never said that I was."

"No." I put my other hand in his hands too. "But it's what you think."

Josh shrugged lightly. He didn't reply.

"Let me tell you the truth."

He raised his eyebrows. He was really close, our skin touching. He shifted so that his face was right in front of mine. "And that is?" he asked quietly.

I bit my lip. "You can compete with Nate." The volume of our voices seemed to be decreasing. "You're pretty perfect too."

Josh tilted his head to the side. He moved closer, if that was even possible. "Is that so?"

I nodded. "And just by the way, I like you too." I felt a smile slowly spread across my face.

I moved as close to him as I possibly could. I didn't know what had gotten into me, but I didn't care. My mind seemed to go blank. Josh leaned forward so that our foreheads were touching.

I felt my heartbeat rise; a strange feeling of butterflies spreading through my stomach. What was happening? Josh noticed.

"It's okay," he whispered. He held my hands with one hand and stroked my face with the other. He pulled a piece of hair behind my ear. "Let me try something …"

And then we were kissing. It came out of nowhere. Well, it didn't, but I pretended it did. I felt Josh's lips on mine. He held me, and strangely it felt right. I put my arms around his neck, brushing his face in the process.

I gasped as he pulled away slightly, his gray eyes staring straight into mine. "I like this," he muttered. "I'm much better for you, you know. I'll take care of you. Nate, on the other hand …"

Nate. I panicked, pulling away from Josh and scooting myself toward the other side of the tunnel. He frowned. "What was that for?"

"I … Nothing. I've just … um … you know." I stumbled across my words as they came out, trying to find a decent excuse.

Josh raised an eyebrow. "Have you never kissed anyone before?"

I nodded rapidly. "Yes," I lied. Josh smiled. He believed it.

He crawled over to me. He shook his head as he played with a lock of my hair. "How is that possible? Nate is really missing out." He grinned. "Too bad for him."

Laughing, Josh kissed my forehead. Then he sat next to me and put his arm around my shoulders. I tried to act as calmly as possible. *What was I going to do?*

Josh turned and buried his face in my hair. I felt his warm breath in my ear. "We should go back."

He stood up, pulling my hand and me along with him. He started to walk me back through the tunnel. He held my hand. I was glad he couldn't see my expression in the dark. I had a big problem.

When we arrived back in the tunnel, Nate and Dale were already fast asleep. It made me realize how tired I was. It surprised me, as it hadn't been too long since we last slept. I guess that's what happens when you walk so much.

We sat down against the wall. That's where we slept. Well, Josh did. As soon as I felt his breathing slow, I removed my hand from his. I felt like crying. I could only imagine what would happen if Nate found out. Whatever it was, it wouldn't be good. It would only lead to trouble.

I carefully grabbed Josh's wrist and turned it so that I could look at his watch. It was four in the morning. Nate would be turning back to human soon; the night was almost over. I softly placed Josh's hand back, shaking my head to myself. Our sleeping schedules were being messed up horribly.

I crawled over to Nate. His heavy wolf chest heaved and fell calmly. I ran my hand through his thick fur. Then I lay down and put my head on his side. I dug myself into his warm fur. I lay there for a while, trying to tune out my thoughts. I couldn't manage to fall asleep for a long time. I was too busy thinking about all the problems that I was going to have to deal with. I twisted the necklace at the base of my throat. The cool metal burned my skin. I tried to keep my focus on the texture of the necklace, just so that I could erase the problems in my mind for even three seconds.

CHAPTER 22

The bright sunlight woke me up instantly. I looked up. I hadn't noticed it in the dark, but there were small holes in the roof of the tunnel. Just big enough to let in thin rays of light. It made the cave look alive and magical. I rubbed the sleep out of my eyes. I wanted to run my other hand through my hair, but something was holding it back. Looking down I realized that it was someone's arm. And not just anyone's arm. Nate's arm.

Nate yawned and pulled his arm back. He wasn't fully awake yet, but he would be soon. I turned so that I was facing him. He looked so peaceful. His chest moved up and down, and I could hear his low, soft breathing. He looked slightly drained, as if being a wolf for the night had exhausted him. Heck, we were all exhausted. Running from the government all day drained your energy.

I smiled, remembering a day when we were eight. We had met in a sandbox and been friends ever since. We had both changed so much since then, but we still stuck to each other's side. He had been my first and only best friend.

I had had other friends, girls, but they had always seemed to follow me to get closer to Nate. Either that or get into some elite party that my parents had organized. Josh had been right the night before. Some things do change you. My case was thinking that I had a best friend, and she left me as soon as she had made friends at a socialite party.

So I stuck to the background. Made sure that nobody noticed me too much. Nate had been the only one not to leave me when I needed someone. All the girls were always jealous of me, and I was starting to see why. Nate was one of the only good people I had ever met. Not only that, but he was also good-looking. He made every girl swoon without intending it.

I laughed at the memory, slightly confused as to what had made me think of it, but I let it go. I was stuck in a tunnel, running away from the government with my best friend. I had only learned a few days ago that there was a whole other world living under our noses. You had to look at the bright side.

Stirring, Nate moved his hand up to rub his eyes. He yawned. Then he put his hand under his head and looked at me. "Morning." He grinned. "How come you always look so good in the morning?"

I felt the heat rising to my cheeks. Why was Nate acting so weird? "I … I don't know …" I stammered out. "Thanks." I hesitated. "You changed back?"

Nate nodded. "Yeah, I didn't want to wake you. You looked so peaceful in your sleep; I moved a ways down the tunnel so you wouldn't hear." Then he smiled and sat up. He looked around the tunnel, squinting his eyes at the light. The sunlight reflected off his hair, and I could faintly see the dust particles floating around in the air.

Nate ran his hand through his hair, making it even more of a mess. It really helped him with the just-got-out-of-bed look.

"Where did Dale go?" he asked, looking around the cave. I followed his gaze. The tunnel wasn't that big; I could clearly see that our goblin friend had gone missing.

Then I saw Josh. His eyes were shooting daggers at Nate. "He went a little ways down the tunnel to get better zapper reception," Josh spat out. Then he shifted his eyes toward me. He only glared slightly, but couldn't keep it up long. He smiled awkwardly.

It probably hadn't been my best idea to go and sleep next to Nate after Josh had told me that he liked me. And after we had kissed. I sighed. I had to figure things out myself first before I could think about admitting anything related to Josh or Nate.

We all jumped at the sound of crunching rocks. The footsteps sounded down the tunnel and were approaching fast. The outline of a purple figure appeared in the distance. Then a head as it came closer and closer. It was Dale.

He put his hand on the tunnel wall as he reached us. He stabilized himself by leaning on the wall, attempting to catch his breath. Then he looked straight at me. He swallowed heavily. I could see the beads of sweat forming on his forehead. "We have a problem."

Nate frowned. "What's wrong?"

Dale waved his zapper. He was still breathing heavily and inhaled deeply before he spoke. "There are people. In my tunnels." He gasped for air. "A whole group of them. Guards, a strange figure, and …"he hesitated to look at Josh—"Michael."

It felt like my pulse had stopped. Michael was in the tunnels, and he was hot on our trail. I glanced at Josh. He stood silently, his eyes flaring with anger.

"Is Ben also here?" I asked Dale.

He shook his head. "No, but there are people in my cave. Werewolves. They found it. It's how they're going to find us. They have my zappers.

"How do you know?" Nate said quietly. There was a slight look of relief on his face, presumably because his dad wasn't there.

Dale's face started to go red. "How do you think I know? Haven't you noticed that I'm out of breath?" He exhaled heavily. "I ran all the way back to my cave to make sure there weren't too many of them. There are a bunch of government people, but only a few are coming into the tunnels."

"How'd you manage that? It took us more than a day to get here, and you just happened to run back and forth in ten minutes?" Josh asked.

Dale rolled his eyes. "They're my tunnels, Josh, they adapt to me better. I told you they move, right? They move along with me. And who said it was ten minutes? But that's not important!" His voice began to rise. "There are guards and werewolves in my tunnels!"

Nate crossed his arms. "Guards and werewolves. It makes sense; they're Michael's protection group. But who is this strange figure you're talking about?"

Dale shook his head. "I'm not sure. He's a tall man, dressed in black. I didn't recognize him. Maybe Michael hired him to help find us?"

"Well, then, we have to move!" Josh shouted. "We can't just stand here and let them find us. If he has zappers and werewolves, it will only be a matter of time before they reach us."

"Right. Right," Dale muttered. He wiped some sweat off his brow. "We need a plan."

"We could split up," I suggested. "We have three zappers. That will help at least three of us find our way and communicate with each other. The wolves can't smell all of us out if we split. They don't have enough people for that."

"That sounds good," Nate agreed. Josh only nodded. The news of his dad being here hadn't made him very happy.

Dale also nodded. He had been looking at something on his zapper. "There's an intersection coming up shortly. We can split up there."

We all grabbed our bags and then split up the remaining food. I quickly scarfed down a muffin for breakfast. It was dry and stuck to the roof of my mouth.

"I'll take Renn with me. The two of you split up," Dale said as we hurriedly made our way down the tunnel.

"I can't let you do that," Nate sputtered. Behind him Josh rolled his eyes.

Dale squinted at him. "And why's that?"

"She needs to be kept safe."

Dale sighed. "I'll keep her safe; don't worry. If she goes with you, there's only a higher risk they'll find her. No one is going to come after the goblin. They suspect you have the marble, so they'll come after you."

"Okay," Nate replied hesitantly. "But take care of her. There are some bad people working for the government who'll do anything to get what they want. Don't let them hurt her."

I shifted my bag uncomfortably on my shoulders. Dale rolled his eyes. "Don't worry."

After another minute or so of walking, we came across the intersection. We all took our spots. Nate would go left, Josh right, and Dale and I straight. The tunnels looked like a never-ending gulf of darkness. I couldn't make out the end.

"All of these paths lead to a cliff with a gorge. We can set that as our meeting point. Just make sure you keep taking turns toward the middle. You can see it on your zapper. It's a big canyon. Can't miss it. The tunnels are old in this area, so they probably won't adapt. If they happen to, your zapper will notify you."

Nate caught my gaze. Our eyes met, and he smiled, as if he was trying to comfort me. "It'll be okay," he mouthed. I nodded with a slight smile. I couldn't let him see how scared I was. He would never agree to split up if he knew.

Josh just stood in his tunnel. I glanced over at him, but couldn't get myself to meet his gaze.

"We must be off then," Dale said next to me. "Good luck, and don't get caught."

Both Nate and Josh raced off, leaving dust in their paths. We watched as they turned into little dots in each of their tunnels. Then they disappeared. Dale and I went straight and started to make our way down our own tunnel. We had the shortest route to the ravine, and Dale didn't seem to be in much of a hurry. Josh and Nate had a whole maze to go through; we didn't.

"Shouldn't we at least speed walk too?" I asked him.

Dale shook his head. "This tunnel is marked as destroyed on the zappers. It was, once upon a time, but I fixed it and never got around to marking it on the zapper. I made a new path next to the gap where it collapsed."

We walked in silence. After a while our tunnel started to curve to the side. Dale gave me his zapper, and I played around with it. There were different features on it; it was actually quite remarkable. There was a flashlight, GPS, and even a communication service between zappers. I pressed another button, and it showed me a map. It had small red dots on it. I zoomed in on one. It was the letter R—Nate's zapper. The dot moved down the tunnel it was in and curved from left to right, with multiple turns. Whenever he came across a crossing, he took a right. Toward the middle, just like Dale had said.

I backtracked the tunnel Nate was in to the intersection where we had started. No one was following him. I zoomed in on the next dot. It said J, which meant it was Josh. I gasped as I spotted another dot that was following him. Slower, but definitely on his trail.

"How come this one doesn't have a letter?" I asked. My voice came out unevenly.

Dale looked over my arm at the zapper. "It's the heat signal the sensors in my tunnels are picking up. It must be a werewolf, because the color is different than it would be on a human. Warmer. A werewolf's temperature is usually raised. The wolf doesn't have a zapper, but it must be on Josh's scent. That's probably not a good thing, but Josh has the leading hand.

I zoomed out of Josh's current tunnel route. I looked at the map and noticed two letters, one almost right behind each other. Probably a mile or so. I zoomed in on the letters. One was the letter E, and the other was D. D was Dale's zapper.

I felt the hairs on my skin rise as the goose bumps ran over it. "Who is zapper E?" I asked shakily.

Dale looked at me. His eyes narrowed. "Extra."

My mouth fell open as realization dawned on me. My voice came out in a bare whisper. "Someone's on our trail."

"Crap." Dale grabbed the zapper from me. He threw it on the ground and stomped on it. It crackled under his foot as sparks came out of the wires. The screen died instantly.

"Dale! What are you doing?"

Dale started speed walking down the tunnel. It wasn't quite running, but it was close. "The person that has zapper E is following our zapper. If we kill the signal, it will be harder for them to know where we are. If it's not a werewolf, which I'm assuming, he is relying on the zapper. A werewolf would go on scent. The only option this person has is to keep continuing straight forward and hope that he finds us."

I sprinted after Dale. "But that's our only way of knowing where to go too! Don't you get it; we don't know the way. And what about Josh and Nate? We won't be able to find them."

"We're in a straight tunnel, sweetheart. We won't get lost; don't worry. I know the way. They're my tunnels, remember?"

"They'll think we're dead!" I shouted. Dale was starting to pick up more speed. "And what about our follower? Can't he see our heat signal just like we could? He can still make out every person in the tunnels, just like we could. Won't he be able to do that too?"

Dale hesitated. "Yes."

"Then why aren't you worried? This person is after us! He's going to kill us."

"No, he's not."

"How do you know that?" I sprinted up behind the goblin.

I ran into Dale as he stopped in his tracks. He turned to me and grabbed my hand. He squeezed it reassuringly. "Because I won't let him. Everything is going to be okay, sweetheart."

CHAPTER 23

We turned and ran down the tunnel, sprinting at full speed. The gravel crunched beneath my feet. I could hear Dale breathing heavily next to me. I felt my own sweat start to stick to my skin. We kept going. Step after step. Wheezing breath after wheezing breath.

After what felt like ages of running, we came across a branch in the tunnel. We either went straight or slightly left and then straight.

"Which one do we take?" I asked as we stopped in front of the crossing.

"I don't know," Dale replied quietly.

I turned to him. "What?"

"I said I don't know."

I stared at him. "You don't know? So you just broke our zapper without actually knowing which way to go? We're going to get lost!"

Dale rolled his eyes. "Calm down and stop fussing. I made the tunnels, remember? I know where they lead to, just don't know which one is …"—he hesitated before speaking the rest of his sentence softly—"destroyed."

I narrowed my eyes at him. "Destroyed?"

"Yes. One has a gap in the floor. Some parts of the tunnels are old, and this particular part crumpled. No big deal. We would have to jump the gap." Dale sighed. "The other tunnel just goes around and joins back into this main tunnel."

"Well, that's great!" I threw my hands up. "Which one are we going to …"

Dale put his hand up. He held his finger to his lips, as if to shush me. I frowned.

"Stop shushing me; we have to make a decision here. We can't just stand around waiting for the guards to catch up with us."

"Shut up!" he hissed at me. He cupped his ear, trying to listen for something that my ears couldn't catch.

Then I heard it. Light tapping sounds and crunching dirt. I started to see the faint outline of a figure in the distance. Someone was coming, and coming fast.

Dale tugged my arm. "Come on!"

We jumped into the left tunnel and ran. I could still hear the feet of the figure behind us; he had probably seen which tunnel we had taken. The hollow sounds of his steps were coming closer and closer. He was gaining on us.

Then I saw what was coming up ahead. A black hole in the ground. You could see the other side, but it was a big jump. A jump that was hard to make.

"We're just going to keep running," Dale gasped next to me. "If we have a good running start, we'll make it."

I nodded. Dale probably couldn't see, but he should know that I understood. The gap was coming closer. I looked at the ground and started to determine how many steps I still had. Twenty. My last foot would be my right, and I would leap. The walls of the tunnels passed my sides in a blur.

"Jump!" Dale yelled in front of me.

I watched Dale jump. He launched through the air. He would make it. If he could, so could I. I took my last step and leaped up. I would make it.

The wind was knocked out of me as a force slammed into me from behind. It yanked me backward into the tunnel. Away from the gap.

I landed with a thud on the ground. Pain shot through my body, making everything ache. I gasped for air, my lungs momentarily empty.

I shook as I tried to get a good gulp of air. Black spots danced in front of my eyes. I forced myself not to pass out. I urged myself to get up. I leaned onto my elbows and went up on my knees.

I shuddered as a dark shadow loomed over me. I looked up. A tall man stood over me, his dark shadow making my surroundings dark. He was wearing a trench coat with a badge. It gleamed in the light. He was one of Michael's guards. He also held a zapper in one hand. I watched as he clipped it onto his belt.

His coat moved slightly as he clipped the zapper into place. A piece of metal caught the dim light of the tunnel from the inside of his coat pocket. A gun. Chills spread through my body. I tried not to show it. I could be brave and live through this.

"Look who we have here," the man said, his voice deep. He knelt down so that his face was level with mine. "Do you have what we're looking for, Ms. Daniels?"

I glared at him, but stayed quiet. I needed to get rid of this guy. I tried to form a plan in my mind, but no thoughts were willing to form themselves together. I needed to plan my attack carefully, but how?

The man laughed. "You might as well tell me." In one swift movement, he flicked out a small knife. "Or you're not going to live long."

I looked over my shoulder in search of Dale. He was nowhere in sight. The gap in the ground was deserted. The gap. If I could just get the guard close to it …

I shook as he put the knife under my chin. The cold metal burned against my skin. For a moment I thought he would cut off my necklace, but I tried not to budge. Instead, he traced my jawline and put the blade to my cheek. My eyes stung as he pressed it in. It wasn't a deep cut, but I could feel the blood start to trickle down my face.

I let out a shaky breath. The man turned the knife over in his hand and held it up. Some of my blood lined the otherwise clean blade. I jumped as the man looked straight at me. "Where is it?"

"I don't know," I sputtered.

I screamed as he grabbed my hair and pulled me up. He banged my head on the side of the tunnel. Pain exploded through my skull, like a cannonball on repeat.

"Where is the marble?"

Tears began to stain my cheeks. I wasn't strong like Nate or Josh. This guy was going to kill me.

"I don't know!" I sobbed. My head exploded as he banged it again. I crumbled to the ground as he let go of my hair.

I took a shaky breath. I watched as he walked over to the gap. Dale had disappeared on the other side. The man stared for a second. He twisted the knife around in his hand. Then he grunted as he stuck it in the wall. I stared. He had stuck the knife in a rock without any effort.

I eyed the knife for a second, still attempting to catch my breath. Ideas slowly started to formulate in my head. If I could just make it to the knife and injure the man, maybe he would fall into the gap. I didn't know how deep it was, but it was worth a shot.

With one eye on the guard, I started to crawl toward the knife, trying to make the least amount of noise possible. I saw the man grab a walkie-talkie and speak into it. He didn't seem to think of me as a threat anymore, so he looked the other way. I tried not making a sound as I inched toward the knife.

"Daniels doesn't have it," the man said into the device.

A voice crackled on the other end. "We have Larson's son captive. He doesn't appear to have it either."

I stopped in shock, my limbs frozen. They had Josh. That wasn't good. I couldn't put up much of a fight, but Josh would. He had enough anger inside him to let out. They would hurt him if he tried.

I tried to set my mind on getting the knife. It wasn't far. I could see the handle sticking out of the wall. But my mind kept going back to Josh. They had him. Who knew what they would do to him to get the information out? Josh wouldn't budge, but he would fight.

I eyed the guard. He was occupied listening to his walkie-talkie. A third voice spoke. "We can't find Mannaro. Any word on the goblin?"

The man paced to the side, still faced away from me. "The goblin was here minutes ago, but ran. Our priority is to find Mannaro."

I looked up. The knife stuck out of the wall right above me. I slowly stood and grabbed it by the handle. I got a firm grip and yanked. The knife didn't budge. I gasped and tried again. It didn't move in the slightest.

I froze as a third voice spoke over the walkie-talkie. I didn't know what it was, but there was a dangerous tone to the person's voice. I couldn't help but listen. However, at the same time, it made me want to run.

"You idiots better find the marble, or you're all dead." The voice sounded familiar, but I couldn't place from what.

Images of Josh's illusion ran through my head. That's where I knew the voice from. The man with the red eyes. The sorcerer. Moros. It couldn't be him. How had Josh even known what his voice sounded like? How did his voice sound the same in the illusions? It couldn't be him.

But deep in my gut, I knew that it was him. There was something about the way he spoke. Even through one sentence, I could see him in front of me. He was a powerful occult and would stop at nothing to get what he wanted. Josh was right. Moros had gotten into contact with the government somehow. He had risen again. And he was after the marble.

I continued to try to pull the knife out of the tunnel wall. The strange figure Dale had seen wasn't just anyone. He was going to kill us all in order to find that marble.

I jumped as a cool metal touched my temple and something clicked next to my head. My hands started to shake as I slowly let go of the knife handle. I glanced over.

"What do you think you're doing, little missy?" the guard said. He held his gun up against my head. "Trying to kill me? I can tell you now that it's not going to work, so there's no point in trying. If anyone's going to get killed, it'll be you."

I trembled as the bulled clicked into place. The man's finger started to move toward the trigger. "Honestly, I don't see your value anymore. You're just a useless human. A weak, defenseless human. What's the point of keeping you alive if you can't help me?" The man grinned. "So before you start worrying about how to get rid of me, I would worry about yourself. Because your end is closer than you think."

His finger started to push the trigger. His determination showed in his eyes. Then he hesitated at the sound of someone yelling.

"Get away from her!"

Dale ran out of the shadows and attacked the man's legs. He lost his balance and fell to the ground. So did his gun. It flew to the edge. I scrambled over to it. My head ached, but I ignored it. This was my chance."

The metal of the gun was cool to the touch. I held it up. "Come on, Renn," I muttered to myself. My hand shook. I couldn't focus on my target.

Dale was on the ground, still fighting the man. The guard was obviously taller, but Dale wasn't doing too bad. But even I knew he would be overpowered eventually.

I tried to aim the gun, but my vision blurred. Dale was in the way. I was going to hit Dale.

"Shoot," Dale screamed at me. He was being thrown around by the guard. But he wasn't letting go.

"I said shoot!" Dale yelped as he was thrown against the rock. The man puffed on the ground. I pointed the gun at his head.

"Go ahead," the man shouted. "See, you can't kill someone." He spat blood. "You're too weak. You can't take a life."

I aimed the gun. "You wish."

The guard screamed as the bullet landed in his shoulder. Just like I had intended. I kicked his side. He attempted to roll away, but only ended up on the ledge of the gap. He looked me straight in the eye. Blood poured from his wound, darkening his coat. It dribbled down his chin from an injury Dale had given him.

"Moros is going to kill all of you. You won't know what's coming. It'll be an horrible end."

I raised the gun again and aimed. I wouldn't let him distract me. I pulled the trigger. Nothing happened. I tried again. No bullets came. The stupid thing was empty. I threw it into the gap.

"You're going to follow your gun right down into the ravine."

I kicked the man's injured shoulder, and he shrieked in pain. He rolled over. Right into the ravine. I squeezed my eyes shut and turned away. His screams were swallowed up by the darkness. Before I knew, it was over.

I dropped to my knees, my hands scraping the rough ground as I landed. I had killed someone. I wasn't that kind of person. Even though he was trying to kill me, I couldn't do that. I had taken a life. My mind blanked, and my vision began to spin.

I felt Dale's arm around my shoulder. I didn't know where he had come from, but I didn't care. I held on tight. At least he was there. I saw him put the knife in his pocket. "You okay?"

I shook my head. Tears rolled down my cheeks. "I killed him." My words came out in short gasps.

"You did great, sweetheart. It's all going to be okay. He was trying to hurt you, and you acted appropriately. We're okay now. You saved us." He stroked my hair. "One guard down, four to go."

I wiped away some of my tears. Blood came off onto my hand. The cut had stopped bleeding, but blood was on my face. Dirt streaked my hands. I was covered in sweat, blood, tears, dirt—everything. It was gross. My clothes stuck to my body.

Dale grabbed my hand and pulled me up onto my knees. Then I stood.

"We have some people to save," Dale said as he led me back through the tunnels. I didn't have to jump over the gap, so apparently we had just taken the wrong way. Once we came back into the main tunnel, we followed it to the end. It opened up into a huge canyon.

Dale pointed to a huge rock at the edge of the cliff. We ran to it and hid behind it. I could faintly hear people talking on the other side.

"I'm going to see what's happening. Stay here." I watched as Dale ran over to another rock before I could utter a protest. He sprinted to another. And then another. Then he was gone. I was alone, hiding behind a huge rock. I looked over to the edge of the canyon. I looked down. A dark shadow represented the bottom. It seemed an awful long way down.

I heard people shouting. The voices were coming closer. I pressed my back into the rock. They couldn't see me. I was a wreck and had no energy left. If they found me, they would be able to kill me without any problem.

I jumped as a strange figure grabbed me. He clamped his hand over my mouth to stifle a scream. Once I had calmed down enough, I let my eyes examine who it was. I jumped into his arms. He hugged me tightly.

"Thank god you're okay," Nate whispered in my ear. "I saw your zapper disappear from the map, and I thought they had gotten to you."

I sobbed. "I …"

"It's okay. Calm down." Nate squeezed my hand. He was covered in dirt and sweat, but he looked unharmed. "Listen. I need you to hold onto something for me."

CHAPTER 24

I watched as Nate took the marble out of his pocket. It was slightly more oval then I remembered, and it was dented on one side.

"I dropped it, and the clasp broke," Nate muttered as he pressed the marble into my hand. The ring was gone, and the marble was terribly dented. I turned it over, running my thumb over where the crescent symbol was. Or used to be. The marble was so scratched up that the symbol was no longer visible.

"I need you to keep it for me. There are some strange people here, and they'll do anything to get it. Moros is a dangerous man with some harmful tricks up his sleeve. I'd rather not see him use them."

I turned the stone over in my hands. "It's not much safer with me either, Nate. You just said that they'd do anything to get it ..."

"That's the thing." He smiled painfully. "They won't expect you to have it. I overheard them talking on their walkie-talkies;

they think that guard searched you and didn't find anything. They believe I have it. You'll be fine as long as I distract them."

I hesitated. "But they'll do anything, Nate. They'll hurt you."

"I don't care about that right now. All I care about is keeping you and that marble safe."

I stared at Nate. His forehead was creased with worry, and his hair stuck to the sides of his head with sweat. He looked exhausted, but he still managed to look calm and convincing. He covered it up well.

A shrill laugh echoed through the canyon behind us. Nate and I scooted ourselves backward, pressing ourselves into the rock. We sat side by side, quietly listening to the people on the other side.

"You were right, Michael." The voice laughed again. "An opportunity does always present itself when you need it. I didn't make a mistake by sending my men to find you. You were the best person for the job."

"Glad to be at your service, sir." Michael's voice echoed through the cave. He sounded slightly strained, scared almost. It was strange for Michael. And he never called anyone sir; he was always the one being called it.

I turned slowly, trying my best not to let the dirt crunch beneath my feet. I grabbed a crevice in the rock and pulled myself up just so that I could see what was going on in the cave.

Michael stood to the side with his back turned to me. Standing at the edge of the ravine was a man that I wished I didn't recognize. He looked exactly like Josh's illusions had portrayed him. The tall man was dressed completely in black. He looked out of place in the badly lit cave. I watched as he bent down and grabbed a rock. He tossed it around in his hand a few times and then chucked it into the canyon.

"Any word on Mannaro yet?" Moros said while looking down into the canyon. His deep voice gave me goose bumps. It gave you the feeling that you had no other option than to be afraid of him. Michael had this too, but with Moros, it was different. Stronger. More dangerous.

Michael stayed still on the spot. "I'm afraid not, sir. We had word on the girl and the goblin, but we've lost contact with the guard that had them."

Moros turned toward Michael. I thought I saw Michael flinch. I had thought Michael wasn't afraid of anyone.

"Are you saying that they took that guard down?" Moros spat at Michael. I saw some of his spit fly down to the ground.

"It's not positive … His walkie-talkie might just have lost contact."

The man raised his hand. "Whatever. I don't care. I just need word on Mannaro."

"I don't know where he is, but he's somewhere close." Michael hesitated. "Don't you have a way of um … finding people?"

Moros sighed. "Yes, but that is so exhausting. Ever since the illusionists tried to erase my memory, spells have been hard for me to do. But I guess they have been coming easier with more practice." I could tell by the annoyed tone in Moros's voice that he was rolling his eyes. "Very well. Can't rely on others nowadays. I made that mistake last time. You have to do everything yourself."

I felt a tug on my leg. I ignored it. I watched as Moros spread out his hands and started to mutter to himself. I didn't know what he was doing, but it didn't look good.

Another tug. I swatted at my leg and hit Nate's hand. I looked down at him.

"What?" I hissed as I lowered myself down to his level.

"I have to go." Nate was speaking so fast that I could barely make out the individual words. "He's a very powerful sorcerer. Even when he's weak, he's stronger than most. He can summon his power to do a spell that is going to let him find me. I have to leave you; otherwise he'll find you too."

"No, please, stay here," I pleaded. I felt fresh tears spring into my eyes. "You can't leave me alone. You heard what Josh said. He's dangerous. We have a better chance of getting through this by sticking together."

"No, we don't. Renn, I'm sorry." My heart broke as Nate's face fell at my reaction. His mouth opened, but he hesitated before he spoke. He grabbed my hand and squeezed it tightly. "I can't let him hurt you. I won't let anyone hurt you."

Then Nate grabbed my face and kissed me. It all happened very fast. His lips crushed against mine. Before I could react, it was over.

"Stay safe." And then he was gone. I watched Nate speed to the next rock and then out of sight. Just like Dale had done. I let out a silent sob. He had kissed me. Nate. My thoughts blurred together like the tears did to my vision. I couldn't even think straight anymore.

The kiss was filled with something strange. A strong emotion, full of intensity and passion. Like it was his last chance to do so.

Nate knew that Moros was going to get him. It was his way of saying good-bye if anything happened. It made me want to curl up in a ball and cry. Sob away from the world. If Moros got the chance, he would kill Nate. He was going to kill all of us until he had that marble. The marble that I now had. Our fate lay in my hands.

I jumped as Moros's shrill laugh rang though the canyon.

"Come out, come out, wherever you are!" Moros yelled. "I know you're here, Mannaro, I can sense it. There's no point in moving. I'll find you anyway; it might just take two seconds longer this way."

I heard the sound of crunching rocks. Then the tapping of feet. I turned around and pulled myself up the rock again, just so that I could see but my body was still hidden. A ball of strange colored mist was floating around. It moved every so often, pointing in a different direction. It was searching for Nate, as if it could smell him out.

Moros stood silently, watching the ball of energy. I had never seen a spell in action. It was weird to see, a ball of bluish mist floating around. He practiced dark magic, and according to the stories, he was the most powerful one to exist. If he already had so much power, then why did he need the marbles to take over the occult? He already had power over Michael—wasn't that enough? Moros spoke up as if to answer my question.

"I know you're here, Mannaro. I need the power of that marble."

"Why would you want that? It doesn't do anything. It's just a ring," Nate shouted. His voice came from a huge rock on the other side of the cave. It was a few steps away from Moros. He only had to move forward to find Nate.

Moros chuckled. "Don't act like you don't know what's going on. You and I both know that the marble you have is important to controlling the occult races. And even if you didn't know that, I'm sure little Larson told you. I noticed that he was snooping around. He's too curious for his own good. It could harm him in the future, unless of course he decides to help me with it. He would be of great value to me."

"He would never do that," Nate replied from his hiding spot.

Moros ignored him. "Your specific marble, on the other hand, represents the werewolf race. Anyone would kill for that power."

"I wouldn't."

Moros started to pace forward. "Of course not. Because you act so good-hearted, just like your daddy." He laughed. "Too bad you showed your true colors when you killed your mom. It's only proof of who you really are."

"I did not!" Nate raced out from behind the rock. He launched up toward Moros but was thrown back. It looked like he had hit an invisible barrier. Nate grunted as he landed with a thud on the ground.

A guard sped out of the shadows and locked Nate's arms behind him. Moros casually strode toward him. He clicked his tongue.

"Have you learned nothing from your father? Don't mess with people who are stronger than you."

Nate tried to launch again, but the guard held him back. He flinched as Moros flicked his chin.

"Give me the marble."

"I don't have it." Nate spat in Moros' face. Moros wiped his eye in response and then shook the spit off his hand. He grabbed Nate's jaw.

"Give it to me, Mannaro," he hissed.

Nate clenched his teeth. "I don't have it."

Moros let go of Nate's jaw. He took a few steps back. "Very well. Suit yourself. I guess we'll just have to use a more persuasive manner to get some answers." He walked toward the entrance of a tunnel and snapped his fingers. "Let's see how good Mannaro's heart really is. Will he react to seeing others in pain, or does he not care? Bring him out!"

CHAPTER 25

Another guard walked out into the cave. He was carrying a figure, which he threw out onto the ground. The figure landed with a painful smack.

"You don't treat your prisoners very well," Josh grunted as he elbowed himself up.

Without hesitating Moros strode over and grabbed Josh's hair. He yelped in pain.

"Don't act so cocky, Larson." Moros laughed. "Your fate lies in Mannaro's hands. Let's see how long it takes him to crack under pressure, shall we?" He dropped Josh on the ground. "It's you or the marble."

And then he kicked Josh. He pulled back his foot and lashed out. It was the least supernatural thing to do, but I could see the pain it caused. I bit my lip to stifle a scream. The metallic taste of blood filled my mouth. I looked back at Josh. He was gasping for breath and clutching his stomach.

"Don't give it to him!" Josh screamed out in a raspy breath as Moros landed another kick. This time on his face. He clutched his nose as blood welled up on top of his lip.

I looked over at Nate. His expression was dark, his forehead creased. He looked away as Moros kicked again. He ran his hand through his hair as he averted his gaze. He didn't know what to do. What was there to do? Get Josh killed, or give the powerful marble to the bad guy?

Moros chuckled. "Look, Mannaro's already debating whether or not to give in. How sweet. You might as well. I'm just getting warmed up."

I watched in horror as he strode over to Josh and grabbed his collar. He put two fingers on Josh's neck. He narrowed his eyes, a devilish grin appearing on his face. "Enjoy."

Then Josh began to shake uncontrollably. It was just a slight tremble, but it overtook his whole body—like he was being electrocuted. A look of terror was frozen on his face. I squeezed my eyes shut and felt a tear roll down my cheek. I could feel the pain it caused.

I opened my eyes again when I heard Josh drop to the ground with a loud smack. Moros had removed his fingers and let Josh remain in a heap on the ground. He lay still and unmoving. I covered my mouth to silence my own sobs.

Moros turned to Nate, a satisfied look on his face. "Do you see what I am capable of? I can do much worse than that. I can do a million times worse than your darkest thoughts. You wouldn't even be able to imagine the pain I could cause you or your loved ones. I don't care. I will find them. And I will hurt them all if you don't give me that marble."

Nate struggled against the guard that was holding him back. His face was flushed with anger and disgust. He stayed quiet, but continued to fight the guard. The man had a blank look on his face, like it was costing him no strength to hold Nate back.

Opposite him, Josh was starting to elbow himself up. He was apparently still conscious. Sweat gleamed on his face. "Don't give it to him!" he shouted as he tried to stand up. He took a few steps before collapsing back onto his hands and knees. Josh wheezed loudly and then attempted to stand up again. Sweat and blood dripped down his face.

Moros didn't so much as glance back before making a simple movement with his hand. A blue ball of energy shot out of his fingers. It launched back and hit Josh square in the chest. He was thrown back and smashed into the rock wall with a grunt.

Josh sputtered on the ground as he tried to catch his breath. He coughed, and blood sprayed onto the ground next to him. He pushed his back against the rock and pulled himself up by the crevices. It seemed like the millionth time Josh was trying to stand. I felt like ripping my hair out. He was conscious, but barely. There was a stagger to his walk as he stepped forward.

I touched the marble in my pocket. Nate wouldn't even be able to give in if he wanted to. He could only keep the act up for so long. If he spoke up about it, Moros would kill him for lying. Their fate was in my hands.

Josh inched forward with the little energy he had left. The sparkle had disappeared from his eyes, and it was replaced by anger. He tried to broaden his shoulders, attempting to act brave.

"I'm not afraid of you." Josh shook as he spoke. "Go ahead; kill me. Not like it's going to get you anywhere."

Moros shrugged, the side of his mouth curving upward. "It'll give me the pleasure of killing you."

Josh staggered a step closer to Moros. He spread out his arms. "Take a shot then."

"Josh!" Nate yelled from his restraints. "Don't do this."

My heart beat fast. This could not be happening. Josh wouldn't do this. If not for himself, then for me. A pain shot through my hand, and I looked down. A long cut on my hand was starting to well up with blood. The rock underneath it was stained red. I squeezed my hands into fists.

Josh shook his head, ignoring Nate. He stood facing Moros, his face masked with determination. He tilted his chin up. "Take the satisfaction then."

"Josh!" Nate yelled again, kicking the guard behind him. He didn't blink.

Moros narrowed his eyes, a gleam to them. "Very well. If you so desire to end your silly, useless, unimportant life."

He took a step back and started to move his hands, one on top of the other a little ways apart. He swirled them around until a ball of energy started to form. As Moros spread his hands apart, the ball started to expand in size. It was the same type of energy mist as before, except this time it was a glowing red. I didn't know if I was imagining things, but I thought I saw a hint of red to his eyes. The ball hovered in between his hands. He looked back over his shoulder. "Say good-bye to your friend Mannaro."

"Stop!" Nate shouted. I watched in horror as he started to fight the guard restraining him. He lashed out, swinging his arms in attempts to land a punch. He started to kick, but the guard didn't budge. Only the muscles in his jaw tensed, but other than that, the guard was unmoving. As if nothing was happening.

Nate's eyes started to turn yellow as he screamed, "Let go of me!" He swung his arms again, but it didn't help. A low growl escaped from his lips. Canines slowly started to produce from his teeth.

Moros removed one of his hands from the energy ball. Without as much as a glance, he snapped his fingers. Nate's rope bracelet snapped and fell to the ground. Nate immediately stopped moving, the terror stuck on his face. His eyes turned back to green, and his canines pulled back.

Moros let out a shrill laugh. He returned his hand to the energy ball, and it turned a darker shade of red. "Can't change anymore now, can you? Too bad, Mannaro. You overplayed your luck. If you were cooperating, I might have let you change, but not if you're fighting us. Wouldn't want you biting the guards now, would we?"

Moros turned back to Josh as Nate fought against his guard again. But it didn't do him any good. Along with losing the bracelet, it seemed as if he also lost his strength.

Josh stood fearlessly in front of Moros. His expression was blank, but there was an emotion behind his gray eyes. He hid it well. Everyone around watched as Moros put one foot forward. I held my breath as he pulled the energy ball back, like he was pulling back the elastic of a slingshot.

Josh's eyes flickered my way. I ducked. It wouldn't be good if Josh saw me. That would only bring trouble. But I had to do something. If I didn't, Josh would die. And I couldn't have that. Not without having done something.

I inched my gaze back over the top of the rock. Josh hadn't seen me. He still wore the same blank expression, facing toward Moros. If anything, Josh's actions showed he was trying to protect all of us. He wanted to be the brave one. The savior.

"Here we go." Moros laughed. He spread his fingers as the energy ball expanded once more. It started to spin. The veins in his hands went rigid, almost black.

"Stop!" someone yelled from the side of the cave. A man came stumbling out of the shadows, pain in his eyes. His suit was covered in dust, and his hair stuck out in different directions. He looked like a madman.

Moros rolled his eyes as he looked over at Michael. His face filled with rage. He let the energy ball falter as he strode over toward the government lead. I glanced over at Josh. A breath escaped through his lips that I hadn't noticed he was holding. Nate closed his eyes and sighed, a look of momentary relief on his face. It disappeared as Moros's screaming voice echoed through the cave.

"What do you think you're doing?" he screamed in Michael's face.

Michael flinched backward. He glanced at his son. "You can't kill him. He knows things. He could be useful.

"You just want to save your son," Moros spat. He turned in Michael's face and started to form the energy ball again as he walked toward the center of the cave.

"No, that's not it." Michael sprinted in front of Moros. Again Moros let the energy ball fall, an annoyed look on his face.

I looked over at Josh. Mixed emotions showed on his face. He looked over at his father with an emotion of gratefulness and despisement.

"He knows Nate and many other occult people," Michael continued. "You could use him to find the other marbles. I'm sure one of his friends has heard of one."

Moros considered this. He stood silently. I looked over at Josh and Nate. They were attempting to signal to each other, but the guard was watching them closely. Nate was mouthing something and nodding his head backward.

I ducked as the guard turned to look my way. I pressed myself into the rock, and the sharp edges poked through my shirt. I could only hope that he hadn't seen me.

I turned back around and slowly started to pull myself back up so that I could see over the rock. The muscles in my legs ached from crouching. I pushed the cramps away.

My mouth fell open in shock as my eyes caught sight of the cave. Nate and Josh stood side by side, and the guard lay unconscious on the ground. Unmoving; his eyes closed. I couldn't help but grin. They had taken the guard out without a sound. Maybe Nate was holding back on some of his werewolf strength. Josh seemed back in better spirits as well. However, exhaustion clouded both of their faces.

I looked over at Moros and Michael. Moros was talking rapidly, and I couldn't make out what he was saying. It looked like he was scolding Michael. He was standing with his back toward Josh and Nate. They jumped as Moros quickly turned toward them.

He didn't seem surprised by what had happened, and he ignored the unconscious guard on the ground.

"You thought I wouldn't notice?" His voice was filled with amusement. Then he strode over to Nate, reaching him in a few short seconds. He grabbed his sleeve and dragged him to the middle of the cave. Nate fell over his own feet and landed with a thud on the ground. Moros pointed to a guard standing at the side of the cave. I hadn't noticed him until now, and it surprised me that the guard hadn't moved until now.

"Search him." Moros's low voice echoed through the cave.

The guard walked over and started to search Nate. He yanked off Nate's jacket and shoes and searched them thoroughly. He wasn't even being careful, and Nate winced every time the guard pulled at him. He took Nate's bag from behind a rock and searched its contents. Nate's stuff scattered around the dirt floor, making dust rise. One of the objects that fell was a familiar sheet of paper. The photo was slightly crumpled now and torn at one corner.

My gut sank as realization dawned on me. The guard wasn't going to find the marble because I had it. The guard could search all he wanted, but he wouldn't find anything. And if I had to make a guess, Moros wouldn't be happy when he found out.

I crouched silently behind the rock. I had been watching all this time and not doing anything. Why couldn't I be the savior? I could at least do something. I had to take action. I looked around the side of the rock. Two eyes gleamed at me from the darkness opposite me on the other side of the cave.

I stared at the eyes straight ahead of me, trying to make out who it was. The longer I stared, the clearer the image became. I could just make out a small figure kneeling in the shadows. Dale held his fingers up to his lips, as if he knew what thoughts were running through my head. He wanted me to hide. And not just me—both of us. He wanted us to hide during the unfolding fight. But I couldn't do that. I had to help Nate and Josh. I couldn't let them get hurt without trying to help. But what could I do without exposing the marble?

I returned my gaze to the group in the middle of the cave. The guard was searching Nate's bag again, ripping it up in the process. The zipper already lay strewn to the side, and a loud tearing sound rang through the cave as the guard pulled apart the thin material. He was seconds away from coming to a conclusion.

Josh wasn't paying any attention to the scene unfolding in front of him. He was staring at his dad, observing his every move. He was obviously still surprised that Michael had spoken up for him. His dad had saved his life. Maybe Michael did care about Josh after all.

Josh let out a short gasp when he shifted his weight onto his other foot. When I looked at him more closely, I started to notice the small signs that he was defeated. He was clutching his side, and a bruise was starting to form on his face. He was caked with dirt and blood from small cuts all over his body. If Moros decided to strike again, Josh wouldn't be able to fight back.

Nate, on the other hand, looked more stable. He was also covered in dirt and sweat, but didn't have any apparent injuries. But who knew what Moros was capable of? If the electrocution was the least he could do, I didn't want to know what was the worst. And if there was anything Moros didn't lie about, it would be his powers. He would use any excuse to show off.

Lastly there was Michael. I had no clue as to whose side he would take if it came down to it. Nate and Josh wouldn't switch sides. Michael was worried about Josh, but working for Moros. He feared him. The guy that everyone feared feared someone else. He looked small and a lot less scary when standing next to Moros. He would be overpowered easily.

"And?" Moros asked the guard, an impatient tone to his voice.

The guard glanced at his boss. His hands had the slightest tremble to them as he stood to face Moros. "He doesn't have it." The guard spoke quietly.

Moros tilted his head. "Excuse me?"

The guard gulped. "He doesn't have it."

"Liar!" Moros yelled. His face turned bright red. A ball of energy shot off his fingertips and hit the guard in the chest. He crumpled to the ground with a sickening smack. His chest stopped moving. He was dead.

Moros didn't bat an eye. He only shook his head. He knelt down and started to search Nate's belongings. He yanked open everything that had a zipper and spread everything else around the floor. Little sparks of energy shot out of his fingers. A mist hovered over Nate's belongings, also searching. But it found nothing.

After the mist had returned to him with no success, Moros stood back up. He straightened his coat calmly. He turned to Nate.

"Where is it?" he shouted. Spit landed on Nate's face.

Nate wiped it off without even the slightest wince. "It's there."

"No, Mannaro, it's not. You hid it! Where is it?"

Nate shrugged. "Maybe you're just as bad of a searcher as that guard."

Moros's eyes narrowed. He turned to the remaining two guards. "Apparently Mannaro here isn't the dumbest. He hid it. Search for it; one of you go back into the tunnel he came from. Find it."

Moros turned to Michael, making him flinch. "Who else was with them?"

"A goblin and Ms. Daniels, sir," Michael replied carefully.

"A goblin and a girl …" Moros muttered. "Where are they?"

"The last thing we heard was that the goblin was gone and the girl was with the guard, but we have lost contact with that guard since then."

Moros turned to Nate. He chuckled softly. "Did you give it to your girlfriend?" He pointed from Nate to Josh. "Or is she yours?

Nate crossed his arms with a *humph* sound. Josh also stayed quiet. He turned his gaze away to avoid anyone's eye contact. He looked behind him. That's when I realized they were free of a guard. Their guard was gone, so they could strike if they wanted.

But that was the problem. They had their hands free, but Moros had powerful spells. He even had some sort of invisible force shield that he could put up as soon as anyone got too close.

"I see the problem here," Moros continued. "You both want the girl, and you want her safe. Which must mean she is safe, or at least you think she is. That also leads me to believe that she must have the marble."

Nate pursed his lips together as Josh spoke up. "She doesn't have it." He glanced at Nate. "We hid it somewhere else. Renn is already out of the tunnels. Safe and away from you."

A dark expression clouded over Nate's face. That's when it hit me. Nate had told Josh this when they had escaped from the guard. I hadn't been able to make out what it was because they were mouthing words across the tunnel, but this was it. Nate had told Josh I was gone. It was the only thing keeping Josh sane, the fact that I was out of the cave. But I wasn't, and it wouldn't take long for Moros to find out. It was only a matter of time before he found me, and he would be able to use me to turn Nate and Josh against each other. I had to do something.

I glanced at Dale's figure on the other side of the cave. I could just make out his face coming out from behind the rock. He was waving his hand to the side. What did he mean? He mouthed something at me, but I couldn't make out what. I squinted my eyes, trying to see him more clearly. He was waving his hand rapidly, and a look of fear was starting to spread across his face. I heard Moros say something in the background, but I couldn't make out what. I was too focused on trying to see Dale.

I jumped as something grabbed my arm. I let out a scream. I felt myself being dragged across the ground. Pebbles dug their way into my leg as I unsettled the dust around me. Then I stopped moving. I coughed and waved my hand to clear away the dust.

Two pitch-black eyes were staring down at me. My heart raced, making my body tremble on the ground. The eyes showed power in them. It felt like the eyes were staring into your soul. There was a strange red gleam to them.

Moros clicked his tongue, a grin appearing on his face. "Found you."

CHAPTER 26

"No!" Josh screamed as he collapsed onto the ground. His eyes shot daggers at Nate, his face turning red. "You told me she had left! You said she was safe. You're an idiot. A liar, just like the rest of them. I never should have trusted you. You just want her to yourself!"

Nate took a step back. His face fell. "I'm sorry. I had to lie to you; I had no choice."

"You always have a choice, Nate. I thought we were in this together. We were going to keep her safe. She's only human. He's going to kill her …" His words slowly trailed off, quieter and quieter. He looked over at me, his gray eyes piercing into mine. They were filled with grief.

"Josh, I'm sorry," Nate sputtered.

Josh ignored him and slammed his fist into the ground. Gravel and dust flew in different directions from the impact. He grimaced as the skin on his bones split and started to bleed.

I pushed myself up. I stood in front of Moros, who was watching all the commotion with a satisfied look. I took a step away from him, but he didn't look very bothered by it. He knew that he could defeat me with the flick of a finger.

He advanced a step toward me when I tried to back up again. I continued backward, step after step, trying to escape the sorcerer. But he followed. Every step I took backward, he took one forward. I tripped over my own feet as I tried to get away from him; he wouldn't let me escape. I jumped as I ran into the cave wall. Pain shot through my back from where I ran into a sharp ledge.

Moros eyed me curiously. "Who do we have here?"

I clenched my fists to stop them from shaking, but I said nothing. Moros smiled. "What do you think you're doing here? Did you stumble into this mess by accident? Humans aren't supposed to be involved in the occult."

I glanced around Moros's head at Nate and Josh. Nate stood quietly, but he was motioning something to me. One hand was running through his hair, but the other was signaling something. Telling me to keep calm and that everything was going to be okay. Josh, on the other hand, was still collapsed on the ground. He had his head in his hands and was rocking slightly. His lips were moving, muttering almost, but I heard no sound. It looked like the ball of energy had done more than physical damage.

"In case you were wondering, which you are"—Moros licked his lips—"that energy ball wasn't a normal spell; no dark magic spells are. Its purpose is to play with the mind." He twirled his finger next to his ear. "Along with the physical pain, it brings along a wave of emotional pain, exaggerating the emotions you have felt before and hitting them over your head again and again. You just need something to"—Moros hesitated with a smile—"trigger it." He motioned toward Nate.

"So, that's your plan?" I tried to hold in a sob. "You're going to use me to turn Josh into an emotional wreck so that he'll force Nate into surrendering?"

Moros's eyes gleamed. "You could put it that way, I suppose. In non-occult language." He smiled. Moros's strength was spells. Dark magic spells. Ones that involved messing with human nature and the mind. Spells that could be used to trick someone.

No wonder he was feared. He turned people against each other to get what he wanted. Turning people into wrecks worked in his favor, along with his wicked manipulation.

"It does work in my favor; yes, you're right. You're a smart girl; too bad you're useless. Useless people don't live long, you know." Moros ignored Josh's scream of protest in the background. I tried to look over Moros's shoulder, but he sidestepped to block my view. "In a way, you are correct about my plan. Too bad it's only a small part of the plan."

"What's your master plan then?" I glared at him, trying to come across as confident and strong. I could tell by the tremble in my hands and the satisfied look on Moros's face that it wasn't working too well. "My master plan is none of your concern. You shouldn't worry about it; by the time I succeed, you'll be long gone. You might be able to guess what it is if you and Mr. Larson over there brainstormed a bit more, but there's no point. I won't confirm your suspicions, just in case you do make it out alive. Wouldn't want any loose ends threatening my master plan now, would we?"

Moros started to pace, a smirk playing on his lips. "You're a smart girl. Too smart for your own good. Too curious. And, yes, my manipulation works on whoever I desire."

I swallowed hard. "Can you read minds too?"

Moros laughed his shrill laugh. "No, but I can, like anyone else, read expressions. You make such bold ones that they become easy to read. There is something about you though, even if you are a silly little human. Something about you is different. Something's up, and I can't quite put my finger on it."

"What if I'm powerful?"

Moros laughed. "There's a chance, Ms. Daniels, but I doubt it. It's unlikely for a small little human to be special. But there's something about you that I do like. Maybe you could join my side and help me out? I could use someone like you—haven't had help from a human before." He traced his finger along my jawline, leaving a cold trail behind. I quickly shrugged him off.

"Don't do it, Renn!" Josh yelled from the middle of the cave. The muscles in his arms tensed as he pushed himself off the ground. He charged at us, staggering as he went. Moros didn't have to bat an eye. He flicked his finger, and another spark of magic shot out. It seemed like a small wave of mist, but as soon as Josh touched it, he was sent back flying. He collapsed on the ground next to Nate, who hurriedly helped him up.

Moros just laughed. I turned to him. "Maybe that's why you failed last time. Because you didn't have a human on your side."

I jumped as Moros's eyes started to gleam red. Sparks shot out of his fingers, his veins turning black. "My failure had nothing to do with you stupid humans. They tried to kill me, that stupid little government, but of course they failed. I am Ker Moros. No one can stop me. I'm too powerful. A silly little human wouldn't have helped with that."

"But what if I am helpful? What if I am that one silly little human that has power? You should let me go." I stared at him. "Maybe I can defeat you."

"That's it!" Moros grabbed my arm and dragged me toward the middle of the canyon. His grasp was firm, and I could feel the bruise already start to form. "Ms. Daniels, there's no way you can defeat me. I'm the most powerful sorcerer you'll ever meet. You are not special, or you would've done so by now." He spit to the side. Then he set me in the center of the cave and pushed the others away. Right before he turned around, he looked me right in the eyes. His pupils had gone back to black, but they still looked dangerous. Evil expelled through them. "I tried being civil, but you annoy me too much. I do like that you're trying to be optimistic, but it doesn't help."

He signaled at a guard as he walked away from me. The guard grabbed my arms and started to search my jacket pockets.

"Turn around, missy," he said from behind me. He was going to search my pants pocket. That's where the marble was. I glanced at Moros. He had his back turned to me and was busy towering over Nate and Josh. Josh looked like he was going to faint.

"I said, turn around," the guard repeated forcefully behind me. He yanked my arm, trying to get me to turn.

I glanced over my shoulder. He wasn't that much taller than me. "If you really want me to," I muttered. So I turned.

I bent my arm and jammed my elbow into the guard's face. He let out a scream and crumpled to the ground, clutching his eye. Blood stained his fingers. It made my elbow tingle with pain.

"What are you doing, human?" Moros yelled from the other side of the canyon. He started to stride toward me, advancing quickly.

"Don't you dare fight us. We're more powerful, if we haven't made that clear already. I might as well take you out now. I don't need you alive in order to search you." He spit his next words. "I've had enough of you."

I put my hand in my pocket and pulled out the marble. I held it up, and the stone twinkled in the dim light. "That might not be a good idea."

Moros stopped in his tracks. His eyes widened as they flew to the marble. "You need to be very, very careful with that." He pointed at the marble. "You don't have the slightest idea what you're doing. I would put some wise thought into your next step."

It was the first time I had seen a hint of fright in his eyes. He rapidly turned to look for another guard, but there were none. The only one left had gone back into the tunnel to go find the marble. The guard I had injured lay unconscious on the ground. My eyebrows knit together. I hadn't hit him that hard, had I?

Another bruise welled on the guard's forehead. Then I looked up at Nate. Blood stained his knuckles, and he was massaging his hand. He had knocked out the guard. Of course he had.

Moros turned to Michael, but made no effort to call him. The occult government leader stood in the shadows next to a rock. Dale was next to him, although I doubt Michael had noticed the goblin. He was too busy pressing himself into the rock wall, trying not to be seen.

What happened next occurred in a blur. Time seemed to slow. Moros started to race toward me at full speed. My brain processed it slowly. It looked like he was moving through water. Out of the corner of my eye, I could see Nate jumping up and down, waving his hands. He was mouthing something, but I couldn't make out what. I couldn't hear anything. Blood rushed through my ears. Moros was getting closer to me, and a ball of red energy was forming in his hands. It turned his face black and his eyes red.

I softly heard Nate shout Josh's name. It was a desperate, begging scream. Then Josh raced through my vision as he jumped between Moros and me. Moros kept running. They would crash any second.

Then in an instant everything returned back to normal speed, and my hearing returned to me. There was shouting everywhere. Dale had jumped out of his hiding space, and Michael was yelling. Nate was shouting at me, but I still couldn't make out what. I was too focused on Josh. Moros's steps echoed loudly through the cave as he approached Josh and me. I couldn't see Josh's face, but his shoulders tensed up, ready for impact.

Nate was still jumping. Then I realized why I hadn't been able to hear him. He wasn't shouting something, just mouthing something. Letters. My mind was racing to make sense of the letters. I wasn't good at these types of games. My mind wouldn't focus enough to let me try.

Nate was throwing his right arm back and forth. Signaling to do the same. But what did that mean?

Then it all clicked in my brain. Throwing. He wanted me to throw him the marble.

So that's what I did. I felt the stone release from my fingers and race through the air. Moros stopped mid-sprint, skidding to a halt inches away from Josh. Everyone's eyes closely followed the small, blue marble through the air.

Nate caught it without any trouble. He glanced at it once and then threw it on the ground. My mouth fell open in a gasp, which never came out. My eyes widened as Nate did the last thing I would ever expect him to do. The marble lay on the ground, unmoving. Nate glanced at Moros once more. Then he stepped on it.

A cloud of dust flew up around Nate's shoe as the marble cracked. It was gone. Crushed onto the ground. All the power Moros wanted disappeared into thin air.

"Fool!" Moros's scream filled the air. "You have no idea what you just did, Mannaro. Strong power like that doesn't just disappear …"

"I know that." Nate smiled. Sweat gleamed on his forehead. "The werewolf race's power has now transferred itself to a new token. Presumably far away. It will take you decades to find it again. So I wouldn't bother."

"You are going to pay! All of you!"

I watched in horror as Moros pulled a knife out of his trench coat. It gleamed in the cave light. It was so sharp that I could barely see the blade. Michael stepped forward out of the shadows. He had his hands up.

"It's okay, Moros. We can figure something out." He gulped, putting his hands down. "I'm sure we can find the power again. It's not lost; the replica will appear. These kids aren't stupid; they know that."

"Do you know how long it took me to locate these artifacts?" Moros raged. He turned the knife over in his hands. "You of all people should know that. So now, you're going to pay."

He turned and grabbed Josh's shoulder. And then he stabbed him.

I screamed as Josh crumpled to the ground. He collapsed into a nonmoving heap. "Josh!" Hot tears ran down my face. Something grabbed me from behind. I struggled, trying to move toward Josh, but the force was too strong.

"He'll be all right," Nate whispered in my ear. I don't know how he had gotten there so fast, but I didn't care. A bloodstain was starting to form on Josh's shirt. He had been stabbed in the stomach. It could kill him. This time he really was unconscious, and he had taken the worst beating of us all.

Moros staggered toward us, drunk with power. "Now for the two of you," he sneered.

Nate stepped in front of me, pushing me back behind him. I tried to see what was happening, but Nate had his hands out, holding me back. I could barely see over his shoulders. All I could see was Moros's figure, looming closer and closer toward us.

Moros stopped in his tracks as Josh let out a piercing scream. He was conscious again and had shot up into a seating position. Blood seeped out of the wound in his stomach. He gasped as his hand stained red when he touched his shirt, pain spreading across his face. He started to cough. He exhaled loudly, gasping for air that wouldn't come to his lungs.

Then he lurched to the side in another coughing fit, blood sputtering out through his lips. He whimpered loudly as spit and blood stained the ground. I watched in horror as his eyes rolled back and he fainted.

"Josh!" I heard my own scream echo through the cave. I pushed myself toward him, but Nate was there blocking my path. I had to help him.

I watched as Dale came running out of the shadows. He was holding a piece of cloth and some medicine. Moros ignored him.

"Good luck saving him." He shrugged. "What you just witnessed were the effects of harpy poison making its way into his bloodstream. The knife was soaked in the substance. It makes for a poisoned, hard-to-heal wound, you know. It prevents the cut from healing and will stop your heart if the poison isn't extracted immediately. He's dead, Mannaro, just like you and the girl."

"Come on and fight me then," Nate said, taking a step forward. "And not with that knife. Hand-to-hand combat. No spells. Strongest person wins.

Moros smiled, twirling the knife around in his hand. It was stained with Josh's blood. "Very well. We all know who will win, but if it gives you a satisfactory feeling before your death, why not?" He launched the knife to the side. It disappeared down into the depths of the canyon.

"Nate, don't do this," I warned, my voice shaking. Nate only pushed me back farther, making me stumble into the rock wall behind me.

Moros laughed again. "Bring it on, Mannaro. We all know that you want to show the girl how strong and brave you are and that you deserve her. Too bad you'll be dead, and so will her other love, and she'll be left all alone." His eyes glistened in the light. "If I don't decide to kill her too, of course."

"Not if I can help it," Nate spit through clenched teeth. And then he launched.

As soon as Moros caught Nate's movement, he also started to move. The two sprang forward and tackled each other, both falling onto the hard ground. A dust cloud came up from the cave floor and covered them. It surprised me that Moros wasn't using any sorcery. Even though he had said he wouldn't, I suspected that he would. But he seemed to have his morals. He wanted to win so that he could prove that he was stronger. He wanted his pride.

I heard a whistle coming from the side of the canyon. I felt the urge to turn toward the sound, but I couldn't pull my gaze away from Nate and Moros. Grunts came from where they were fighting, and I feared Nate was getting hurt. He was going to lose. I knew it, Moros knew it, and Nate knew it too.

I turned at the sound of a second whistle echoing through the cave. Dale was working on Josh's side. He was wrapping a cloth tightly around the wound, and he had some sort of ointment that he was applying. He didn't even look up. I could see the sweat glistening on his face from where I stood.

He glanced at me and whistled again. So Dale had been the one to whistle. He pointed at the ground with his free hand before quickly returning it to pressure Josh's wound as he wrapped the cloth. I followed his gesture down at the ground. A small knife lay there. It was stained with a few spots of blood on one side, but was otherwise clean, aside from some dirt. The blood on it was my blood. I recognized it instantly. It was the knife that the guard had stuck into the wall earlier. My mind started to race. What did Dale want me to do with it? Only one way to find out.

CHAPTER 27

I dropped to my hands and knees. Without trying to stir up Nate and Moros, I slowly crawled toward the knife. I tried not to pay too much attention to the fight going on. I could see bruises starting to form on Nate's face, and blood streamed out of his nose. Moros looked perfectly fine. His suit was stained with blood here and there, but it wasn't his. It would only be a short while before Nate would be left for dead.

Halfway there. I crawled forward, trying not to make the slightest sound. If Moros saw me, he would come after me for sure. I cringed as Nate yelled out in pain. I squeezed my eyes shut, trying to tune out the noise.

Out of the corner of my eye, I could see Michael crushing himself into the rock wall. He was trying to hide, but at the same time see what was going on. He had his phone out and was punching in random buttons. Trying to call more guards? I didn't know. I was certain Dale's tunnels weren't ones with cell phone reception. Every now and then, Michael would cast a worried glance in Josh's direction.

Dirt crushed beneath my knees. Pebbles dug into my skin as I arrived next to Dale. I slipped my hand around the handle of the knife. Its weight hung heavy in my palm, the silver weight out of proportion for the size of the knife. But how could I use this knife to help Nate?

"You have to find the chink in his armor," Dale whispered from next to me, answering my unspoken question.

I turned to look at him. He glanced up once; he was busy trying to fix Josh's wound.

"What do you mean?"

"Pressure." Dale hesitated, gesturing at Josh's wound. It looked worse than I had thought. The skin around it was starting to go a shade of black, and the blood didn't look clean. Dale had already bandaged up most of it, so I pressed my hands there, trying not to stain them with blood. I tried to close the wound slightly as Dale grabbed some more of the ointment.

Josh stirred, letting out a low whimper of pain. My heart felt like it was breaking into a million pieces. His skin had paled a few degrees from its original tone, and he shook slightly, even though he was unconscious.

"Careful," Dale said as he applied some of the ointment. As soon as it touched the wound, it started to sizzle, bubbling like an acid. Some of it spattered onto my skin, and I winced as it stung. The spots it had touched turned red.

"Sorry," Dale muttered as he grabbed another bandage. My eyes widened as the skin around the wound started to clear. It was still bleeding, but no longer the ugly black color. Like the poison was being sucked out of it. The acid ointment turned the black color instead, and it soaked itself into the bandage as Dale applied it.

"What is that?" I looked at Dale.

"It's an antidote. But that doesn't matter right now." He waved off my comment. "You have something else to do." He stopped working on Josh and pointed at the knife in my hand. "Like I said, you have to find the chink in Moros's armor. His weak spot. You noticed he has an invisible shield, right?"

I nodded. The side of Dale's mouth curved upward in response. "See, smart girl. Well, it's like a piece of armor. Find his blind spot. Everyone has one, even people as powerful as him. Find his Achilles' heel."

I glanced at Moros and Nate. They were still throwing punches, but Moros was clearly winning. Nate lay on his back, trying to get in whatever hits he could. I could tell that they were getting less powerful.

"How do you suppose I find it?"

"You've figured out everything so far; I'm sure you'll find this too." Dale continued, "Pay close attention to what Moros does. That's all I can say. I'm sorry, but I can't be more help than that."

I turned the knife over in my hands and trailed the top of the blade with my finger. "Let's hope for the best hone."

Dale smiled reassuringly. "You'll find it, sweetheart. The good guys always win."

With a last glance at Dale, I crawled to the side of the canyon. I pulled myself up onto a rock. Everything in the middle of the cave was a horrible sight. Moros, the most powerful dark sorcerer, was in a fight with Nate. It wasn't very hard to determine who would win.

I noticed that Nate's pupils were starting to turn yellow. He was trying to change. Forcing himself to become a werewolf. But it wasn't working, and Moros noticed. "Can't change without your bracelet and the full moon now, can you?" Moros sneered. "Told you you were a useless little wolf. At least your daddy can change whenever he wants without that stupid token."

Moros laughed as he dodged one of Nate's punches. "Your dad would be a good person to have on my side. He's strong. That's why he's the pack leader. He could bring all his little pups with him."

A slight shimmering caught my eye. It was coming from Moros's back. I looked closer. Nate was attempting to punch again, but none of his punches were hitting home. They were being stopped by Moros's shield.

I watched as Nate hooked his arm around and hit Moros in the back. To my surprise the sorcerer cringed in response. He had felt that. He only seemed to feel the punches hitting him in the back. And not just anywhere—one specific spot.

Nate had figured it out. He had found Moros's weak spot. Dale was right; he did have one. It was on his upper back. When he lost focus, the spot would grow bigger, but if nothing was distracting him, Moros could get it down to the size of a pea.

He had to be focused on something else, not paying attention to who was coming at him from behind. His focus needed to be away from his force shield so that the open spot would grow wider.

I glanced at the shimmering light again. The puzzle pieces slowly started to connect together in my mind. If the shimmering light was the outline of the unprotected part, I needed to get his focus away from his force shield so that the open spot would grow wider. If I could just hit it …

Nate screamed out in pain. His shrill shout echoed sickeningly throughout the canyon as he clutched his leg. I bit my tongue in response and immediately felt the blood well up in my mouth.

"When are you going to get it, Mannaro?" Moros stood up shakily. "You can't win. I'm too powerful for a weak wolf like you."

Nate lay on his back. He pushed himself partly up on his elbows. His green eyes came in contact with mine. His eyes widened as he saw the knife, and then he looked at Moros. A smile started to play on his lips. "I guess you haven't learned anything either."

Moros took a drunken step toward Nate. "And what does that mean?"

"Well," Nate spit to the side. The ground spattered with blood. "The good guys always win."

Before I knew it, the knife was flying out of my hand. The instant I noticed Moros had been caught off guard by what Nate had said, I acted. Moros wouldn't see it coming. The gap in his force field had widened. It was our only hope.

Those three seconds that the knife was hurtling through the air were the most terrifying I have ever experienced in my life. Everyone's eyes followed the weapon, all of us momentarily holding our breath. My heart raced.

Moros's scream pierced the air as the knife hit home. The throw had been perfect. It had hit right in the center of the shimmering light. I stared at my hand in surprise. It tingled with energy. My mouth fell open at my perfect aim.

Moros dropped to his knees. He groaned loudly, cringing as the blood started to seep through his jacket.

We all watched the sorcerer. It was a horrible sight. The blood that dripped off his jacket was such a dark shade of red that it almost looked black. Moros paled, and the tint of red in his eyes vanished.

Moros screamed as he bent his arm backward awkwardly to pull the knife out of his back. I wasn't a doctor, but I could tell it was close to his heart. It was the same height. If it hadn't hit his heart, then why not another organ? Why wasn't he dead? A shot like that should have killed him. The amount of blood that gushed out of the wound wasn't safe. He wasn't supposed to be alive.

Moros pushed himself up off the ground, dropping the blood-soaked knife. It landed with a loud clang. Blood spattered off it and onto the dusty ground.

Moros staggered slightly, but seemed fine otherwise. His powers were stronger than I thought. Were they trying to save him?

Moros pointed a bloodstained finger at me. Some of it dripped onto the ground. "I'm not done with you yet. Something's up, and I won't stop until I get what I want." He turned to face Nate, who had been inching away slowly. "I'll be back for all of you.

"You think you can get away with this? A knife shot doesn't kill me." He spun around. Anger flashed in his eyes. "I'm Ker Moros. A dark sorcerer. I will heal. And when I do, I'll be back, as strong as ever, ready to kill and take over all of these marbles. And once I have them, the first person I will come after"—he looked at me, his black eyes staring into mine—"is you.

"There's something you're hiding. All of you. I will find out what it is." He walked over to the edge of the canyon. He opened his mouth to speak, but stopped when he noticed Josh starting to stir on the ground.

Moros tilted his head to the side. "You have an antidote? Maybe you are smarter than I assumed." He looked at Dale. "But I can't let young Mr. Larson get away with it so easily, nor his father."

He turned to Michael. "You will pay for what you've done. You failed me, and anyone who fails me will be found. I threatened you when I found you, and what I said will happen."

He glanced at Josh as he moved again. Josh's eyes were still closed, but I could tell he was close to waking up. A sickening feeling spread in my gut.

A smile spread on Moros's face. "Maybe I'll just follow through on that threat now."

He spread out his hands and looked up at the ceiling. He inhaled deeply, letting his power ride through him. When he opened his eyes, they were red. Just like in Josh's stories. Pure red, not a hint of black left.

Mist started to come out of Moros's fingers, sparking with energy. A red energy ball started to form. He took a step forward and started to extend his hands.

But then he coughed, and the energy ball faltered. Sweat started to drip down Moros's head, along with the dark blood. Moros lurched to the side coughing, and blood spilled from his lips and onto the ground. Moros wiped it with his sleeve.

"Harpy poison!" Moros snarled, his nose wrinkled up and his veins popping out next to his temple. His hands balled into fists, his eyes wide.

"I'll be back next time; don't you worry." A drool of blood and spit dripped to the floor. It was disgusting, I looked away. When I looked back, his red eyes were looking straight at me. He inched himself over the edge so that there was no ground under his feet. "And when I come back, none of you will be safe."

Then to my surprise, he winked. His plan wasn't foiled; we had only slowed it down. Then he let himself fall backward. I gasped as he plummeted into the canyon, the wind whooping as he went.

I ran over to the edge. A strange black mist was racing through the bottom of the gorge. Wind blew up into my face, pushing my hair back. Moros was nowhere in sight, and his body was definitely not on the floor of the ravine.

The ghostly mist started to move. It was Moros. Of course it was. His spells were faltering due to the poison, but to no surprise, he had found enough power to escape. I'm sure he had reserved energy just for it.

I watched until the mist was out of sight. But then everything came flooding into my brain, washing over me like a tidal wave. Moros was gone; we had done it. But he would be back. He could hit unexpectedly, and he wouldn't hesitate to do so. It would only be a matter of time before he healed.

I turned around and sprinted to Nate's side. He had taken a seat on the cave floor, his leg stretched out in front of him. His knee was starting to swell and was twisted in a sickening direction. Blood was smeared on Nate's cheek, and bruises covered his body. I flung myself into his arms. He grunted, but made no effort to move me. I felt a lump form in my throat, and hot tears started to stream down my face.

"It's okay." Nate stroked my hair. "We're all right. He's gone. We did it." He pulled me away so that he could see my face. "You did it."

I sat on my knees. "He'll come back, Nate. We're all doomed. He could have killed you, and he won't hesitate to do so next time." My words came out in short sobs.

Nate squeezed my hand. "But we'll be ready. There are enough occult in town to help. If we convince them to fight, we can go against him with an army when he returns."

I shook my head. Hair fell in front of my eyes. "But I'm not occult."

Nate shrugged as he pulled a piece of hair behind my ear. "No, but you are special. What you did today—you saved us all.

Not just anyone has the courage to go against an evil sorcerer and chuck a knife at him. You were brave, and you helped us defeat him. If he had gotten the marble, it would have been a whole new story with huge amounts of trouble."

I watched as Nate stood up shakily. He pulled me up lightly and started to limp over to Dale. I jogged up next to him and pulled his arm over my shoulders. I let him lean on me. His weight was heavy to hold, but he sighed in relief instantly. He was in more pain than he was letting on.

We arrived next to Dale. Josh was still unconscious, but breathing peacefully. Michael had silently made his way over too.

We were all hurt in one way or another, but at least we were still alive.

CHAPTER 28

"He's gone, but he's definitely alive." Dale spoke softly. He was the first of our little circle to speak up. It must have been a horrible picture. We were all covered in sweat, blood, and dirt. I grabbed my necklace and started to trace patterns on the ground with my foot. I ran my fingers over the engraved letters. I frowned when my hand came away wet. When I looked down, I saw that the charm was spotted with blood, and my fingers had stained red because of it. I must have grabbed it sometime during the fight or when we were with the guard. I didn't even know. It was such an automatic habit for me to grab it that I barely noticed it anymore.

Michael rubbed the sides of his mouth. "I guess I have some guards to fire …" He trailed off as he looked at his son. "Will he be all right?"

Dale nodded slowly, a hint of annoyance in his eyes. He wasn't quite ready to forgive Michael just yet. None of us were, for that matter.

"He'll be just fine, Mr. Larson," Dale replied hesitantly.

I frowned. "I thought he was stabbed with some kind of poison?"

"Harpy poison?" Nate asked.

Dale looked at us. "That's correct, but he'll be fine. The ointment Renn helped me apply was an antidote. It will clean his blood of the poison. We still have to take him to the healer to fully clean and bandage the cuts, but he's not dying anymore."

"Antidote for harpy poison is very hard to come by, goblin. Why do you have it?" Mr. Larson towered over Dale, but it didn't seem to bother the goblin much. After seeing Michael with Moros, I couldn't picture him as the scary man he set out to be anymore either. But he was still the occult governor after all.

Dale rolled his eyes slightly. "Goblins have hobbies." He stood and brushed the dirt off his knees. "After I completed my tunnels, I had all the spare time in the world. When I'm not busy with them, I look into antidotes and stuff like this. Harpies fascinate me; wonderful creatures they are."

"Until they get the poison in your blood," Nate muttered from beside me.

Dale narrowed his eyes at him. "That's why I make the antidote, Mannaro."

We all stood quietly for a moment. I turned my gaze to Josh. I had thought I saw him stirring earlier, but he seemed to have fallen unconscious again. His breathing was even, making his chest heave and fall slowly. I heard Nate exhale loudly through his nostrils. He was the first to speak.

"Shouldn't we address the elephant in the room here?"

Michael glanced at him. He seemed annoyed that he was stuck in this situation with a bunch of teenagers. "Which is?"

"You, of course!" Nate took a limping step toward him. "Why were you helping Moros? How did you ever get it into your head that it was a good idea to help someone as evil as him? What did my dad say about it? It's not like he thought it was a good idea to come after us."

A look of sadness crossed over Michael's face. He paced a few steps. "I never wanted to help him." He looked back at us over his shoulder. The back of his suit's coat was covered in dirt. "Especially as head of the occult—do you have any idea what that would do to me if the public found out? It would put me in a horrible position. People would want me gone and start to go against the government. There would be no control or trust left and throw the occult races into chaos, which as you might be able to imagine, would not work out well for the humans."

"Then why did you do it?" Nate said through clenched teeth. "We were almost dead because of you."

Michael sighed and rubbed his temples. "Moros came to me one day knowing I had some information on the marbles. I don't know how he knew that I had these facts, but he was right. I had collected all the separate information and compiled it into one record for the pure safety of the occult. I had tried to take precautions in case Moros rose again.

"But alas, I didn't do it right. He came after me and told me to dig further and find out who had the marbles that I knew of. Once I did, I told him and thought that was that. I couldn't imagine anything as bad as from those stories. I didn't think it was possible. My predecessor had told me, but I barely paid attention." Michael looked down at his son. "But of course Josh knew all of it. He did a better job than I did.

"Then Moros threatened me. He told me to find you and get the marble from you. When I refused"—he hesitated—"he threatened to kill Josh. I convinced myself to do it just to make sure I could keep you safe while Moros did his job. I worked as I always do. I didn't want to raise any suspicion, so I tried to find an excuse to go after you. The excuse came, like I thought it would, but things got complicated. I thought we would be able to catch you, but you met Dale and got into the tunnels. We lost your trail, which only …"

"Angered Moros," I finished softly.

Michael nodded in response. Dale shifted on his feet, adjusting his purple jacket. I had gotten so used to it that I barely noticed the neon color. Or faded neon color. It had already been faded when we met him, but was even worse so now. There were holes in different parts of the material.

Dale sighed. "So did you need my tunnels for him too?"

"No, that was for occult reasons."

"What reasons?" Dale exclaimed. Color turned his face a shade of pink. "Why would you do that?"

"It's a dangerous thing to have, goblin. People could leave through them, but more importantly enter through them. I'm surprised Moros didn't use them. It would be perfect for people like him to hide out in and only come out when they want."

"I saved your son."

Michael crossed his arms. "So?"

"Maybe I deserve a favor."

Michael pondered this. Then he rolled his eyes. "Fine, goblin. Your tunnels will be returned to your possession by the end of the week. Give my men a few days to disable the alarms. But be warned—one wrong move and you'll lose them, no matter what it is. Even if they are misused and it was not your fault, it is your responsibility to look after them."

Dale nodded, a smile starting to form on his face. "Of course."

I grinned at the thought. Dale could easily tell Michael the truth about why he lost his tunnels. About what Josh did. But he stayed quiet. Goblins weren't as bad as they seemed. Well, at least Dale wasn't.

We all jumped as Josh launched up gasping, his eyes fluttering open. Then he sank back onto the ground. He rubbed his eyes. "What was that ...?"

"Sorry." Dale scratched his head. "It's a side effect of the antidote. I haven't fully worked out the mix yet. It seems to give a little energy boost when you awake, but you'll be unstable on your feet for the next few hours."

Michael's eyes widened. "You gave my son an antidote that you weren't sure of yet? You could have killed him!"

Dale rolled his eyes. "It needs to be worked out some more, that's all. The important thing is that I saved him. He would have died otherwise, and it was worth the try."

Josh pushed himself back so that he was leaning against one of the rocks. His gray eyes looked up at Dale. "Thanks." He chuckled. "So, Moros is gone? The last thing I remember is the marble being destroyed. What a bummer."

Nate shifted on his feet.

"So now what? Moros can't do anything until he finds a hint as to which new object the power transferred to. Without it, the marbles aren't complete, and he can't take over?" I asked, speaking out loud my own thoughts. It made sense to me. "We won't hear from him again for a while, right? I mean, wouldn't it take really long for him to find out where this new marble is?"

"I wouldn't be so sure ..." Nate's voice trailed off.

I narrowed my eyes at him. "What is that supposed to mean?"

"He'll find a way. There will always be a way for him to find the marble without going through lots of trouble."

Dale cleared his throat. "What I can't believe is that the marble broke so easily. With the mist swirling inside, I would have suspected the power it held would protect it from breaking. Whoever made it didn't think that through."

"Strange …" Nate agreed. He was nodding slowly, a disturbed look on his face. His green eyes kept flying to look down at his pants pocket. He had his hand in there, and it was balled up into a fist.

"I was thinking the same thing; the power in the marble should have kept it intact," I commented with a glance at Nate. "What surprised me was that it broke when you stepped on it. It was a piece of stone, right, and it vanished into thin air—only little dust particles remained."

Nate nodded distractedly. "I did what I had to do."

"You know, I was wondering. When you gave me the marble, it was really banged up. You must have really dropped it."

"I did; I tripped on my way through the tunnels."

"Huh." I considered this. "I get how it could have broken out of the ring, but even the crescent symbol had disappeared. Like it was scratched out or was never there in the first place. And I thought the marble exerted off power when it wasn't in the clasp, but it didn't do so this time. Isn't that strange?"

"Strange indeed."

"Nate!" I shoved his shoulder. He staggered on his injured knee. I quickly grabbed his arm before he fell over. "Tell me what you did!"

"What do you mean?" Nate shrugged. "I didn't do anything."

"Nate!" I shouted in his face. "I know that look. You're hiding something."

"Fine! Shut up already." He ran his hand through his hair before reaching into his pocket. "I gave you a fake."

Then he took an object out of his pocket. He opened his hand, and there lay a marble ring. It was perfectly intact, as shiny and radiant as ever. There were no dents, and I could faintly see the crescent moon symbol from where I stood.

I took a step back. Josh's eyes widened beside me. "How did you manage to do that?"

"Well"—Nate cleared his throat—"remember when we were in the cave with the bridge? The soft crystals on the wall reminded me of the marble; they even had the same color. I had taken a spare just in case—who knew when it would come in handy? Coincidentally I was able to use it today. I was trying to find a way to avoid giving Moros that power and thought it would be worth a shot."

"So this was all for nothing?" Josh threw his hands up. "I got stabbed for nothing!"

Michael sighed. "That's not true, Josh. Nate did the right thing."

"Of course he did. He's just so much better."

"That's not true either." Michael turned to Nate. "It was a good idea not to give it to him, but Josh is right. Moros will come after you again if he finds out you have the marble, and it will not be a good thing."

Nate nodded. I turned to him slowly.

"So, how did I end up with a fake?" I asked.

Nate shrugged. "I never gave you the real one. You had the fake all along. It was a soft crystal, easy to smash. At least Moros believed it."

"So now what? Michael is right. If Moros finds out, he'll be pissed."

"You get rid of it," Michael said. "There's no place you could keep it safe from Moros. The only way is to try to destroy it; get rid of it at the very least."

"I'll throw it into the canyon." Nate looked behind him. "It'll fall with a great enough force. If it'll break or not, I don't know. But at least we'll be rid of it."

"Very well. We'll leave you to it." Michael turned to Josh. "We have to get you out of here and to a healer, but I'm afraid I'm going to have to carry you."

Dale laughed.

Josh just looked disturbed. "I can walk myself."

"No, you can't," Dale smirked. "You're shaking of exhaustion just by sitting there; there's no way you can walk."

With muttered protests, Michael lifted Josh up, much to his son's dismay. They walked into one of the tunnels. Dale followed closely behind to give directions. Apparently we weren't that far away from an exit. I was about to follow when I noticed Nate standing at the edge of the canyon. He was tossing the ring around in his hand. One simple throw away from destroying his mother's ring.

CHAPTER 29

I jogged up to Nate. He started to speak as he noticed me approaching. "I can't do it, Renn. It's the only thing I have left that's my mom's. I can't …"

I slipped my arm around his waist. "I understand," I murmured softly.

"But I have to. It's the only way Moros won't come back. He can sense these things. He'll come back, and I can't let that happen to us. To you."

"We'll be ready for him." I looked down at the ring. The blue shade of the marble matched the silver accessory perfectly. "We can get the occult to join us. Convince them to fight. Just like you said."

It was funny how quickly things could change. Not an hour earlier, Nate was telling me the same thing trying to comfort me. All I was doing was repeating his own words back to him.

"It's just … I can only choose one thing. I can only keep one safe." He spun the marble in its clasp with his thumb. It spun slowly, revealing the crescent etched into it. "Either I keep this ring safe—or you."

We stood silently for a minute.

"How did you manage to hide it from the guard?" I asked, thinking back. The ring had been in Nate's pocket; there was no way the guard could have missed that.

"You mean how I hid the ring from them?"

I nodded.

"I'm still not exactly sure. I tried acting like it was in my bag, just to get the attention away from my pocket. It was in there the whole time." He shrugged. "I guess it was pure luck. That, and the guard that searched me was a good friend of my father's. Maybe he didn't want to see me get hurt. He probably didn't search very hard."

I squeezed Nate's waist. "We've all been lucky today."

Nate stared out over the canyon. "Very. I wouldn't know what to do if anything had happened to you."

I smiled slightly. "I was hurt least of all."

"Yeah, but still. It's a lot to go through in a few days." He sighed.

I leaned my head against Nate's shoulder. He wrapped his arm around mine, his firm grip giving it a tight squeeze. "You must have known I would find out about the werewolf thing eventually."

Nate chuckled to himself. His green eyes laughed with him, but he looked tired. Dirt streaked his face, along with some hardened blood around his nose. His eyes were the only bright thing about him.

"I told you, I would have told you the moment I met you. My dad just doesn't think that way." He cringed as he shifted onto his non-injured leg.

"Does your dad know about the marble? Or about the power it possesses?" I asked, even though I could probably guess the answer.

"No," Nate replied, confirming my suspicions. "He knows that I have the ring. He was the one who gave it to me when my mom passed. It was the day of her funeral. He even joked that I should give it to a special girl. It was the only smile I saw from him that day …" He trailed off.

"Whatever that means, right?" I smiled, attempting to lighten the mood.

"Yup, whatever that means," Nate muttered. "I'm sure he doesn't know that the marble possesses power, but he will know soon. Michael will probably tell him." He laughed. "I wasn't even sure about its power, but I had my guesses. My mom used to tell me stories before I went to bed. Similar to the one Josh showed you in his illusion. When I heard rumors of Moros's uprising, I looked into it, just like Josh did. I found out about his previous attempt and the marbles, which only confirmed that the stories my mom had told were true."

"Crazy things," I muttered, a cold laugh escaping through my lips. I hesitated. "What now?"

Nate pressed his lips together. "We have to get rid of it. The marble is dangerous. We can't keep it."

"But you want to keep the ring." I finished his thought. There had to be a way. I held out my hand. "Give it to me."

Nate handed over the ring, a hesitant look on his face. I had no idea if this was going to work, but it was worth a shot.

I put as much pressure as I could onto the clasp. The marble would only exert its power when it came out of the clasp. If I could just separate the clasp from the ring …

I gasped as the ring snapped and broke in two. Exactly where I had intended it. The clasp was still stuck to the marble, and the rest of the ring was still intact. It remained as a shiny silver hoop, as if the marble hadn't even been there in the first place. It would look perfect if a diamond or something was attached onto it.

"What did you do?" Nate asked, trying to see the palm of my hand.

"Don't worry," I whispered as I pressed the ring into his hand. "Now you can keep your mom's ring, but throw out the marble. It won't exert power if it's still in the clasp. It'll look like an ordinary marble."

Nate shook his head. "Smart," he said softly. He admired the ring for a few seconds, running his thumb over the thin silver band. When he caught me looking, he quickly stuffed it in his pocket, brooding with a manly huff.

"What do we do with the marble?" he asked after he had cleared his throat. He scratched the corner of his eye.

I looked over at the ravine. I could barely make out the bottom; it was all rock and dirt. "We throw it in, just like Michael said we should do."

Nate frowned. "Are you sure that will do any good? It's not the crystal; I'm sure there's some kind of spell on it to keep it from breaking."

I squeezed the marble, the clasp digging into my skin. "Even so, it'll be away from us. It's the safest thing to do at this point. There's no other way, Nate."

"I know ..." he muttered, taking a look over the edge of the canyon and down into the black gorge. "Are we sure that it will be gone though? What if it lays at the bottom of the canyon for Moros to find?"

"It's better than if we have it." I undid the clasp, and the marble instantly started to give off a faint glow. The blue mist inside started to swirl, and I could feel the power vibrating in my hand.

Nate grabbed the marble from me. "Crazy, isn't it?" he said, echoing my exact thought.

I nodded as I touched the clasp to the marble. With a slight push, it clipped into place, the mist stopping its swirling instantly.

"I guess I'll do the honors then?" Nate took a step forward. He looked down into the gorge. "Here goes nothing …"

With one last look at the marble, Nate launched it into the air. It gleamed in the faint light of the cave. For a moment it caught the light, reflecting the rays off it, lighting the gorge up. It sparkled, making the dust particles clearly visible. Then it dropped out of sight. Out of our lives.

Neither of us spoke as we walked back across the cavern. Nate grabbed my hand, and we slowly walked through the tunnel, Nate limping by my side.

Ben showed up at the entrance of the tunnel. Apparently he had been there all along, but had refused to come in the tunnel with Michael. He didn't know about Moros, but had had bad feelings. Nate muttered a few words to his father, but told him he would save the in-depth explaining for later.

Ben gave me a quick hug, squeezing my shoulders reassuringly. He asked me how I was, but I only nodded. Everything seemed to be happening in a slow soundless blur, like they show at the end of an action movie.

I faintly heard Ben tell us that Michael and Dale had gone ahead to get Josh medical attention. He told us that he had heard everything and was sorry for getting us into this mess. Nate told him it wasn't his fault. I didn't react. Since I had watched the marble go down into the gorge, everything that had happened had started to flood back to me.

When we arrived in Manhattan, we were taken to some government building. It had a Latin saying on the wall, which according to Ben said something about the occult.

He chuckled coldly when I asked what specifically it said. "It's too ironic for my liking."

Nobody was allowed to come into this section, with most people believing it was just another company building. Nobody knew of it. Only the occult. The occult and I.

We stepped into an elevator and rode it up to a floor that I didn't pay attention to. The only thing I was aware of was Nate's hand gripping mine. Never letting go. I didn't want to let go. It felt like if I did, I would fall.

I was seated in a room that looked like the waiting room of a hospital. A giant oak door at the end of the hall was labeled with Michael's name. His office, I could only assume.

Ben had taken Nate to the healer's wing or something to get his knee fixed. Or leg. I hadn't even asked what was wrong. Nate had wanted to stay by my side, but his dad had pulled him away. Nate had looked over his shoulder back at me while limping away, a look of sorrow in his green eyes. We both felt the same way; it was a pain to have his hand ripped out of mine.

I was told someone would come get me, but it took an eternity. There was a clock on the wall opposite me. It was the only piece of color on the otherwise white background. I watched the hands tick slowly, without actually processing the time. I didn't even know how long I had been sitting there.

"Renn Daniels?" a voice creaked. I looked up at an older stubbly man approaching. He pushed his glasses up the bridge of his nose when he reached me. He wore a name tag, which read "Hello, my name is …" The name Hector had been hastily scribbled onto it.

The old man pushed some thin strands of graying hair away from his face. "Mr. Larson would like to see you now."

The man, Hector, led me to the end of the hall, which I could have easily found myself. He opened the door for me with a pained smile.

"Good luck."

CHAPTER 30

I entered the cold office. The air conditioner was on so high that the goose bumps exploded on my skin. Everything in the room was a shade of gray. Typically Michael. It screamed out his name. The office had a look to it like it was meant to be modern, but failed and gave a cold, unwelcoming feeling.

He sat behind his desk, staring out the window. I stood on my toes to look down over his shoulder. I chuckled softly to myself at the sight. It was a typical place for Michael's office to be. He could see exactly who was coming in and out of the building.

"You got yourself into some trouble, didn't you?" Michael said as he turned around in his chair. I quietly took a seat in the chair on the opposite side of his desk. It squeaked slightly as I sat.

I shrugged. "I guess you could say that."

The side of Michael's lip curved upward, giving him a wicked look. "Why don't you tell me exactly what happened, from beginning to end."

And so I told him. I started off at the party and worked my way to finding out about Nate. I told him what I knew and what Nate had told me. How we had run and eventually thrown the marble into the chasm. Michael listened patiently, lifting his eyebrows every so often.

"Very well," he muttered to himself after I had finished. He picked up a stack of papers and straightened them neatly. "What did Josh tell you about me?"

"Why is that important to you?" I asked hesitantly. "He only told me that you were the head of the occult government."

"No, that's not true. And I'm sure if Josh didn't tell you, Nate did. But I know my son. What did he tell you about my excuses?" He air-quoted the last bit.

I shifted in my seat. "He told me that you always find a reason to go after people to get what you want." I hesitated. "And he doesn't like you very much for it."

"Of course that's what he said." Michael sighed coldly. "My son doesn't understand why I do the things that I do. I have a reason for everything, yes, but not in the way that he thinks."

"Mind telling me the way that you do things then?"

An unexpected laugh escaped him. It sounded strange, like a laugh without humor. "I can tell you that I know things. I know, for example, that Josh was the one that started the riot, not Dale, just as I know that you aren't what you think you are."

My mouth fell open. Michael only looked at me sympathetically. "You have a lot to discover about yourself, young lady."

"What is that supposed to mean?

Michael didn't reply. He picked up a different stack of papers and scanned through them quickly before putting it back down.

"What is that supposed to mean?" I repeated through clenched teeth.

"Nothing important." Michael waved it away. "I just meant that all the information you have perceived over the past few days makes it feel like you are part of the occult, while you are in fact just human. A figure of speech, some would call it."

I narrowed my eyes at him. "I don't think that's what you meant."

"Oh, that is exactly what I meant." His eyes sparkled. For a moment they resembled Josh's; there was even a slight tint of gray to them. "Now on another note, I didn't come after you under false pretenses. No, not at all. I never do; that would be illegal." He hesitated. "People of the occult are not supposed to tell humans about our existence—it's the law—and Ben Mannaro did the right thing to tell me. I may have used the information to my advantage, but when it comes down to it, Nate did break the law.

"Therefore I have to punish both of you. Usually we have a sorcerer come in and perform a mind-wiping spell. That way you would not remember what has been told to you of the occult, and you would no longer be a threat to the system.

"But after the events of today, you have proven to be capable of handling the information. You do not seem like the type that will panic about feeling powerless. I would actually argue that you are quite powerful, even though you might not realize it. So I have come to the conclusion that I will not bother to arrange a memory wipe for you."

I let out a breath that I hadn't even realized I was holding. I hesitated before speaking. "But there's a catch?" I snapped stubbornly.

Michael caught my gaze. "There is always a catch, Ms. Daniels." He straightened his tie. "Even though I trust you with the information, I cannot risk sending you out and having you blab random occult facts to your family and friends. Plus, because the law was broken, I cannot do nothing about it. So you have a choice. You choose your family and leave everything related to the occult behind, or you choose the occult and become one to help fight Moros."

I frowned.

"To clarify, choosing your family would include leaving Mannaro behind. If you choose the occult, it would ban you from having any contact with your family. Someone will be assigned to you to make sure you don't break this promise."

A sob hung in my throat. I gasped as someone grabbed my arm and pulled me out of the chair. I didn't even see who it was. I stared at Michael. He had a slightly sympathetic look on his face, but it didn't seem to bother him that much.

"How could you?" I whispered. The tears were starting to well up in my eyes and slowly stream down my face. I couldn't choose between my family and Nate.

Michael didn't hear me. He grabbed a pen and started looking through a stack of papers. "Let me know in an hour," he said without looking up.

The grip on my arm dragged me out of the room. I tried to scream and shout in protest, but no sound came out. The door slammed shut, and the image of Michael disappeared. I was pulled along and taken into the elevator. I rode down and was taken to a place outside with a fountain. I could barely see through my tear-filled eyes. Everything was blurry.

Nate was sitting on the edge of the fountain and immediately stood at the sight of me. He took me from the strange person and led me toward the fountain. I collapsed onto the cold stone, the rough texture of it poking through my pants. I didn't care anymore. My mind had gone completely blank. I didn't even realize I was sobbing until Nate put his arm around me.

"Hey, it's okay," he murmured, holding me close. The scent of his cologne filled my nostrils, and his heart drummed in my ear. If everything had been okay, I might have enjoyed it.

I sniffed and separated myself from Nate. I kicked off my shoes and shifted around. I shivered when my skin touched the water. It felt cool against my bare feet. Birds chirped in the background. Everything seemed so simple.

"Are you going to tell me what happened?" Nate's voice interrupted my thoughts. Reality came crashing down.

"You seem really upset," he said, not meeting my gaze. He winced while pulling up his leg. It was tightly wrapped in a piece of cloth. Nate followed my gaze. "I needed stitches and some spells for the cuts and bruises. The healer did it all. I guess that's what they're for." He chuckled coldly. I watched as he twisted a rope bracelet that hung around his wrist. It looked the exact same as the one he had before except a little less dirt-covered. "They gave me a new one. It kind of sucks that I lost the old one; I've had it for forever. But at least now I can be in control again without hurting anyone."

I eyed him for a second. Nate was right; all of the bruises he had had were gone. I stayed quiet. A bird hopped on the ground before taking off into the city. Cars honked in the distance. I wished I was out there. Out there back at the party. Back at the party with Nate and Colin, before anything had changed. Before everything had become so complicated.

"Renn, talk to me." Nate grabbed my hand. His touch felt warm on my skin. "Tell me what Michael told you. What did he tell you to make you so upset?"

"He's making me choose," I said quietly. My voice came out rough, and my throat was dry. I coughed. "He's making me choose," I said again, louder this time."

Nate's eyebrows knit together, his green eyes filled with worry. "Making you choose what?"

"Between you and my family!" I blurted out in a sob. All the tears came rushing back. I pulled my feet out of the water and turned back around. "I can't do that, Nate. I just can't. You or my family!"

"I'm so sorry," Nate muttered softly. He put his arm around me. "What are you going to do?"

I huffed. "What do you think, Nate?" My voice came out louder than I had intended, and Nate recoiled when I spoke.

"I have no choice," I said softly. "I have to choose my family. I can't leave them. I don't care about leaving the occult behind. I just need them."

Nate's expression hardened. "The whole reason all of this happened was because you were in a fight with them. You wouldn't be happy." He quickly pulled his arm back.

I pushed myself off the fountain edge. "I can't just leave Colin behind, Nate. And even through all the hard times, they're still my parents. They raised me. I owe it to them."

"But I'm right, aren't I? All of those times you cried in my arms. You would rather live alone than with them." A look of hurt crossed Nate's face. It made me realize what this looked like to him. Why couldn't he see how hard this decision was for me? Just because I was choosing my family didn't mean he wasn't important to me.

"You can't do that, Renn. We've known each other for ages. You're my only friend." Nate blinked and looked away, avoiding my gaze.

The words were stuck in my throat I didn't know what to say. I could only feel the tears slowly making their way down my face.

Then Nate's expression changed. It turned softer, like he had thought of something. He stood and grabbed my hand. "Come with me. I'm going to warn the people of Moros. I know some guys that have heard of him, and we can work with them to fight. We can find a way to defeat him."

"Nate …"

"I wish I could help you find a way around this. But I know Michael. He'll keep an eye on everything. But that doesn't mean you can't choose me. Just look at everything we have been through in the past few days. We need each other, Renn …"

"Nate, I'm sorry," I cried. I had to lie. It was the only way he was going to let me go. I had to say something to get Nate to leave. As much as it hurt, I had made my decision.

I swallowed hard. "I wouldn't be fair of me to choose you. I have feelings for Josh." The lie stung as the words came out of my mouth. My mind was spinning. It was the only thing I could think of to get Nate to believe.

My heart broke into a million pieces when I saw Nate's reaction. He scowled, his eyes alight with fury. "Renn, don't do this. Don't lie to yourself. You can't let me go. Admit it! You're a mess without me."

The tears made tracks in my dirt-covered face. It was true. I wanted to run to him. Tell him he was right and that I would take off with him. But I couldn't. It would work out. I had to stay with my family. There was no other way. I shook my head, the tears spilling from my eyes, my vision starting to become blurry.

Nate threw his hands up. "So, you're giving up? After everything that's happened, all we've been through, you're giving up? Decided the occult life was too difficult for you?" He glowered at me.

"I can't just leave my old life behind."

"I don't care, Renn." He rushed over to me and took my hands in his. "Stop with this nonsense. We can get through it," he whispered, staring into my eyes. I forced myself not to get lost in his gaze. "My life meant nothing to me. I had killed my mom, had nothing to live for. Not until I met you. The day I met you, everything changed. You can deny it all you want, but we both know that you feel the same way."

Pain filled my body. Everything ached, my heart most of all. "Nate, stop it," I pleaded. I couldn't keep my act up if he kept going. I would crack. I grabbed my necklace and ran my thumb over the charm. When I was younger, it would always help calm me, but not this time.

"You mean the world to me, Renn. Every day we are together is the greatest, and I want it to be every day for the rest of our lives. Don't you get it?" Nate leaned his head in so that his forehead was touching mine. "I love you."

I couldn't help but gasp. It came out in a ragged sob. Deep inside, I had known how he felt. But even then it hurt to hear the words out loud. His green eyes met mine, and I wished I could just give in.

"I want to be with Josh," I blurted out. I didn't know what to say anymore.

"Stop lying to yourself!" Nate exclaimed. He caught me off guard. Why had I thought he wouldn't notice if I was lying. Of course he knew.

"But I do, Nate. I'm sorry," I continued. I could hear the tone of desperation in my voice.

Nate snorted and shook his head. "I thought you were different. I thought you weren't like everyone else. You were the girl that didn't care about what other people thought and did what your gut told you to do. That girl wasn't afraid to choose what she wanted even though it probably wasn't the right decision."

"I'm still that girl," I whispered.

"No, you're not. But that's okay." He glared at me. "It's not the first time I've been wrong."

"I'm so sorry," I sputtered through the tears

"Good-bye, Renn. I'm leaving, just like you wanted. You've made your choice, so I've made mine. If you need me, don't expect to find me," he said harshly. His expression softened the slightest when he traced the line of my cheekbone and down to my jaw. "I'm just afraid you're making the wrong choice," he finished quietly. I watched as he turned around and stomped off toward the exit.

"Nate, listen!" I yelled after him. I sprinted toward him, the dirt bits sticking to my damp feet.

He stood with his back toward me, his gaze off into the distance. "No, Renn. Just because we can't be together or you don't want to be together doesn't mean I don't love you. Remember that. I have and always will be there for you."

Nate glanced over his shoulder at me. He turned and pulled me toward him. He kissed me lightly. Electricity ran through my body. His touch felt warm as he ran his hand along my cheek. "I love you."

I sobbed as he pulled away. He sprinted off toward the exit. He hesitated when he reached it and looked back, meeting my gaze. He looked hurt. Turning away hastily he sprinted off away from the city. Away from New York. Away from me.

I shuddered as I took a breath. My heart ached. "I love you too," I whimpered after him, but he was long gone and away from earshot.

I tripped my way back to the fountain. I collapsed onto the edge and put my shoes on, even though my feet were still damp and covered in dirt bits. I couldn't care less.

"You look heartbroken, sweetheart," an approaching voice said.

My heart skipped a beat, hoping desperately for those few seconds that Nate had come back. I was disappointed at the sight of Dale. Josh was following close behind.

"I don't know what to do," I said quietly. I sniffed, wiping tears off my face. Except they were only replaced by new ones. "I don't know if he'll be okay."

Josh stopped when he reached me, but Dale kept walking in the direction Nate had gone. "I'll follow him, keep an eye on him for you," he said with a wink. He gave me a reassuring smile.

"How will you know where he's going?"

"I won't, but he still has a zapper. I'll be able to follow him." Dale walked down the steps. Instead of going down the road Nate had followed, he turned toward the bushes. "I'll see you later, sweetheart. He'll be okay, don't you worry," he said with a last smile, and then he was also gone. Gone to follow the boy I had just hurt terribly.

I heard the sound of rustling bushes and a loud creak. Dale had tunnel entrances right under the government's nose.

I rubbed some of the dried tears off my face. New ones were right at the surface, but this time I forced the lump in my throat away.

"He'll be okay. My dad reopened the tunnels to the West Coast, so he'll be in his own comfort zone," Josh said. He pulled me up off the ledge and into a hug. "I wouldn't worry about Mannaro though; he had it coming."

Josh's words stung me like a knife. He hugged me close, but it felt different than it had with Nate. I could feel the bandage under his shirt. I ran my hand along the covered wound.

"It hurt like crazy, but I'm okay now," Josh muttered. "Harpy poison does something to you; I could have died. Dale saved my life." Josh chuckled. "I guess I owe him another favor now."

I shrugged, not taking his words in fully. It all seemed so distant.

"My dad told me what happened," Josh continued. "It was cruel of him to make you choose between the occult of your family. However I was able to make him see that he couldn't take everything away from you. So, he assigned me to be your bodyguard." He laughed. "My purpose is to keep you away from the occult world, and I take this job very seriously. However, I see it more as a gift than a curse."

I gasped. This couldn't be happening. It made no sense. Michael had assigned Josh to look after me. I looked up at him. "Why's it a gift?"

"It lets me keep in contact with you of course." He smiled.

I couldn't help but let my mouth fall open. I couldn't believe this.

"But enough of that," he said as he ran his hand along my cheek. I shuddered. It was the same place Nate had touched.

"You okay?" Josh asked in concern. I only nodded.

He smiled. "You made the right decision."

I looked off into the distance. "I did what I had to do."

"That's what you told Nate, but secretly you needed an excuse to get rid of him. We all know your true feelings were towards me. Which is a good thing. We belong together. I love you."

"I love you too," I replied. It would take time to learn, but I would love him eventually. It was definitely the right choice. I couldn't just leave my family.

"Good." Josh smiled. "Now let's go tell my dad of your decision."

Before turning around toward the entrance of the building, Josh leaned in. I met his gaze, his gray eyes sparkling. He kissed me softly.

No electricity, no feelings; just emptiness and regret. I felt nothing.

EPILOGUE

Wesley stood, frozen in shock, at the bottom of the ravine. He was leaning against the rocky wall, trying to process what had happened. It couldn't be true. The most feared and mysterious being was alive. Ker Moros was alive. How could this have happened? How did he come back to life?

Wesley shuddered. He had grown up with scary stories about Moros. No one knew which ones were fake; in fact, everyone expected the tales to be made up. Made-up stories to warn the occult kids of messing with dark magic. But no. This was not a fairy tale. This wasn't just some scary story. Ker Moros was alive and plotting some sort of plan.

Wesley took a step forward and looked up at the edge of the gorge. The sounds of the people that had been there were long gone. It was safe. No one had even been able to acknowledge his presence.

"What the hell is this?" he muttered to himself as he examined the blue marble-like stone. It glowed in the dim light. Wesley didn't know what it was, but it had been what the people above him had been fighting over.

Wesley had been exploring the tunnels when he came across the ravine. The gorge had branched off into two different directions. He had gone one way, and his companion had gone the other. He was curiously searching around when the sound of people shouting had made him hide in the shadows.

When the fight seemed about over, the blue stone had been thrown into the ravine. Even though there was probably a very good reason for the people wanting the marble to be destroyed, Wesley's curiosity got the best of him, and he had speedily gone to catch it.

He turned the marble over in his hands. "Ow." He yelped as a small metal clasp cut his finger. He sucked on the wound while examining the clasp more closely. It was a small metal clasp with ridged edges. It looked like it had been broken off a ring or necklace of some sort.

Wesley decided to take off the small piece of metal. As soon as he did, a mist started to swirl inside the marble. It started to glow blue. Wesley jumped as it started to vibrate, exerting some kind of power.

"Holy!" Wesley dropped the marble onto the ground. It rolled around a bit before lying still.

"This is crazy!" he exclaimed softly. He got on his knees and crawled over to the object. He reached out a finger and touched it. The stone buzzed with power. He carefully picked it up and turned it over in his hand. It was completely smooth except for a small symbol carved into the bottom. It reminded Wesley of a moon.

Grabbing the metal clasp, Wesley tried clicking the stone back into it. The marble fell into place without any trouble and spun around loosely in its holder.

Wesley turned the marble over once more before putting it in his pocket. He had to keep it safe. He stood and started walking back the way he had come. He had to find his brother and get out of there. They had to get back to Seattle as fast as they could. They had to tell their leader about Moros and this strange marble. Wesley and his brother had been allowed to go on a short trip exploring the caves, but their leader probably hadn't expected them to find out about all of this.

"Connor!" Wesley shouted through the gorge. Where was his brother?

A strange lump was lying against a rock in front of him. Wesley broke out into a sprint. He knelt down next to his brother, who was just regaining consciousness.

"Connor, are you okay? What happened?" He felt his brother's pulse. It felt like it always did. "Connor?"

Connor groaned as he tried to sit up. Wesley grabbed his brother's arms and hauled him up. Connor's eyebrows knit together. "Get off me!" he said, a strange tone to his voice. "Dude, don't touch me."

Wesley frowned at his brother's strange reaction. What had gotten into him? "Connor, just tell me what happened."

"I don't know!" Connor glared at the ground. "I was walking along when a strong gush of wind came. It was this strange, ghostly mist, and it knocked me out."

Wesley gave his brother a strange look. "Are you sure you didn't hit your head? Do you have a concussion? When's your birthday?"

Connor madly pushed himself up. "What does it matter when my birthday is? Same as yours, you idiot." Connor staggered on his feet. He had been a bit too eager to stand up. He shakily decided to sit down on the rock. "I don't know, Wesley! It was probably just a strong wind."

Wesley was still staring at his brother. "Are you sure you're okay? You're acting strange."

"I'm fine!" Connor's eyes flared at his twin. He rubbed his head. "If I do have a concussion, I'm sure it'll heal."

"Okay," Wesley said, changing the subject quickly. "Did you hear that fight going on up there? The whole Ker Moros thing?"

Connor nodded. "Yeah. Right when I heard Moros surrender, the gush of wind came and knocked me out. Strange, right?" He sighed. "We should probably go back and warn them."

Wesley nodded. The two brothers stood up and sped away, out of the gorge faster than any other person would. The speed of a cheetah, Wesley used to call it.

They stopped when they reached the train tracks. They didn't have to wait long before the light of a train grew larger on their right.

"One … two … three!" Wesley shouted. The brothers pushed up and jumped on the train with incredible strength. They landed steadily on the top.

"You know what's funny? When I was listening to that whole fight, I thought I heard Nate Mannaro's voice. I think he was the owner of that marble." Connor chuckled. "You know, Leo's werewolf friend."

Wesley looked doubtful. "Leo as in leader of our house? Are you sure?"

Connor nodded. He sat quietly for a second, enjoying the breeze as it blew past him. "You know, that marble that Nate had, which we now have, looks really similar to the one Reed has. It even has the same type of symbol carved into it." Connor laughed, slowly coming to realize the same thing as his twin. "Reckon the marbles are related?"

Wesley looked off into the distance. "I'm afraid so."

ACKNOWLEDGMENTS

First off, I would like to thank my family for being so extremely supportive of my writing. Even at the start, back when I was scared to share my stories, you were there for me. You helped me realize how much all of this meant to me. Thanks for pushing me to do this, even when I doubted.

Thanks to my closest friends, you know who you are. The amount of outpouring support was more than I could have ever imagined. I never expected people to be so interested in my writing. You guys are awesome.

Thank you to everyone else who has been involved in this adventure. Thanks for helping me through this process, introducing me to the publishing world, and answering all my questions. Without you, this book would not have been possible.

And lastly, thank you. A book would be nothing without its readers. It means the world to me that you took the time to read my story.

STEFANIE MULDER

Stefanie is a high school student. She started writing when she was twelve. As part of a school project, she decided to take her hobby to the next level.

Originally from the Netherlands, Stefanie has lived in the United States and Singapore. She loves traveling and exploring new places.

Follow her journey at http://www.stefaniemulder.com.

ABOUT THE BOOK

Living in the Upper East Side can be hard, dealing with the demands of socialite parents and barely any friends you can count on. Renn Daniels doesn't think it can get any worse. When she accidentally stumbles across her best friend's biggest secret, her world turns upside down. She starts to find out more and more about things she never knew were possible. To make things more complicated, Renn's and Nate's relationship gets pulled to its limit as unexpected trouble arises. Can their friendship survive? And what happens when Renn is left with a choice she never thought she would have to make?

Printed in Singapore by Markono Print Media Pte Ltd